Before her mind started to cope, Ryan was in motion. He struck the water to Krysty's right, heading for the spur of rock that marked the sunken entrance to the redoubt.

J.B. was a moment behind him, followed immediately by Dean. Krysty drew breath, ready to duck dive after them, when Doc exploded into the sea only a yard away from her.

A moment later Doc's head broke the surface, his white mane pasted to his thin skull. "No sign," he bellowed.

"He'll be..." Doc began, striving for a note of reassurance, the sentence dying stillborn as Dean, J.B. and Ryan appeared from the cavernous redoubt. With no sign of Michael.

"Oh, Gaia!" Krysty's voice was harsh with shock. She stood, pointing toward the western horizon, her face frozen. "Look out there!"

There was a massive eruption about three hundred yards from shore. White froth and a burst of spray soared into the sky. All that they could make out, writhing at the core of the thrashing disturbance, was a giant, sinuous shape.

"Sea snake," Ryan said. "And—" He broke off as the creature crashed back into the water again, rolling to reveal, for the first time, its hideous head.

And the limp body of Michael Brother clasped in its blunt, hoglike jaws....

JAMES AXLER

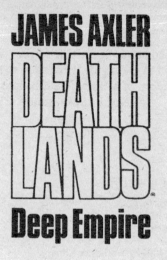

DEATH LANDS

Deep Empire

A GOLD EAGLE BOOK FROM

WORLDWIDE.

TORONTO • NEW YORK • LONDON
AMSTERDAM • PARIS • SYDNEY • HAMBURG
STOCKHOLM • ATHENS • TOKYO • MILAN
MADRID • WARSAW • BUDAPEST • AUCKLAND

This one has to be for Chris Priest who has succeeded in taking me, gibbering, to reveal the singing chasm of infinity. Well, he knows what it means! Thanks, squire.

First edition January 1994

ISBN 0-373-62519-7

DEEP EMPIRE

Printed in U.S.A.

There are those who see the future as a place of sunshine, honey and sylvan glades. Others see it as a time when eggs moulder in their shells, corpses lie rotting in the streets and the little children weep. Who is to say which is correct?

From *Smiley Smile Or Breaky Heart?*
by Jeremy Christian, Ortyx Press, 1992

Chapter One

Coburn and the pursuing posse were closing fast through the snowy Colorado evening, but Ryan Cawdor and his companions had made it to the massive locked sec doors of the redoubt. All of them were close to the ragged edge with fatigue and the effects of the altitude. Doc Tanner was on hands and knees, breath rasping in his throat, shoulders shaking with exhaustion.

"By the three Kennedys, my brothers and sisters," he panted, "but somewhere to lay this old gray head would be most damnably welcome to me."

Ryan reached up and pressed the control panel at the side of the right-hand door, punching in the familiar code of 3-5-20.

"Open sesame," Mildred said.

The whole group was filled with a tense energy, knowing that the horrors of the past couple of weeks were safely behind them and security lay just ahead.

"What?" J. B. Dix asked.

Ryan pressed the numbers again.

And again.

Nothing.

He tried a fourth time, though he was only too aware of the futility of the gesture. If the comp lock hadn't worked the first time around, then it wasn't going to work at all.

Nothing happened. The vast sec-steel entrance remained immovably locked against them.

"Fireblast!" Ryan swore.

There wasn't time for much of a discussion or argument. J.B. summed it up in his usual combat-wise, concise way. "Coburn won't risk coming closer. He knows we're well armed and hold the high ground. Can't get behind us. Can't get above us. He'll figure we're stuck up here, like hogs on ice. So, we got the dark hours on our side."

Ryan nodded. "They can't easily get up at us. We can't move down from this place. Only hope is for one of us to climb up the cliff face. In through where the earth slip opened the interior corridor walls. Try and open up the sec doors from inside." He paused a moment. "Have to be me."

Dean's face was a pale blur in the icy gloom. "But, Dad. The worms."

"Yeah, son. I know."

None of them could forget the worms.

THE TRADER USED TO SAY that if a man was going to get hurt, then waiting wouldn't make it any better.

Ryan left the walnut-stocked Steyr SSG-70 bolt-action rifle behind with the others, taking the SIG-Sauer P-226, snug in its holster, and his old and trusted eighteen-inch panga in its oiled sheath on his left hip. His thin-bladed flensing knife was concealed in the small of his back.

The snow was falling again with a serious intent, settling on the rocks all around him, on the faces of his companions and on the flaming hair of Krysty Wroth.

"Take care, lover," she whispered, kissing him once on the cheek, her lips like fire on his skin.

"Don't I always?"

"What if you can't get in? Or you can't make it to the main doors? Or you can't work the lock from inside?" Michael Brother bit his lips. "What then, Ryan?"

"Then, young fellow, you'll all have some tough decisions to take."

Doc shook him by the hand, his grasp surprisingly powerful for such an old man. "Test every foot and handhold, there's a good chap. Some mountain-climbing fellow told me that, back in about 1890. Or, was it 1980? I fear that I disremember, Ryan."

"I get the message, Doc. Thanks." He looked at the circle of friends, nodding to Mildred, who gave him a thumbs-up sign. "Right. Here goes."

ONCE HE WAS OUT of the shelter of the plateau, Ryan encountered the full force of the wind, biting in from the north. It plucked at his long coat, ruffling the white fur that trimmed it, and made his good right eye water, probing under the patch across the raw empty left socket.

Despite the bitter cold, Ryan knew better than to try to climb with gloves on. Though his fingers were cold, he kept moving them, fighting off numbness. In the shrieking maelstrom of the blizzard he couldn't see how far he'd climbed, nor how far there still was to go up the jagged face.

His memory put the ascent at two or three hundred feet. He moved cautiously, making sure that every foothold was secure before shifting his boots to the next one, testing the crevices and outcrops of granite with his fingers. Ideally he knew that he should always have either a foot and two hands on, or a hand and two feet.

Logical advice didn't always help.

Ryan was losing track of height, space and time. He hadn't checked his wrist chron before leaving the others, but he guessed he'd been working his way up the side of the mountain for the better part of a half hour.

Twice he'd slipped as icebound chunks of rock came loose under a foot or hand, sending him sliding yards down the cliff.

The noise of the wind was constant, filling his ears, blurring his concentration. All around him there was a whiteout, snow swirling into his mouth and eye, the force of the blizzard threatening to pluck him into the abyss.

Ryan paused and flattened against the stone, fighting for breath. It had occurred to him several minutes earlier that there was a serious risk of his climbing past the cleft in the granite face, going on up and up, like a blinded, bottled spider, trapped in the storm, doomed to scramble on until exhaustion and the weather brought his lonely ending.

He tried to replay in his mind the look of the hillside when they'd stood outside the entrance doors of the redoubt and stared upward. It seemed to him that it might have been a little more to the . . .

"Right," he whispered.

But he knew well enough how conditions like this could totally addle a man's sense of direction.

There'd been a motor mechanic from War Wag One, somewhere near the big lakes of the northeast. He'd been plagued with a virulent dysentery and had disdained the common latrines, choosing instead to go a few yards into the surrounding forest.

And the snows had swallowed him up.

Only when the blizzard ceased, thirty-six hours later, had they found his frozen corpse, less than fifty feet from safety.

Ryan steadied his breathing, trying to use the power of Gaia, the Earth Mother, that Krysty had taught him. But it was so hard to concentrate.

Just for a moment the memories of the old war wags brought a fleeting thought of Abe, his old friend who had chosen to go off into Deathlands to try to find whether the Trader was dead or alive. That had been . . .

But Ryan's memory wouldn't function.

All there was in the universe was cold and wind and an infinity of white.

HE WAS OUT of the blizzard.

Ryan found himself lying down, knees drawn up under his chin, a thread of frozen spittle linking him to stone. To concrete.

It was entrancingly comfortable.

Warm.

It felt so good that there was a temptation to simply lie there for a few more minutes and rest. Surely that couldn't do too much harm, could it?

Maybe even sleep.

"Fuck, no!" Ryan shouted, his voice hardly reaching his own ears.

There wasn't a lot of sensation left in his hands, but he pummeled himself in the face, eye closed, kicking out with his frozen feet, forcing the pain of recirculating blood, mouth open in a rictus of agony.

Finally he found that he could see, make out the dim shape of passage walls on either side of him, and a domed roof.

He'd managed it, blundering into the redoubt by a heady mixture of luck and judgment.

Ryan pulled himself upright and stared into the curving darkness of the corridor.

That was the easy part done.

Chapter Two

While he regained control over his body, Ryan checked his chron, shaking it and bringing the tiny numbers closer to his face, unable to believe what they showed.

The whole climb had devoured less than forty minutes.

It took him nearly as long to be certain that his body was back to something approaching full combat readiness. He flexed his fingers and moved his head from side to side, falling to a crouch and then jumping up and kicking sideways.

To anyone watching, he knew that he'd have presented a bizarre sight. But J.B. had once said that it was better to look stupid and stay alive than be crucial-cool and dead.

Finally, feeling as ready as he could be, Ryan drew the panga from its sheath and readied himself to move toward the heart of the complex.

It was still bitingly cold, his breath feathering out in front of him, and he could hear the distant roaring of the gale, fading away behind. Crystals of ice crunched under his boots as he picked his way along the sweep of the passage, taking the greatest care to stay in the center, away from the pitted walls and their lethal inhabitants.

Now he'd reached a point where some of the overhead lights were functioning, casting a sepulchral pallor over the place. One or two of the tiny sec cameras were also working, their lenses flicking from side to side, miniature ruby lights glowing.

From his memory, Ryan knew that he would soon be reaching the region where the walls had been honeycombed by the white worms. If he could get past that section in safety, he would pass the entrance to the mat-trans unit, then on into the heart of the military redoubt and down to try to open the doors to his waiting companions.

He stopped and glanced behind him.

There had been a small noise, like a footfall, or metal touching the ice-sheathed walls. But the curve of the corridor was enough to limit his vision to less than fifty yards.

Ryan waited for a moment, then carried carefully on, occasionally glancing behind him.

If he was lucky, then he might not disturb the murderous worms.

Now he could see the first signs of their activity.

The surface of the concrete, already pitting and seamed by age and by the shifting of the earth beyond, had begun to show a different texture—larger holes, accentuated by the shadows from the overhead lighting. Ryan had never actually seen Swiss cheeses with their smooth holes, but he'd occasionally come across pictures of them in the brittle old mags that still littered the wrecked malls of Deathlands. That was what the walls of the redoubt corridor were starting to resemble.

Ryan stopped, knowing that a combination of speed and silence was his best hope to get past without disturbing the lurkers within the walls.

A yard ahead of him, the brittle stone exploded in a burst of powdery shards. The sound of the gunshot was almost simultaneous, roaring out, filling the arched passage.

Most men would have stood still for a frozen second of time, shocked into immobility.

And they would have died.

Before the second round slashed past him, gouging another crater from the concrete, Ryan was in motion. His combat-honed mind racing like a comp in overdrive.

The blaster was an M-16 A-5, the sound unmistakable, despite the distorting effects of the rounded walls.

That meant it was Coburn, the rangy sec boss of the late and unlamented Baron Nelson.

Coburn was a tall and laconic man, with the face of a boxer and the voice of a gentle poet, someone Ryan could have befriended in another place and at another time.

But he was also a man who had taken his lord's salt and now saw his task as to hunt down his lord's killers—Cawdor and his friends.

All of that raced through Ryan's mind even while he was still diving sideways, dropping the panga, fingers grasping for the familiar butt of the SIG-Sauer.

From what he'd seen of Rick Coburn, his guess was that the sec boss had come alone, made the infinitely dangerous climb in the blinding snow, figuring that was what Ryan would have done, skirting the sheltered plateau where Krysty and J.B. and the others were waiting.

With a rifle Coburn had a notional advantage, but the poor lighting and the disorientating curve to the passage had saved Ryan's life.

He flattened himself against the wall, his automatic drawn and ready.

The sweep of the corridor was deserted.

"Nice, try, Rick," he shouted, "but you don't get to win the gold apple."

"Used to say a Kewpie doll in the old detective vids, Cawdor."

The voices echoed and rolled through the still, cold air of the redoubt.

"Seems like a standoff."

"Yeah."

"How do you want to play it, Coburn?"

"Any way you like. Better make it fast. It's colder than a whore's conscience here."

"Knives?"

Coburn laughed. "Full of tricks like that one, Ryan."

"What?" He was grinning, despite the razored tension of the moment, wishing that there was some better way out of this confrontation, knowing that there wasn't.

The sec boss laughed again. "I got me a seven-inch blade that I use to slice my ham. You got that big sticker that you used to butcher the fucking pig!"

"Count three and both step out and start blasting?"

"No, Ryan. Don't care much for that one, either. I like tec vids, not cowboys. None of this gunfight-at-high-noon shit, thanks. Try again."

"Hand to hand?"

There was a long pause, while the sec boss weighed all the odds.

"You trust me?"

"Believe I do."

"Believe I trust you, too, Ryan. No blasters and no steel? That it?"

"Why not?"

Out of the corner of his eye Ryan could see slow, roiling movement in the shadows of the wall.

Coburn shouted again. "Now?"

"Why not?"

He eased a little away from the wall, opening up another few yards of the long corridor.

The blaster was still cocked and ready. Ryan might have said that he trusted Coburn, but that was because he couldn't see any other quick way out of the impasse.

If there was an opportunity to gun down the sec boss without too much risk, then Ryan was going to take it. Survival wasn't some sort of role-playing game.

"Come on," he shouted.

Coburn appeared, holding the M-16 A-5 at the hip, finger snug inside the trigger guard. "Now what?"

"We both put the guns down on the floor, slow and easy. Step away from them. Then lay down the knives. Then we get to it. How's that sound?"

"Not so good as sitting together for a talk and a drink. But right now it'll have to do."

The rifle and the automatic hit the icy concrete at the same moment, followed by the panga and a horn-hilted hunting knife. Both men stood and looked at each other, less than thirty paces apart.

"Halfway?" Coburn called.

"Sure." Ryan tried to calculate at which point he could turn and make a dive for his own blaster, figuring, from what he'd seen of Rick Coburn, that there wouldn't be too much in it. Not enough to bet his life on.

Every nerve was stretched for the tall, lean figure to spin around and grab at the old rife.

But Coburn second-guessed him.

Instead of going for the gun, Coburn suddenly dug in and powered his way *toward* Ryan, arms pumping, closing the distance in a moment, sparks flying from the steel-tipped heels of his boots.

It was a good move, which took Ryan by surprise.

There was time to swing a short clubbing right that landed with a satisfying thud under Coburn's ribs, but the sec boss's momentum and weight drove Ryan back a dozen staggering paces, and he nearly tripped over his own automatic and knife as he went.

The men fought with frightening intensity. There were flurries of clawing, kicking and punching, larded with long moments of strained stillness. Muscle against muscle, each of them striving desperately for a glimpse of a potential advantage, a second when one of them might manage a grip or a blow that would open up the other's defence.

Ryan succeeded in snapping the little finger on Coburn's left hand, and nearly got in a killing blow to the front of the throat with the heel of his hand.

But the sec boss parried it with his right forearm and they broke apart for a few seconds.

Ryan was in the center of the corridor, flexing the big hamstring muscle at the rear of his left thigh, where Coburn had managed to numb it.

"Son of a bitch, Cawdor!" The tall man was panting, the veins prominent in his forehead. "Knew it wasn't a good idea. I'm real sorry about this."

"What?"

"This," he replied, pulling a small over-and-under derringer from beneath his jacket.

Chapter Three

Ryan had been about to draw the slender-bladed knife from his own belt to kill Coburn, and there was a certain grim humor in the realization that, for once, someone had been faster and meaner than him.

"Anything we can say?"

Coburn shook his head, and spoke in a whispering voice so quiet that Ryan could barely hear him, like a black velvet ribbon being laid across green baize.

"Not a thing."

"What about the others, Rick?"

The sec boss was leaning casually against the wall, breath hissing between his teeth as he glanced at his crooked little finger. "Hurts like a real bastard, Ryan. The others? Krysty, Doc and the kid?"

"All of them," the one-eyed man replied, beginning to let his hand crab toward the concealed knife.

"No." Coburn waved the pistol. "Keep real still, Ryan. This holds a pair of .44s. Useless above twenty feet, but we're closer than that."

Again, Ryan noticed a slight blur of movement from one of the myriad holes above the sec boss's head. "You'll let the rest of them go? Appreciate it."

"Hell, why not? Blood feud's between you and me. Sure. You got my word on it."

"Like I had your word on no blasters?"

Coburn grinned. "Yeah. Life's a bitch and then you go to buy the farm. Real sorry. Want to turn around?"

"No. Want to see it coming."

"Sure. So long."

The muzzles were like miniature railroad tunnels, aimed at Ryan's eye.

Coburn held the gun granite-steady.

The white worms boiled from the pitted walls all around him, like an eruption of albino death. The gunshots must have disturbed them and also scared them for a while. Then, sensing no great threat, the nest of worms came out to feed.

The tall sec boss had time for only one stifled scream of shock and mind-closing horror.

Ryan was moving to his left as the man's finger tightened on the trigger of the derringer, the bullet bursting into the wall a yard to his right and bringing an instant response from more of the writhing worms.

When Dean had been attacked by the malevolent creatures, there had seemed to be dozens of them. Now there were hundreds, vomiting from every crack and crevice in the walls over a length of twenty paces, all of them making for Coburn.

Ryan froze, close to his discarded blaster and the panga, not daring to make any movement that might draw their attention to him, watching helplessly.

The worms seemed to have layers of teeth within teeth, set in circular, needled jaws. Once they'd fastened onto the man's flesh they burrowed into him, just as they'd excavated the solid walls of the redoubt. Their bodies thrashed to and fro, making Coburn look as though he were covered in a shroud of white cords.

After that first strangled cry, the sec boss fought his futile battle in silence. Several of the blanched creatures had struck at his face, one delving, as Ryan watched in horrified stillness, directly into his left eye socket. Two more wriggled between Coburn's lips.

A fine spray of blood dappled the struggling figure, like a ruby mist.

The only wonder was that the sec boss had the physical strength to keep on his feet for as long as he did.

But less than a minute had slithered by since his finger had begun to squeeze the trigger of the derringer.

Finally, like a slab of meat dropping from an iron hook, Rick Coburn fell to the floor of the passage.

The worms seemed to sense the moment of death, and they instantly became less frantic in their attack.

In the slowest of motions Ryan stooped and picked up the blaster, sliding it into its greased holster, taking the panga in his right hand, wiping the film of sweat from his palm before gripping it tightly.

Now the thrashing had ceased, and Ryan realized, to his gut-churning disgust, that he could actually hear the worms at their feeding. It was a moist crunching sound, tiny and soft, but repeated endlessly.

Already most of the dead man's clothes had gone, along with much of his skin. In places, between the feeding creatures, Ryan could actually glimpse the ivory whiteness of stripped bone.

He took a deep breath and steadied himself. Still more of the worms were emerging from the rotten concrete farther along the passage, crawling down the walls and along the ice-frosted floor toward the fresh meal.

"Go!" he urged himself.

Ryan sprinted past the charnel feast, jumping to avoid a few of the creatures as they struck at his boots. But his speed carried him through, away from the treacherous corridor walls, past the entrance to the mat-trans unit and toward the controls of the main sec doors.

It was one of the smallest redoubts that Ryan had ever visited. The military complexes had been established in conditions of great secrecy during the last few years of the twentieth century, mostly, but not entirely, in areas of natural solitude, though Ryan had encountered urban redoubts as well as at least two outside the old United States.

Many had been stripped in the panic conditions that existed once the accidental nuke holocaust had been triggered, early in the twenty-first century. But some had held caches of food or supplies or armaments that had been helpful to Ryan's group.

This small Colorado redoubt had been stripped, containing only a few metal-framed beds and miles of empty shelving. From the scant evidence, Ryan and J.B. had deduced that the underground complex had to have been used for radar surveillance of both Earth and outer space.

The only section that had been left in full functioning order was the mat-trans unit and its control area.

Ryan picked his way quickly to the main entrance. If the door locking system had collapsed on both sides, then it would be the devil's own work to get everyone up the sheer face of snow-coated rock. And past the white worms.

The digital number code for closing the sec doors was still showing 2-5-3.

Ryan pressed the reverse 3-5-2 and waited for a few breath-stopping moments. He was reaching out to press the numbers again when he caught the faint sound of movement from within the surrounding walls.

Gears whirred and compressed air hissed, overlaid with an ominous grinding noise, as though grit had worked its way into the control mechanism.

With an agonizing slowness, the ponderous doors began to open.

A draft of even colder air came feathering into the already-freezing redoubt. A few flakes of snow were blown in through the widening gap and Ryan, crouching back with his gun drawn, was able to see feet.

Dean was first inside, his nose red, his eyes watering.

Mildred Wyeth was next. The black woman doctor was shivering as though she were suffering from an ague, and her skin had taken on a gray pallor. "Good to see you, Ryan," she said through chattering teeth. "I figure another hour or so out there and you'd have needed to chip us from the ice."

Doc came third. Despite his age, he was in surprisingly good spirits. "Chipper as a new-minted dollar, my dear Ryan," he boomed.

Fourth was Michael Brother. He was wearing the all-black assortment of clothes that had replaced his monastic gear—parka, quilted vest, shirt, pants and boots. On his right hip was the blaster that he'd initially been so reluctant to take, a Texas Longhorn Border Special, which was a small center-fire revolver that held six rounds of .38s. He was rubbing his hands together, his long black hair streaked with diamond beads of ice.

Krysty was last but one.

She looked anxiously at Ryan. "Had a bad feeling about a half hour after you left us, lover."

"Yeah. Coburn."

"Where?"

"Worms got him. Chilled."

"Rick Coburn's dead?" J.B. said, the last of the group into the complex. "Shame. Liked the man."

"Me, too." Ryan pressed the code to close the sec doors. "Wasn't my choosing."

The doors closed even more slowly than usual, the noise of grating metal growing louder. They finally stopped less than three inches from the floor.

"Take a thin man to get in after us," Dean said with a grin.

Now that they were out of the blizzard and safe from the threat of the posse of sec men, everyone was in better spirits. Even Mildred had warmed up, her double-lined denim jacket unzipped as they moved quickly toward the gateway, ready to make yet another jump into the unknown.

THE WALLS OF THE CHAMBER were armaglass, tinted a deep cobalt blue. Ryan stood by the door, ready to close it.

A mat-trans unit was found in almost all of the redoubts the companions came across, and they had been designed to transport people instantly from one gateway to another. Sadly the control codes to utilize the unit safely had been long lost. All that Ryan and the others knew was that the slamming of the heavy door would trigger the mechanism. They would become briefly unconscious, and then they would be somewhere else.

After he'd been time-trawled from November, 1896, Doc Tanner had been allowed brief access to research on Operation Cerberus, which had dealt with spatial "jumps." This had been a small part of the Overproject Whisper, itself a cog within the complex organization known as the Totality Concept. But he'd proved so stubborn and difficult that he had been jumped forward in time, from December 2000 into the anarchic horrors of the future world of Death-lands, where he'd met Ryan Cawdor, Krysty Wroth and J. B. Dix.

But even he knew nothing about how to work the comp controlled mat-trans units.

It was totally random.

"Everyone ready?" They were all sitting on the floor of the six-sided chamber, backs against the walls, ready for the unpleasant strain of the jump.

"I confess that I am never ready for this brain-scrambling exercise, but let us to it. Mayhap to somewhere a mite warmer than this place."

Ryan nodded at Doc, clicked the door shut and sat alongside Krysty.

Metal disks in the floor and ceiling began to glow, and a faint mist appeared, swirling like an ecto-plasmic shroud about them, closing over their bodies, clouding their minds.

Ryan shut his eyes and allowed the darkness to rise about him and draw him down.

Chapter Four

Dean Cawdor, Ryan's son by the amoral Sharona, was just eleven years old.

He was sitting at a round table, its top scarred by knives and burned by ancient fires. The room was dark, but it looked like the eatery of a frontier gaudy. But there was no sign of any jack sluts, so perhaps it wasn't.

Torches guttered and smoked in sconces around the earthen walls, making the atmosphere smoky and thick. The floor was crusted mud, scattered with a layer of filthy rushes, and Dean could see the glint of bones among the straw.

There was a wooden dish on the table, crudely carved, with a patina of grease around its sides. It held a dark and noissome liquid that could once have been some sort of soup. Now it wasn't anything at all.

As the boy turned his blue eyes to the dish, the surface stirred. Rancid platelets of dusty grease shifted, and the twin antennae of a large cockroach broke through, waving from side to side.

"Oh, fuck…" Dean thought for a moment that he was going to be sick, but he swallowed hard, forcing the bitter yellow bile back into his gullet.

The bug worked its way out of the gruel, its coppery flanks streaked with tiny gobbets of white lard. Immediately it was followed by another, and another, and another, each growing larger than the previous one.

It was screamingly obvious that the wooden bowl couldn't possibly hold so many roaches.

Dean tried to stand up and run away from the gibbering horror, but his legs were paralyzed, filled with icy lead, making it impossible for him to move.

He struggled to cry for help from his father, but his tongue was like a length of wet string, flopping uselessly between his dry lips.

The mat-trans jump wasn't going well for Dean.

KRYSTY WROTH WAS DEAD. She knew that because her brain was working all right. Trillions of electrical impulses were racing inside her skull, bringing messages from her body.

Her dead body.

Every single part of her was oozing into a liquid corruption. Krysty could actually feel her fingerbones pushing through her fingertips, feel her eyes melting back into their wind-washed caverns of bone.

The jump wasn't going well for Krysty.

J. B. DIX WAS WALKING along a narrow highway that stretched ahead of him like a ruled line. In the distance, thirty or so miles away from him, he could see irregular buttes and mesas, twisted and distorted, like a nightmare landscape from one of the old Western vids set in the valley of monuments.

The sun didn't move, hadn't moved during the hours that the slight figure, known as the Armorer back in the days of riding the war wags with the Trader, had been plodding across the empty wilderness. His beloved fedora was perched on top of his head, preventing his brains from boiling. Apart from that he was quite naked.

His body was covered in weeping sores where blisters had erupted and burst. Every single step was white agony on J.B.'s raw and bleeding feet.

And he was aware that he was starting to lose his sight to desert blindness.

It wasn't a good jump for J.B.

MICHAEL BROTHER WAS BACK in the reclusive community of Nil-Vanity, in the snow-tipped Sierras above Visalia, back in the communal dining room, with its scrubbed pine benches and tables. Outside, through an open window, he could hear the chanting of a group of novices working at the martial art of Tao-Tain-Do.

Michael had been an oblate, committed to Nil-Vanity almost from birth, spending virtually all of his nineteen years in the isolated settlement.

The leader of religious thought, Brother Font, sat opposite him, interrogating him on traditional questions of philosophical theory. This happened at frequent intervals, and Michael wasn't at all surprised to find himself back there in old California, reliving the experience.

"How when is up, Brother Michael?"

But he'd forgotten the answer.

The older man, face seamed by ninety summers and winters in the high country, waited patiently.

"I do not remember."

"Ah. Then the price must be paid for your foolish lack of attention, Brother Michael."

He reached out onto the table and took up a chromed tool that glittered in the sunlight. It had a hatched handle for ease of grip, and a honed blade five inches in length. The steel tapered toward a point.

Brother Font placed the needled tip against his own cheek and slowly pushed it through until it emerged the other side of his face. Blood flowed copiously from both wounds, trickling over the protruding tongue, filming the brown teeth.

"Don't do that, Brother!" Michael cried. "The fault is mine, and the punishment should also be mine."

The scalpel was withdrawn and laid again on the table, a ruby bead staining the white wood.

"I shall ask you a different and much easier question, my brother," said the old man. "I am sure you will know the response and I shall not have to draw the blade across my eyeball. Are you ready for it?"

"Yes." His mouth was dry, his palms sweating. "Yes, Brother, I'm ready."

"How when is up?"

The gnarled hand reached and took up the surgical blade again, bringing it toward the rheumy eyes.

Michael was having a bad jump.

MILDRED WYETH WAS at her own birthday barbecue and she was twenty-six years old, which meant it had to be the seventeenth day of December in 1990.

The garden of her home was filled with people that she knew, friends and relatives.

Her father beckoned to her from under the shade of a flowering cherry near the picket fence—her dead father, butchered by the Klan when she was less than a year old.

Much later Mildred had been allowed, by her mother, to watch the vid-news reports of the killing—a Baptist church, south of the Mason-Dixon line, smoldering ashes, smoke rising into the magnolias. For the rest of her life she couldn't stand the heavy scent of magnolias.

"You aren't alive, Daddy."

His hand stretched out to greet her, his face wreathed in a smile, just like in the photo that stood on the upright piano.

"I'm fine, my little honey," he replied. "Do I look to be dead?"

"No." Mildred's face was touched by tears. "No, Daddy, you look real good."

"That's 'cause I am. I'm 'fraid it's you who's dead, little girl."

Mildred was having a real bad jump.

Doc Tanner was deeply unconscious, mind and body floating in a bizarre limbo, barely connected to each other.

His inner eye kept receiving flashes of disparate images, like a child's revolving toy.

A saloon on East Forty.

Sawdust on the floor.

The unforgettable scent of naptha flares.

Beer and nickel cigars.

Sweat and fresh rain on tweed jackets.

Pickled eggs and knucklebones.

A raddled whore offering penny bunk-ups.

Spilled liquor on the metal bar top.

Fingers on the silver lion's-head handle of a cane.

But not one of the flickering flames of the memory film would remain long enough for Doc to grasp them.

Still, all things considered, it wasn't that bad a jump for the old man.

Ryan Cawdor was shaving, his face reflected in a polished convex mirror, distorting the room behind him, magnifying so that every pore gaped like a canyon and every hair was like a black cable.

The deep scar that ran vertically from the corner of his chillingly pale right eye to the corner of his mouth puckered the top lip so that it looked as though he were always on the verge of smiling.

There were deep lines etched around his eyes, nose and mouth, more furrowing his forehead.

Ryan was struck by the resemblance to his father, the late Baron Titus Cawdor, of the powerful ville of Front Royal up in the blue Shens.

When he'd been a young boy it had seemed that his father was a stooped old man. Yet he realized with something of a shock that he was now older, in his mid-thirties, than Titus had been at that time.

The straight razor appeared in the bottom of the mirror, moving toward the dark stubble that overlaid his skin.

Now there was reflection within the reflection, his face in the steel of the blade, showing again, distorted, in the polished mirror. Reflected again, in microscopic miniature, back into the razor.

He felt himself being drawn into the line of endlessly repeating visions of himself, sucked in so that his brain began to whirl and lose its focus.

Faces inside faces.

His empty eye, raw, threaded with capillaries leaked blood into the mirror, onto the razor.

Part of himself, the core of his soul, suddenly realized that the process was going to continue until there was nothing left, nothing that could be called Ryan Cawdor, just the spreading chasms of blackness that lie between the stars.

It was the worst of jumps.

Chapter Five

A far place away to the west, where the ocean and the mountains meet.

That was what the old Indian wisewoman, Sees All Ways, had told Abe weeks earlier in her tiny, dream-filled home, promising him that the rumors were a possibility. No more than that. Certainly not anywhere close to a probability. She wouldn't tell him that.

But the message was enough to give the ex-gunner from War Wag One real hope.

"Possibility," he whispered to himself, alone under a blanket near a narrow stream in the high peaks of the Sierras. "Possibility that Trader's still this side the dark river."

Abe had been the last one to see the Trader alive, when the legendary leader, ravaged by what everyone assumed was an insatiable cancer, had taken his final solitary walk into the shadows of the forest.

But, like Ryan and J.B., Abe hadn't necessarily believed that he was gone forever.

All three of them had ridden plenty long enough with the Trader to know that you never took anything that he said or did at its face value.

Not ever.

"Man believes his eyes and ears without raising a question's already gotten his ticket booked for the last train out to the coast" was one of Trader's almost infinite list of sayings that they all remembered.

Twice there'd been clues that had lifted Abe's hopes even further. He'd come across a half-breed with a dog sled ten days earlier, hauling the results of six months' trapping, and they'd shared a mutually suspicious night camp, neither trusting the other enough to want to fall asleep. Both men had eventually dropped off from sheer exhaustion.

The trapper had heard the stories and had a special interest in them.

"Met Trader once. Shit, he'd never remember a nothing fucker like me. But the old bastard sprung up from a Comanche trap out on the Platte River. Came in with his wags like the Almighty and all the angels. Wouldn't recall me, but I heard tales. Yeah, fucking right I did. Met a girl who said she'd been washing dishes in a hash cabin way over east in the greasy grass. Said a man had come in, wrapped up, face hid. Spoke low. Grizzled hair."

Abe had pressed him over the description of the lone stranger.

"Weapon?"

"Old Armalite. She said that it looked like he'd been using it as a crutch through a cesspool."

And the stranger hadn't been able to read the menu written up on the wall. The Trader had never got around to learning his letters and numbers.

The girl also said that a couple of Mex toughs had given her mouth. The old man had rested his half-smoked cigar on the edge of his plate, stood up, slow like it pained him, and thrown them both through the window.

"Without opening it. One bled to death. Other ran and never come back." The trapper had nodded. "Way she told it, friend."

It could have been the Trader.

The second clue was less positive.

This time the story wasn't filtered through another person's retelling, and it came from the lips of a dying man.

Everyone knew that a dying man would always tell you the gospel truth.

Believe that and you could believe just about anything.

Abe had been walking his stolen bay mare along a goat trail in the mountains when he heard a sound that was familiar enough in Deathlands. Someone was calling for help.

Abe took no notice.

The shout was repeated.

"I hear... hear you! For the sake of sweet charity help me. I'm done for."

The Trader had never really been all that big on the concept of charity.

"Charity's something that stupes do for losers."

Then again, Abe could think of dozens of times that the Trader had gone against his own inherent cynicism, using the discipline and firepower of the war wags to come to the lost, the weak and the abandoned.

"Please. I'm near done."

Abe carried a big stainless-steel Colt Python, and he drew the blaster, knotting the reins of the horse over the low branch of a wind-blasted larch.

"Triple-crazy doin' this," he muttered, as he picked his way cautiously down through the trees toward the river.

As soon as he saw the man, Abe knew that this one wasn't a trick.

Nobody destroyed their right leg in a massive, rusty bear trap just to try to fool a traveler into helping him.

Abe paused, still behind cover, glancing around to make sure that the dying man wasn't just live bait. The river beyond was flowing fast, slicing white over huge boulders that glistened with outcrops of mica. It was a beautiful scene, marred only by the sight of the helpless man, head turned toward Abe.

"I see you.... See you! Please..."

He was along to Abe's right, twenty yards or so. The trap was bolted to solid rock with a ring of red iron tethering it by a chain of heavy steel links. The serrated jaws had bitten into the man just below the knee.

Abe walked out into the open, the Colt questing before him like the tongue of a snake, tasting the air for any threat of potential danger.

Across the river a pair of red-breasted jays were clattering into the sky, noisily protesting his arrival. That was enough to reassure him. They wouldn't have been there if there'd been any other humans in the vicinity. He also noticed a huge mutie crow, as big as a white-headed eagle, sitting patiently in a pine tree, waiting for the meal that the dying man offered.

He looked to be in his thirties, with thinning hair, wearing a plaid shirt and jeans. Abe saw first that there was no sign of any kind of weapon.

''What happened?''

''Camping yonder.'' He pointed across the river. ''Four days ago. Mebbe five.''

''Alone?''

''Yeah. Just moving through. Doin' some . . . some hunting. Left my guns and knife in the camp. If I'd had...fuck...a blade I'd have cut my leg off. Rather than . . .''

Abe was close enough now to smell it, the familiar sweet-sour stench of earthly corruption. The rotting flesh was visible through the torn material of the jeans. The skin had blackened, the crusted blood attracting a host of small iridescent flies. The whole leg had swollen, up to the hip, the material of the pants stretched tight.

"Name's Abe," the dying man groaned. "What's your name, mister? Odd that. Seem important to know."

"My name's Abe, as well. You know I can't do..."

Something that resembled a laugh came croaking out. "Sure. Don't want salvation, Abe. All that's way in the fucking past. Want a bullet from that cannon you got on your hip. Smack...bang between the eyes."

"Sure."

As he stood over the dying man, the flies buzzed angrily away from the shattered leg.

"Shame you didn't come a few days ago. Might have saved my...my leg. Saved me."

"You got any messages, Abe? I'm heading up west toward the ocean."

The man's eyes rolled in their pain-filled sockets. "Always been a kind of loner. No women and no kids. Didn't see any...need for that. Now...one time around, Abe. Is all. Head north and west. Like he said."

"Who?"

"Never knowed his name, Abe. 'Round fifty or sixty. Like he'd been real sick. Been in dark...dark tunnel and come out other side."

"Describe him, Abe."

"Can't. Just put a bullet in my head and let me go on to rest."

"Soon." The Python was drawn and cocked. "Real soon, friend. Tell me about the man."

It was the Trader. Every painful detail of the description made Abe certain that it was the Trader.

"How long ago?" he asked.

For a moment he thought that the trapped man was gone. He'd slumped back, eyes closed, a thread of gummy spittle edging from one corner of his mouth.

But he rallied.

"Figure it at…two or three weeks…month mebbe. No longer than that. Give me a drink and a bite…bite of food, there's a good mate, Abe."

"Only be a waste," the ex-gunner replied, shooting him carefully through the middle of the forehead.

ABE KNEW that he was closing in on his target, knew it in his heart, felt it drawing him like the magnetic north draws the lodestone.

It crossed his mind that he ought to try to get in touch with Ryan Cawdor, let him know the news of this progress.

But he didn't have the least idea where Ryan and the others might be.

Or when.

Abe carried on north and west.

Chapter Six

Ryan Cawdor opened his eye. He had a filthy headache, and the inside of his mouth tasted as though someone had been sweeping buffalo chips into it. He closed his good eye again, sighing at how down-and-dirty ill he felt. His breath carried the flavor of puke, and he risked a second glance, expecting to find that he'd been sick all over himself during the horror of the recent jump. But his coat and jeans were still relatively clean.

Making a jump always screwed up your head, but this one had been something specially awesome.

"Fireblast," he muttered. "That was a bad jump."

"Bad as they get." Ryan felt Krysty's fingers touch his hand.

"How about you, lover?" He opened his eye and risked a shudder of movement to sit upright, finding that, as usual, the walls of the mat-trans chamber had altered color. The rich cobalt blue had changed to an insipid watery yellow. Ryan winced at that, finding that the sickly hue precisely matched the way that his churning stomach was feeling.

"Not so bad. But the dreams were…Gaia, but I'm glad to be out of them! Like a story that Uncle Tyas

McCann used to tell me back at Harmony ville. By a man called Poe. About a person buried while he was still alive.''

"Can't say my jump dreams were happy.''

"Doesn't feel so cold.''

Ryan took a deep breath. "Looks like the rest had a hard time of it.''

Dean was deeply unconscious, on his back, snoring loudly. There was a fresh bruise on his right cheek and blood at a corner of his mouth.

Michael was huddled up, head between his knees. His eyes were closed, but his lips gaped in a rictus of horror. He had been sick on the metal disks of the floor near his feet. His entire body was trembling.

Mildred was next along. She sat with her back against the armaglass walls of the hexagonal chamber, her eyes blinking as she started to come around from the blackness. Her cheeks were smeared with tears.

J.B. was also recovering. "Bad one,'' he croaked out.

Doc had suffered a nosebleed, crimson dappling his shirt and jacket. He was slumped to one side like a rejected puppet, his sword stick rolled onto the far side of the chamber.

At least everyone was still there and everyone appeared to be still alive.

From that point of view it hadn't been such a bad jump after all.

Doc WAS THE SLOWEST to stage a recovery. Mildred insisted that the old man remain sitting on the floor, legs straight out in front of him, making him take long, slow breaths while he kept his eyes closed.

She knelt at his side, carrying on a whispered conversation with him, reminding him of who he was and what had happened to him, where he was now and who all the others were in the glass-walled chamber. The long-term mind-scrambling effects of his earlier double time-trawling hadn't entirely left him, and it was certain that he would never have a wholly clear mind.

Finally he opened his eyes.

"I am fully cognizant of all of this, madam. I see no reason for you to treat me like some forgetful child. Would you assist me to my feet?"

Mildred smiled and helped him up, stooping to pick up the sword stick and hand it to him. "There you go, Doc," she said. "Ready for action."

Ryan glanced around at his six companions. "Usual condition red when I open up the door."

J.B. and Krysty already had their blasters out, and the others followed their lead.

"I smell the sea," Dean said suddenly, making Ryan pause with his hand already on the lock release.

"What?"

"The sea. Salt kind of smell, Dad."

Krysty moved to stand near Ryan, her head on one side, her eyes half closed. "Could be."

"What do you feel?" Michael asked. "I can't smell anything in here. Except sick and sweat."

"There's things out there. Far off. But..." She looked puzzled, her emerald eyes opening wide. "Sort of strange communication. Not human, but kind of linked to..." Krysty shook her head. "No. Can't get it."

"Danger?" J.B. asked.

"Don't think so."

"Well, everyone on full red alert. Right. Opening up the door now."

It eased silently back, revealing the familiar sight of a small anteroom. Like most of the ones they'd come across in the various redoubts that they'd jumped to, this one had no furniture. A single row of empty shelves stood along one side, and there was another closed door beyond.

But there was one significant difference.

The walls were furrowed with cracks, a network of connecting lines, some of them up to a half inch in width. The ceiling also showed signs of some potentially serious damage. A section in one corner had actually fallen down in a small pile of plaster and concrete rubble.

"I can smell the sea stronger, Dad."

"Think I can, too, son."

"I believe that the temperature is a little higher than in our previous location." Doc was holding his powerful Le Mat in a casual way, as if it were an ornament that had somehow appeared in his hand.

"Concentrate, Doc," Ryan said. "Going to open that door in a moment."

Mildred was examining the maze of crevices, touching them with the tip of her index finger. "Some serious quakes been going on here," she said. "If the gateway section's as deep as usual, then, well, I wonder what the rest of the redoubt's going to be like. How about power, for starters?"

"Most redoubts seem to have had all sorts of nuke backups. Some on direct drive from a master unit. Some had separate generators buried deep in the heart of the system. One thing we've learned about the jumps is that there's a kind of fail-safe."

"How's that, J.B.?"

The Armorer pushed his glasses back up onto the bridge of his nose. "Means we can't jump if the receiving mat-trans unit isn't functioning. It might be that it tries and fails, then relocates us at a second choice."

"I've wondered whether that might be what happens when we get a particularly bad jump," Krysty said.

"Could be," Ryan agreed. "Anyway, talk's cheap and—"

"Action costs," the others replied in chorus.

"Yeah. Keep ready, people. Here we go."

He opened the door into the main control-console room of the redoubt, where the salt smell was so much stronger that everyone could detect it.

THE CONDITION of the mat-trans control area was even worse. There was a fissure several inches deep running across one-third of the floor, exposing torn cables. All of the comp screens in that part of the room were down and dark. Many of the others were only working intermittently, lights flickering and digital displays showing an erratic mania.

The walls and ceiling also demonstrated the evidence of some massive earth movements in the vicinity.

During his life in Deathlands, Ryan had seen the results of the hideously intensive nuking of the continent. He knew that thousands of square miles of what had once been coastal California had slithered beneath the boiling tsunamis of the Pacific. The Great Lakes had changed beyond all recognition, and the old fault lines had opened and closed, destroying cities. Some volcanoes, extinct for ten thousand years, had also burst in terrifying life, spewing forth gushers of molten lava and superheated steam to ravage the land for a hundred miles around.

Even now, a century later, the planet still hadn't recovered from its torturing, and sometimes lurched and tilted in a ceaseless protest.

"Looks like we were lucky to finish up here at all," Ryan said. "State of this part means that it might all close down at any moment. Could be we should jump again."

"Not unless there is absolutely no viable alternative," Doc protested in his deep, booming voice. "I would rather endure immersion in a vat of cold goose shit.''

''I reckon hot goose shit might be worse, Doc,'' Dean said, making everyone laugh.

ONCE, UNCOUNTED MONTHS earlier, Ryan remembered trying to open a pair of sec doors within a redoubt and finding that it released a flood of water.

''I'll ease up the green lever to start the mechanism, J.B., and you watch out for danger.''

''Sure.''

''Any sign of the sea, or anything else tripledangerous, yell out and I'll drop the control again.''

''Right.''

Ryan turned to the others. ''Rest of you get back into the gateway chamber. If it's bad, we'll need to start another jump sooner than now!'' He snapped his fingers to emphasize the urgency of what he was saying.

Now they were ready.

J.B. was crouched, his face to the cold stone, his glasses in one hand, fedora in the other. Michael, back within the sickly yellow armaglass walls of the chamber, was looking after the Smith & Wesson 400 fléchette scattergun, as well as the Uzi.

''Five, four, three, two, one and *now!*''

The dark green lever moved as easily as a razor through a silk thread.

''Dark night!''

At the exclamation Ryan instantly threw the lever into reverse, bringing the sec door grinding down the inch or so it had already risen.

"What?"

J.B. grinned up at him. "Sorry about that, Ryan. Didn't actually see anything. But the smell of the sea was suddenly overwhelming."

Both men peered at the floor, but the dusty concrete was still bone dry.

"Mebbe we're close to water. Could be the redoubt's been split apart by quakes."

Ryan shook his head. "Can't see that."

"Why not?" J.B. looked around. "You figure that someone would've gotten in here? And the power'd probably have gone if there was that sort of damage."

"Yeah. Let's try lifting the door a little way again. If nothing comes in, I'll hold it around eight or nine inches. Take a look under it."

"What's happening?" Krysty shouted from the gateway chamber behind them.

"Nothing! J.B. reckons that we must be close to the sea. Real close."

The green lever raised the curtain of sec steel for a second time. As Ryan halted it, the Armorer flattened himself again on the floor.

"Anything?"

"No. But.... Yeah, I'm sure I can hear waves as well as smell them."

"Lift it all the way?"

"Why not?"

As the sec door neared the top of the entrance, Ryan heard a faint grinding sound, but it didn't check the smooth upward progress.

Now there was no doubt about it.

They could all hear the noise of lapping waves, and the dark green smell was almost overpowering.

The lights in the corridor outside were shining brightly away to the right, much less strongly to the left, where the sound of the water seemed closest.

They checked to the right first, Ryan taking the lead and J.B. bringing up the rear.

It didn't take long.

In less than fifty yards, with no side turns or doors, the passage ended in an impenetrable fall of rock, immeasurably solid, roof to floor, looking like it had been there for all eternity. Ryan turned around and they walked away to the left, around the slight curve of the passage. The sound and feel of the ocean became more overwhelming with every step.

They approached a sharp bend, with all of the lights beyond the corner gone out. The floor also began to slope steeply down.

Ryan stopped in his tracks at what he saw. "Fireblast! That takes the wheels off."

As the tunnel dipped, it disappeared beneath the sullen surface of black water, which filled the passage completely, tiny waves whispering on the concrete. There was a stained line on the floor a few inches above the edge that looked like it might be a high-tide mark.

There was no way forward.

Chapter Seven

"What time is it, Dad?"

Ryan glanced down at his wrist chron. "Few minutes after five in the morning."

None of them had been able to face the grim reality of tackling another jump without some sort of rest. Doc and Michael had been all for lying down right by the dark water and snatching some sleep there and then.

"Surely we shall be safe enough here, will we not? The corridor is sealed, and nobody can come through the gateway at us. Why not rest awhile, Ryan?"

"Suppose something came out of the water, Doc?"

"Ah, the works of the Lord and his wonders in the deep. More things in heaven and earth. I take your point, my dear fellow. Safety first."

So they'd all retreated into the control room of the mat-trans unit to catch up on some rest, behind the locked and sealed sec doors.

ALL OF THEM were used to discomfort, but none found it easy to get a restful sleep.

Eventually Ryan had risen, intending to check the high-water mark, finding that his son had silently joined him. He opened the sec doors, still exercising the same amount of caution, drawing his blaster.

"Nothing could get through, could it?" the boy asked.

"I don't know that. Isn't anybody could lay their hand on their heart and say there isn't some bastard mutie creature somewhere around Deathlands that couldn't come through after us."

But the surface was serene, barely showing the tiniest ripples of wavelets. In the darkness of the passage the pool was blacker than black.

"What if we swam through?"

"Where?"

The boy put his head on one side. "Well, Dad, if the redoubt used to be above land, then the corridor must go along farther. Some place."

"Could be a mile under water, Dean. Can't hold your breath that long."

"Yeah, I could. Triple-easy thing for me. Be a real scorchin' hot-pipe deal."

Ryan shook his head in mock sorrow. "There's times I can't understand a word you say, boy. Reckon I must be getting too old for all this."

"Yeah, you are." Dean glanced sideways, grinning at his daring. "But we..." Dean stopped talking, turning to stare down into the still deeps. "Dad?"

"What is it?"

"Thought I saw something."

"Fish?"

"Don't think so. Just that the water kind of swirled around. Like something big had gone by."

"Come on." He placed his hand on the boy's shoulder, feeling a sudden swelling of paternal pride, a momentary flash of what it might be like to settle down with Krysty and his son. It was something they'd talked about a lot over the past year or so, but it was always something for tomorrow.

For the right time.

The right place.

Hadn't happened yet.

EVERYONE WAS AWAKE stretching and moaning, feeling the damp warmth seeping into them.

Doc was leaning with his left hand on the desk, going through the motions of fencing with his sword stick. "Have at you, damnable poxy rogue. What, insult the king's musketeers, will you, fellow? My cold steel will pierce your yellow liver, you gutter-spawned whoreson coxcomb!"

Michael was watching the old man's antics, his jaw slack with utter bewilderment. He turned toward J.B. and Ryan.

The Armorer gave one of his rare laughs. "No, Michael. Hasn't gone trip-crazy. Not this time."

Doc wagged a warning finger at the diminutive figure. "Mock not the afflicted, John Barrymore Dix, lest ye also shall be mocked. I'm going to peruse the blue lagoon before being dragged once more into that hideous box of torture, from which no traveler returns." He pointed with the silver ferrule of his cane toward the gateway chamber.

"Mind if I come along, Doc?" Krysty asked. "Last breath of what passes for fresh air."

"My arm, dear lady."

They walked off together, Doc's stick counterpointing the clicking of the heels of Krysty's elegant blue Western boots.

Mildred took J.B.'s hand. "Let's go see the ocean, shall we? I'm not honestly in that much of a hurry to get my brains into free-fall."

"Why don't we all go?" Ryan suggested.

THE TIDE HAD TURNED, drawing the sea a short distance down the corridor.

"If we were in the Bay of Fundy," Doc observed, "we could rely on a tidal drop of thirty feet or more. Probably enough to get us out." He looked at the others. "I am become a stopper of conversations," he smirked. "Read about the Bay of Fundy in a magazine in a dentist's waiting room. I considered... Was that a light?"

"Where?" Ryan said, looking quickly over his shoulder.

"No, beneath the waves, in the midnight abode of King Neptune. In the locker of Davy Jones. Look!"

Everyone saw it this time. It was like a searchlight, far off and weak, showing itself in the depths of the water and then vanishing again, briefly turning the sea a lighter shade of paler green.

There.

Gone.

There.

"Gone," Dean said. "There's somebody down in the sea, signaling to us."

"Sunlight," Ryan said quietly. "Dawn outside. When we jumped here it was still dark in the world beyond the redoubt. That's the morning sun, showing itself through the waves outside. Filtered down here."

Everyone stood silent, thinking about the implications of that. Krysty spoke first.

"Can't be all that far."

Ryan nodded. "Mebbe."

"Could we swim out?" Mildred looked doubtful. "Shooting's my game and swimming's my shame. Put me in water and you got one big lead balloon."

"Risky," J.B. said. "No way of knowing what's out there. Could be a gap only a few inches wide. All kinds of rubble, metal and shit like that."

"I'll go," Dean offered without a heartbeat's hesitation.

Ryan knew that his son was able to swim like a fish, but the thought of sending him down into those menacing, unknown deeps was simply impossible.

"No," he said, flat and final.

"But I..."

He turned to the boy. "Remember what I've said before, Dean. Time to argue and a time to keep your mouth shut. Right now, it's time to keep your mouth shut.''

''Are we going to hazard our minds and our precious sanity on another of those too ghastly jumps?'' Doc asked. ''Or are we going to join together in a refreshing little morning dip in the breakers of the briny?''

''IF WE WERE CHARACTERS in a movie,'' Mildred said, ''I'd have found a hidden coil of strong, thin rope, and we could've tied it around your waist, Ryan, to pull you back to safety if you got into difficulties.''

Ryan hadn't bothered to strip off. He'd removed his long coat and knotted the arms into his belt, so that it trailed after him like a rejected royal cloak. He'd also taken off the heavy combat boots, tying the laces together and looping them into his belt. The SSG-70 Steyr rifle was hauled tight across a shoulder.

''Why not go through in your pants first?'' Krysty asked. ''Safer that way.''

''If it's safe, I'll get through with the blasters and all. If it's not I'll come back and we'll make the jump that everyone's so keen about.''

There weren't many things in Deathlands that frightened Ryan Cawdor. Fear was something that you learned to dominate, or you let it dominate you and spent your life cringing at every shadow in a dark corner.

But, in his heart, Ryan wasn't looking forward to diving into the unknown.

When he'd been about seven years old he'd been swimming with other lads from his home ville of Front Royal in the lower waters of a millstream. After the turbulence of the race it eased into a shadowed pool, fringed with scrub oak. The rusted remains of an ancient, predark truck rested in the deepest part there, and it was a challenge to swim down, lungs bursting and heart fluttering, to sit in the driver's cab and hold the rotted spokes of the old steering wheel.

His brother, Harvey, had been among the other boys.

As Ryan, the youngest in the group by three years, had taken his turn in the challenge, Harvey had dived after him and pushed the door shut, trapping him in the cab.

Ryan had never forgotten that moment of eye-popping panic, the terror making him gasp and choke in the muddied water. Only by an enormous effort of self-control had he overcome and dominated that fear and wriggled out of the narrow side window, cutting his arm and chest in the escape.

After that, he'd never been too keen on going swimming in unknown waters.

"I get through, and I'll dump some stuff and swim back here. If I don't return..." He let the words fall into the stillness, the echoes vanishing like a candle in the sun.

Ryan patted Dean on the head and nodded to Krysty, then he turned away, closing his good eye and concentrating on filling his lungs with as much air as possible. He drew in long breaths and held them, expelling them and repeating the process until he felt about ready.

Ready as he'd ever be.

He was prepared for it to be shockingly cold, but, to his amazement, the water was relatively warm, not far below blood heat.

His guess was that the corridor continued for a short distance and then the earthquakes must have broken down the outer walls and let in the ocean.

All he could do was follow the shimmering chimera of the light, ahead and above him.

He kicked and pulled, aware of the constricting walls around him. Seeming to close in like . . . like the cab of a long-sunk truck in a pool beneath . . .

Suddenly Ryan was conscious that he'd broken through and was swimming in an immeasurably vaster expanse of sea.

The dawn sunlight was brighter now as he squinted up toward the surface, lightening the dark blue green and promising him safety.

As Ryan thrust his way upward, weighted by the sodden length of his coat and the steel-capped boots, his ears caught a deep rumbling, like an echo of an ancient explosion, far, far off, that he seemed to feel vibrating in the marrow of his bones rather than actually hear.

But the feel of sun on his face and good air in his lungs drove all thoughts of the sound from his mind. He shook his hair from his face, looking quickly all around him.

It was like a vision of paradise.

A golden sun, rising from a perfect cerulean sky, sparkled off a limitless expanse of gentle ocean. About a hundred yards to Ryan's right was a stretch of beach, unspoiled yellow sand, with palm trees behind it. From where he was it wasn't possible to make out anything beyond the dunes. But there was no sign of any sort of life, animal or human.

Immediately behind him stood a tumbled pile of sea-washed stone, a hundred and fifty feet high and a quarter mile across.

Ryan could see that it was obviously the ruins of the remainder of the redoubt, totally destroyed. Generally speaking they'd found that the mat-trans units were in the deepest parts of the military complexes. That was obviously what had saved the gateway from the absolute ruin of the rest of the fortress.

He swam slowly to the nearest section of rock, hauling himself up. A jagged spear of corrode concrete, topped by the rusted stump of a metal girder, marked the place where he'd emerged from the undersea passage, giving him the guide for the return plunge.

Ryan laid the rifle and his pistol on the rocks above the reach of the swell and put the fur-trimmed coat alongside the weapons, his boots on top of it.

With the brighter sunlight piercing the water, it was easier to see his way back, the black circle of the opening clear against the lighter rocks all around it.

He burst into the gloom with a whoosh of air from his lungs.

HE, J.B. AND KRYSTY were the strongest swimmers in the group, though Doc claimed to have been a positive merman in his younger days.

It was agreed that Ryan would lead the way, shepherding Dean with him. Doc would take the plunge next, followed by J.B., who'd help the frightened Mildred. Krysty would then assist Michael through the underground siphon, out into the fresh air.

"Can you swim, Michael?" she asked him.

"Sure. Sort of. Had to at Nil-Vanity. But we never got too much chance to practice it."

She noticed that he was intensely nervous, his fingers knotting like a nest of small snakes. His lips were moving, and she guessed that he was trying to use some form of transcendental meditation technique to calm himself.

Her own heart was beating that small bit quicker, and she also began to fold away the darkness from her mind, washing away all fear and doubt and concentrating on the bright, warm sunshine that Ryan had described.

He and Dean had dived out of sight, and Doc was waiting a minute or two before taking the plunge. His frock coat was buttoned across his chest to avoid it snagging on any jagged outcrop as he swam through to safety.

"Farewell, cruel world, I am off to join Mr. Barnum and Mr. Ringling and... I disremember who the third of the great trio was."

"Get on with it," J.B. said.

There was hardly a splash as the old man dived elegantly into the dappled darkness.

"Nice. Now it's our turn. You ready, Mildred?"

"Long as you kiss me before we go, John."

Krysty found that her breathing had slowed right down. She watched Mildred and J.B., his glasses safe in one of the capacious pockets of his coat, jump hand in hand into the beckoning sea, vanishing immediately in a welter of bubbles.

"Us now," she said to Michael, aware of his hesitation. "Want us to do it holding hands?"

"Yeah. No, thanks. No, Krysty. You go and I'll be right on your heels."

"Sure?"

"Think so."

"Tell you what, Michael."

"What?"

"We'll make the jump together. But I'll let go immediately after we're in the water, and you can just kick out and follow me through and up."

"All right," Doubt made his voice sound high and strained. "Let's do it right away. Before I lose the last bit of nerve. Right *now!*"

Krysty was taken by surprise as he snatched her wrist and pulled her beneath the surface. She hadn't had any time to properly draw breath.

But, as Ryan had told them all, it was amazingly simple. The golden-green sunlight filtering down through the ocean beckoned to her, drawing her swiftly to the fresh morning air like a giant magnet. Just for a second she felt a shifting current beneath her, but it passed quickly.

For a few magical moments Krysty floated on her back in the warm sea, the salinity bearing her effortlessly upward. Her fiery hair floated around her like a halo spun from flames. Since her boots fitted tightly, she hadn't bothered to remove them for the short swim.

She saw Ryan and Dean on the rocks nearby, Doc sitting beside them, wringing water from his coat, his Le Mat already drying in the sun.

Mildred and J.B. were clambering out, still hand in hand.

Ryan was calling something out to her, but Krysty couldn't catch it over the gentle sound of the waves on the boulders.

"What?"

"Where's Michael?"

She turned quickly, but the sea all around her was quite flat and undisturbed.

Michael Brother had vanished.

Chapter Eight

Even before Krysty's mind had started to cope with the puzzle of where the teenager could be, Ryan was in motion. He stood and hurled himself back into the sea, drawing the panga from its sheath while he was in mid-dive. He struck the water in a burst of rainbow spray, right at Krysty's side, heading toward the spur of rock that marked the sunken entrance to the redoubt.

J.B. was a moment behind him, followed immediately by Dean, both of them in the air at the same splinter of a frozen second. Krysty drew breath, ready to duck-dive after them, when Doc exploded into the sea only a yard away from her.

Mildred remained on the rocky slope.

The sea was instantly tranquil again, the sandy beach completely deserted and serene. A large flock of gulls was wheeling and screeching far out toward the horizon, probably attracted by a shoal moving just out of her sight. Mildred watched them for a few moments, seeing them diving, most emerging with silver fish glistening in their beaks.

She stood, the small tight plaits of black hair dripping water down her cheeks and neck.

"Oh, sweet Jesus," she whispered, the light westerly breeze snatching away her words so that she scarcely heard them. "Help me, Lord. For I'm alone."

Doc's head broke the surface, his white mane pasted to his narrow skull, making him look like a bewildered and bewigged goat.

"No sign!" he bellowed, but the woman couldn't make out whether it was a question or a statement. But she shook her head anyway, holding her hands wide.

Then Krysty's bright red hair emerged into the sunshine. "Didn't take enough breath. Others gone back down into the redoubt. Don't worry, Mildred. That's where he'll be. Didn't want to make the dive."

She and Doc swam to the rocks and pulled themselves from the sea, both watching with Mildred for the first person with good news of Michael's safety.

"That's got to be a full minute," the black woman stated. "Got to be."

"He'll be . . ." Doc began, striving for a note of reassurance, the sentence dying stillborn as Dean, J.B. and Ryan appeared from the cavernous redoubt.

With no sign of Michael.

"Hadn't gone back out. Swam through and the stone...stone floor was dry." Ryan started toward the rocks. "Must've cramped up, I guess."

"Unless something took him," Dean called. "Maybe a great white shark."

It was possible.

"About ninety percent of shark attacks take place in less than five feet of water," Mildred said.

They were all out of the sea, staring around at the gently undulating waves. The flock of gulls had disappeared away into the north.

"Oh, Gaia!" Krysty's voice was harsh with shock. She stood, pointed toward the western horizon, her face frozen. "Look out there!"

There was a massive eruption about three hundred yards from them. White froth and a burst of spray soared into the sky. All that they could make out, writhing at the core of the thrashing disturbance, was a giant, sinuous shape.

"The mighty serpent, Uroboros!" Doc exclaimed. "By the three Kennedys, the seventh seal has been opened and the horrors of the grave released."

"Sea snake," Ryan said. "And—" He broke off as the creature crashed back into the water again, rolling to reveal, for the first time, its hideous head.

And the limp body of Michael Brother clasped in its blunt, hoglike jaws.

"Hundred feet long if the bastard's an inch," J.B. said quietly.

"He's not dead! He's waving to us." Dean turned to the others, frantic for them to share his sudden belief that Michael still lived.

"No, son," Doc said, laying a hand on the boy's shoulder. "Just the movement of that serpent's head, shaking him. Like Ahab returned, enmeshed with his great white nemesis, to beckon to us to all join him on his last long dive.''

The monstrous mutie sea snake was moving back and forth, its coils rippling through the white-crested waves. Its body was fully as thick as a stout man's waist, its head a good six feet in length. Its eyes were protected by hoods of bone, and its teeth glinted in the sunlight.

''Can't you shoot it,'' Krysty asked, ''with the big hunting rifle?''

''No point. Even a long 7.62 mm is only going to seem like a pinprick.''

''He's dead?''

Ryan shrugged. ''No way of knowing. If he had a good breath before he jumped in with you, then he could've held it long enough to... well, to have some kind of chance of being alive. For another minute or so, when that long fucker goes back under the sea.''

''Sharks,'' Mildred announced.

They could all see what looked like a dozen or more dorsal fins, slicing at high speed from around the point of the coast, heading directly toward the serpent. But the water was so disturbed by the monster that it was impossible to make anything out with clarity.

''Even if he's still living, they'll finish any chance for him.'' J.B. shook his head. ''Shame. There were some real good things about the kid.''

The great sea snake, looking like some nightmare from a prehistoric past, was still coiling, its head held high with the limp body dangling from its jaws. It seemed oblivious of the fast approach of the group of sharks, almost flaunting its helpless victim to the group on the piled debris.

Ryan was holding the Steyr, a small part of his mind considering whether it was worth trying a shot at the serpent's eye. But it would probably make it clamp its teeth shut on the teenager, or drop him so that the sharks picked up the meat.

The range was well within his capabilities, but the mutie creature was moving so fast, surrounded by a veil of sparkling spray, that it was impossible.

Mildred had also drawn her Czech target pistol, thinking along the same lines. She'd won a silver medal at the Atlanta Olympics in 1996 in the free-shooting, and the AKR 551, adapted to take the Smith & Wesson .38 round, was as good a blaster as you could get.

She caught Ryan's eye and slowly shook her head. "No," she said, her voice barely audible above the sounds of the ocean. "No, afraid not."

"The sharks are attacking the snake!" Dean yelled, standing higher up the pile of tumbled rocks than anyone else, giving him a better viewpoint.

Krysty scrambled up to join the boy, shading her eyes with her hand, holding her mane of sentient hair off her face.

"They aren't... Not sure if... No, they aren't sharks. I reckon it's a big school of dolphins. And

Dean's right. They're going at the snake, ramming it really hard. Serious attack.''

Now everyone could see it.

The Armorer replaced his glasses, then took them off again to try to wipe them clear of the salt mist.

The action was taking place well out to sea, but the violence of the dolphins' assault could easily be heard. They were driving in with their bottle noses, thudding into the heavy body of the mutie serpent. Every cracking blow made it shake. It was desperately trying to dodge the elegant, swift mammals, but they were far too quick for it, sliding past its clumsy movements, with others coming in on the creature's blind side.

"It's bleeding," Ryan said. "There's pink blood in the froth around it.''

The snake was now making a noise, a deep snuffling roar that could have meant pain or rage. It lifted its body high, its questing head turning blindly from side to side, shaking Michael like a little doll.

"Go, go, go!" Dean screamed, jumping up and down, shaking his fist at the monster. "Chill the bastard monster! Sink the fucker!''

"There's more dolphins coming." Krysty pointed behind the ruins of the redoubt toward the part of the coastal beach that was out of their line of sight.

Ryan felt the short hairs rising at his nape. There was something going on that he didn't understand, something that was out of kilter with normal life,

even "normal" life in the bizarre world of Deathlands.

It wasn't the nuke-mutated horror of the giant sea
snake that was so unsettling. It was the sudden arrival of the school of dolphins, seeming to act in con-
cert to try to rescue Michael. Where had they all come
from? And what had happened to unite them?

There were another eight or nine of the intelligent
creatures joining their brothers and sisters. It was
possible to hear their high-pitched fluting and whistling as they communicated with one another above
the distressed bellowing of the serpent.

The great mouth suddenly opened and the teenager's body dropped into the ocean, landing with a flat
splash.

As the mutie snake turned away, they could all see
that its flanks were streaked with blood from dozens
of wounds. It would have been impossible for one or
two of the dolphins to have harmed the giant creature on their own. But sheer force of numbers had
defeated it, driving it away. The loops of its body
coiled and swirled toward the west, driving a vee of
white foam into the water. A quarter mile off it dived
and didn't reappear.

But Ryan and the others were watching what was
happening behind the monster.

"Christ on the Cross!" Mildred's exclamation was
the softest whisper.

Ryan had readied himself to open fire into the
middle of the thrashing crowd of dolphins, suspect-

ing that they might have been victims of some sort of collective chilling madness, a gestalt desire to attack and try to slaughter any living thing that got in their way. If Michael *was* still living.

But he lowered the rifle, as all of them saw what had prompted Mildred's stunned amazement.

The dolphins were working together like a resuscitation team of paramedics, gathered around the drifting, unconscious figure, nudging it, until a pair of them swam beneath it, lifting Michael onto their backs, balancing him there.

"What on earth…" Doc was squeezing water from his frock coat's sleeves, gazing unbelievingly out to sea.

The activity around the slumped body was so intense that the ocean seemed to be boiling, almost as if there were an underwater volcano erupting.

Dean was on tiptoe, jumping up and down, his sodden clothes squelching. "They taking him, Dad. Taking him to the beach, keeping his head out of the sea!" His voice cracked and squeaked with excitement.

"Let's go." Ryan looked behind them. "Up over the top of this rubble. Must be able to find a way out onto the mainland. Get down onto the sand."

It wasn't that simple. The ruins of the redoubt were tangled, filled with a maze of rusting iron and steel, locked into clumps of stained concrete.

By the time Ryan found a clear path to the beach, the dolphins had all disappeared. And the body of Michael Brother lay still, just above the tide line.

He didn't look to be alive.

Chapter Nine

Mildred sat back on her heels, wiping damp sand from the tips of her fingers.

"He'll make it. Strong boy. Got a real slow pulse and respiration. Probably helped him all the time he was under the water with that bastard monster."

"Would have been paying his silver penny to the dark ferryman if it hadn't been for your skills, Dr. Wyeth," Doc said, bowing to her.

She turned to him, ready to snap back if she'd detected a hint of sarcasm. But the old man was solemn, no trace of a smile on his face.

"I didn't do much, Doc."

"Only saved his life, Mildred." J.B. squeezed her hand and kissed her on the cheek.

"Shucks, John Dix, I bet you say that to all the gals. It weren't nothing." Her mock Southern accent failed to cover her embarrassment.

Ryan was lying on the ground, honing the edge of his panga on a handy stone. "I reckon Doc's right, Mildred. Think he would have died if it hadn't been for you."

He licked his lips, tasting the salt dried on them. It had been a lung-bursting sprint, the soft sand sucking at his boots, slowing him. His arms had been working, knees lifting, struggling to reach the motionless figure.

Dean had been there first, his power-weight ratio so much better than any of the adults. But he hadn't known what to do.

Mildred had been running with all of her might, close on Ryan's heels, yelling out to the boy not to touch the unconscious man.

She'd stood over him for a dozen heartbeats, recovering her breath, trying to weigh his physical state. There was a lot of blood around his face and arms, and visible bruising on his throat. Yellow sand clotted in his hair and eyes.

But he was still breathing.

Just.

Mildred had used her fingers to clear his mouth, easing his tongue to one side. Stooping over him, she began to give him the kiss of life, helping his lungs to function after the massive trauma that had so nearly chilled him.

The young man had coughed, bringing up a mixture of sandy water and blood. His eyes had blinked open for a moment, then closed again. But his breathing had steadied.

While they waited for Michael to claw his way back to something approaching full consciousness, J.B. had been taking sightings with his tiny pocket comp sextant, working out where in Deathlands their latest jump had taken them.

"Hawaii," Krysty guessed. "Sand and palms and a warm sea. Got to be."

Doc coughed. "If my suspicions are correct, my dear, then I believe that we might be a good deal farther east than that. Perhaps not all that far from Florida."

The Armorer looked up from his calculations. "Florida it is, Doc."

"I knew it."

"But a hell of a long way south. Some kind of chain of islands heading toward Cuba."

"The Keys," Doc pronounced. "Of course. We are on one of the Florida Keys."

"I DON'T KNOW," Michael said. "I can't remember very much at all."

"Do you not recall the creature snapping you up, like Jonah in the jaws of the great whale?"

"Sort of, Doc. But only sort of. I took a big, big breath and dived in along with Krysty." He looked sheepish. "Truth is I was nearly crapping my pants at swimming under water like that. I was terrified of getting trapped."

Dean touched him on the shoulder. "How about those triple-acing dolphins?"

"No. As I was heading toward the sunlight, I can remember being hit. Harder than I'd have imagined possible." The teenager shook his head. "More power than there is in the world. It gripped my chest. I thought . . ." He hesitated. "I thought I was having a heart attack. I saw Brother Albert die like that, and he said it felt like his body was being crushed.''

He whistled between his teeth. Everyone was gathered around him, sitting in the soft sand. There had been no further sign of either the dolphins or of the wounded monster.

"Blacked out. Next thing, I'm flat on my back here. If it hadn't been for you seeing what happened and telling me, I'd have thought it had been a miracle.''

Mildred stood and stretched. "Way I look at it, Michael, that came as close to being a real honest-to-God miracle as I ever want to see.''

DOC AND MILDRED shared memories of what the Florida Keys had once been like, though neither of them had ever been down there. Both agreed on the extraordinary length of the sinuous archipelago, stretching out into the Gulf of Mexico, its single highway running along the coral outcrops, with dozens of bridges carrying it over the water.

Once Michael had recovered and was able to stand, albeit shakily, Ryan led them inland.

Which didn't take long.

Once they were over the bank of sand dunes, lined with feathery palms, they were able to see clear across to the glitter of the ocean on the far side, less than three hundred yards away beyond the corrugated remnants of the four-lane blacktop. There was a little scrubland, with some stunted mimosas on either side of the road, but nothing else—no stores, houses, churches, gas stations, phone booths, schools.

Nothing but the dusty ground and the palms and the ribbon of highway.

"Look at the ripples in that," Krysty said, as they walked closer to the blacktop. "Must've been a triple-strong quake to do that much damage."

The road looked as though it had been made from saltwater taffy, folded and refolded until it switchbacked as far as the eye could see to north and south.

"Think there's a bridge out up that way," Dean said, pointing toward the mainland.

"Be amazing if there were any bridges left at all after what must have gone down here at skydark." J.B. took off his fedora to wipe sweat from his forehead. "Hotter than nuke red this morning," he commented.

"Can't tell at this distance if it's wrecked or not." Krysty shook her head. "Is there any point in our exploring this wilderness, lover?"

"We don't have much in the way of food. Then again, we can always swim through into the redoubt and make a jump to somewhere else."

"Not me, Ryan," Michael said vehemently. "If people were still saying 'no way,' then that's what I'd be saying. Take a lot to ever get me swimming again."

Doc smiled. "That puts me in mind of an old friend who was terrified of swimming. A gypsy wench once told him he'd die in the water. So he always took a boat. Even to get across the smallest river." He paused.

"Go on, Doc," Ryan prompted, knowing from ample experience that the old man's story would have a sting in its tale.

"Well, I recall he was in a little yacht going across Puget Sound when an airplane crashed on the boat and they were all drowned."

"There weren't airplanes when you were around, Doc," Mildred reminded him.

"Quite right, my dear. Just testing you. It was a hot-air balloon, of course."

Everyone moaned in disgust, including Dean, though he didn't really understand why.

J.B. swatted away a persistent fly. "I'm not sure that the gateway doesn't seem a better bet than this pesthole. All sweat and bugs."

"I reckon we can walk a way farther. Mebbe south. Those dolphins came from that direction. Sort of interested in that. It's only—" Ryan glanced down at his chron "—still hours shy of noon. I say we explore some."

A HALF MILE SOUTH the road flattened and walking became easier. A light breeze sprang up from the west, cooling the sultry air and blowing away the flies and mosquitoes.

Even the Armorer conceded that he'd known some worse places than the Keys.

With no sign of human life, it was a rare opportunity to relax, guns holstered. Ryan and Krysty walked hand in hand, trailing fifty yards behind the rest of the group. She'd picked a delicate hibiscus flower and plaited it into her blazing hair.

"You look triple-ace, lover," he told her. "Beautiful... and happy."

"That's because I don't see us doing any chilling for a while. No blasters pointing around corners. We can sit and relax and not worry about suddenly getting a cold knife in the groin. Place like this comes close to ideal."

"Only close?"

"Yeah. Need some other folks within calling distance. Otherwise you get cabin fever."

Ryan nodded. "Guess so."

"And help in delivering the children."

He stopped and looked at her. "You aren't trying to tell me that..."

She smiled and kissed him on the cheek. "You need a shave, lover. No, I'm not expecting a little Wroth. Or a little Cawdor, come to that."

"One day."

Her smile slipped away like the last thin ice of spring. "One day, lover," she said quietly.

THE ROAD CLIMBED slightly upward, cutting off the view of the south. Dean, eager as ever, had run on ahead and had stopped on the crest of the rise. He turned to wave to his father and the rest of the group, calling for them to hurry up.

Eventually they could all look down.

The chain of islands spread ahead of them like a necklace of gold and emeralds, set in a perfect onyx sea. But what caught everyone's attention was the neat complex of buildings, dazzlingly white and clean, centered in a wired compound about a quarter mile ahead of them. From where they stood it was possible to see a number of people moving around, most of them concentrated in the section of the place nearest to the sea.

"There's dolphins down there," J.B. said. "Close by the quay."

"We going down, Dad?" Dean asked.

"Why not?"

Chapter Ten

The remains of a high wall were topped with the rusted coils of ancient razored wire, and a few white porcelain disks strung at intervals indicated that the barrier had once carried high-voltage electricity. Scorch marks along the tumbled stone showed that it had been attacked by high explosives, but luxuriant growths of ivy and orange-leaved creepers indicated that it had all happened a very long time ago.

A white-painted concrete marker had been erected at the side of what had obviously once been the main gate to the establishment.

"Looks new," Krysty commented. "Not like this boundary wall."

Doc was walking up and down, poking at the dirt with the ferrule of his sword stick, humming to himself, a slow, melancholic tune.

"What's the music, Doc?" J.B. asked. "Sounds kind of sad to me."

The old man nodded. "Sort of sad and sort of solemn, I would say, John Barrymore. It was once a concerto for the cello by a composer from nearly two centuries ago. An Englishman called Edward Elgar, if my memory serves me well."

"It's nice," Mildred said.

"Dull shit," Dean muttered, earning an angry glare from his father.

"Instead of being a double-stupe," Ryan said, "why don't you read what's carved on that stone marker?"

"Why should I?"

"How about I'll kick you flat on you skinny ass if you don't?"

The boy grinned. "All right, all right. Keep your cocksaver on, Dad."

He stopped and followed the incised writing with his finger, his lips moving slowly. A flock of gulls circled between him and the sun, making him look up.

"Come on," Michael said. "Do you want me to read it instead, Dean?"

"Go take a flying..." He stopped himself just in time, knowing how his occasional lapses into bad language upset and angered Krysty.

He read slowly, stumbling over some of the more difficult words on the stone.

"'Diviner'... What's that mean?"

"Just carry on with reading it, son."

"Sure. 'Diviner than the dolphin is nothing yet created. For they were in olden times men and lived along with mortals in their cities.' I don't get it."

"'Diviner than the dolphin is nothing yet created. For they were in olden times men and lived along with mortals in their cities.'" Krysty nodded. "I like that."

Ryan looked across the complex of buildings toward the glittering sea. "Those dolphins that came and saved Michael from the snake," he said. "Thought there was something kind of strange about them."

"Trained creatures, my dear Ryan? Such entertainments were popular for a time, toward the end of the previous century. Until the coming of wisdom that the shows using those beautiful creatures could be cruel."

"We going in, Dad?" Dean's patience level was swiftly exhausted.

J.B. pointed ahead. "Looks like they're organizing a reception committee for us."

Inside the ruined wall was another, newer line of defence. Sun-bleached concrete, salt-stained in places, stood about eight feet high, topped with what looked like either splinters or jagged metal or broken shards of glass. Seven or eight white-clad figures had appeared out of what looked like the main entrance to the place.

"Be fine against dwarfs armed with bows and arrows," the Armorer commented. "Not much against anyone seriously wanting to find a way in."

"They got blasters," Mildred said, her hand on the butt of her own target pistol.

"Let's take it careful." Ryan unslung the rifle from his shoulder and snapped off a quick round toward the oncoming group of people, making sure that the round hit the sandy ground a good twenty paces in front of the leading figure and five paces to the left.

The white coats stopped, some of them throwing themselves dramatically to the dirt. One leveled what looked like an old M-16, its stock bound with silvery wire. But the man who appeared to be the leader turned and snapped a command and the weapon was lowered.

He then called something to his half-dozen followers. Those who'd dropped at the shot now rose, sheepishly brushing orange sand from their clothes.

"You have made your point, stranger!" The voice was calm and gentle, yet it carried effortlessly to Ryan and the others. "Is there to be chilling?"

"Not unless you start blasting away. We don't mean any of you any harm." Ryan whispered to his companions out of a corner of his mouth. "Take them all out at the first sign of trouble. *All* of them, right?"

"Then come on down. I see you have an excellent arsenal of armament."

"We got enough," Ryan replied.

Now that they were closer they could see a rectangular hand-painted sign nailed to the inner wall, at the side of the iron-bound, wooden door. Mark Tomwun's Institute of Peaceful Oceanographic Research.

"Dolphins again," Krysty said quietly.

The man had left the rest of his group, advancing with open arms toward them. He was about six feet

tall, looking lean and muscular. His face was deeply
suntanned and he wore rimless glasses, perched on his
aquiline nose. Ryan guessed that he was about mid-
forty. Like the others he was wearing a knee-length
white coat, similar to those Ryan had seen on old vids
about doctors or scientists.

He didn't seem to be carrying any kind of weapon.

Ryan held up a hand, checking the others. "You
run this place?"

The man stopped, smiling, his head slightly on one
side. "Indeed I do. Oh, yes. My name is Mark Tomwun. They—" he waved a casual hand behind him
"—are some of my assistants."

"We could use some food and drink. Be happy to
work it off for you."

"Wouldn't dream of it. Strangers are welcome."
Tomwun shrugged his shoulders. "Perhaps I should
qualify that a little. Any stranger who comes with
hope, love and friendship in his heart is *very* welcome."

"Guess that's us," Ryan said.

"Your names?"

Ryan introduced them, one by one. There were a
few places in Deathlands where some of the names
could have brought trouble. Certainly he and J.B. had
a blood price on their heads in a scattering of frontier pestholes from Portland, Maine, to Portland,
Oregon.

"I'm Ryan Cawdor, from the Shens. Doing some
traveling. My son, Dean, and my friend, Krysty

Wroth, from Harmony ville. This is John Dix. Dr.
Mildred Wyeth and Dr. Theo Tanner. And Michael
Brother."

Tomwun nodded to each of them, showing particular interest in Mildred and Doc.

"Doctors? You mean you have some grounding in
the sciences or in medicine?"

"I was a specialist in microsurgery and cryogen-
ics," Mildred replied.

"I fear that my own doctorate will be of precious
little use in these parlous times. My science skills are
not truly applicable to this brave new world in which
we live."

"I don't quite catch all of that, Dr. Tanner,"
Tomwun said, "but I think I understand the drift."

"What do you do here?" Krysty asked, but the
man wasn't listening to her. Instead he was staring
intently at Michael.

"Of course. Outlanders that came from under the
sea. You must somehow have found a way into and
out of the old redoubt. I shall be interested, perhaps,
to talk a little about that with you. Perhaps next time
you'll be more careful for the big serpents of the deep,
young man."

"How do you know about that?" Ryan asked.
"Someone with a glass on the dunes?"

"No. There are more things—"

"In heaven and earth than are dream't of in your
philosophy, Horatio," Doc concluded.

The white-coated man's face brightened like the first flush of sunshine after a summer thunderstorm. "Ah, a person of culture, Doctor! Rara avis in these parts."

Doc grinned, rubbing a hand over his stubbled chin. "Mayhap a little hygiene and nourishment before the culture, my dear fellow? What think you?"

"I think that sounds like an excellent idea."

Ryan held up a hand, stopping Tomwun from turning to lead them toward the buildings. "You didn't answer my question. How did you know about Michael and the snake?"

Tomwun held out his hand like a pesthole jolt dealer offering a Sunday bargain. "If you stay with us for a day or so, Ryan, then you'll learn the answer to that and to many other questions. You must trust me."

"Last man who said that to me tried to cut off my balls with an ivory-hilted razor the same evening. Trust's something you earn, not something you offer around like it fell off the back of a trade wag."

"Mea culpa, Ryan Cawdor. Mea maxima culpa. All the blame is mine."

"We going in, Dad?" Dean whispered.

"Look that way. Keep red-eyed, friends."

So they followed the lean figure into the grounds of the Mark Tomwun Institute of Peaceful Oceanographic Research.

Despite the word "peaceful," Ryan kept his hand close to the butt of his SIG-Sauer.

Chapter Eleven

Five days had passed. It was 6:18 a.m., and Ryan had just been awakened by Krysty, blinking awake in the neat, white-painted room that they'd been given by Mark Tomwun.

She had wriggled down between the clean cotton sheets of their double bed, her fiery hair brushing over his chest, across the muscular walls of his scarred stomach. The bright tendrils plaited for a moment in the dark curls that sheltered his groin, then her lips were caressing his penis, arousing it into instant, swollen life.

Ryan felt his love and his lust breaking the surface together, like delighted twins. His legs straightened and gave himself up to the exquisite sensations of Krysty's tongue and lips.

His breathing quickened and there was, for a moment, the desire to let it race on to its ending. She was taking him deeper now, swallowing him, her right hand cupping his balls, one finger probing delicately behind. His hips came up, and he could feel the tension building.

Krysty was pressing herself on him, her nipples hard against his spread knees.

"No," he whispered, reaching down to touch her on either side of the throat.

"No?" Her voice was thick with arousal.

"No. I'm nearly over the edge already, and I want to do it for you."

"You first, lover."

"Together," he insisted.

She eased herself back up him, his diamond-hard erection pushing against her breasts and belly. Her strong fingers insinuated between them, guiding him home into her warmth, sighing with her pleasure.

"Good," she breathed.

Ryan let his breath out slowly. One of Krysty's mutie traits gave her control over her internal muscles, which gave both of them greater satisfaction. They fluttered all around him, tightening and then loosening.

Krysty lay on top of Ryan, flattened against him. She nibbled at the side of his neck, her breath sweet in his face.

Her weight kept him pinned to the bed, giving him little scope for movement. But he could flex his thigh and buttock muscles, lifting himself a couple of inches.

Enough.

THE INSTITUTE HAD its own power generator, operating from a water turbomill linked to a wind-and-tide complex.

Ryan swung his legs out of bed and padded naked across their room to the coffee-sub maker on the wall.

"Nice ass!" Krysty called, giving him a low whistle.

"I bet you say that to all the boys." He switched on the machine, and it began to bubble almost immediately.

"Good loving, lover." Krysty stretched her arms above her head, smiling at him.

"Always is."

"Always?"

Ryan stood for a moment, head on one side while he considered the question. "Yeah. Yeah, always," he said.

"Same for me." She laughed, brushing away a fringe of bright hair. "Only thing about being here with Mark and his merry band, it makes a real nice change to be able to make love in a real bed in a real room without having to keep one hand on your cock and one on my Smith & Wesson."

He spooned out the dark, granular powder into the two plastic mugs and carefully added the steaming water, stirring with a chromed spoon.

"What do you reckon about him?"

"Tomwun?"

"Yeah." Ryan sniffed at a jug of milk. "This smells all right to me."

"You've asked me about him three or four times a day since we got here, Ryan."

"I know. There's something…" He passed her the pale blue plastic mug. "Careful."

"Thanks, lover," she replied, putting it down on the small table at the head of the bed. "I can't *see* anything about him. Can't *feel* anything wrong, either."

"But?" He joined her in bed, sipping at the light brown, bitter drink.

"But what?"

"There was a 'but' in there."

Krysty nodded. "True. I sometimes wish that you'd stop knowing me quite so well, lover."

"I've been thinking about the time here. Nothing to set the danger signals running." He rubbed his chin. "But I still don't feel right." He stretched out flat, biting at his lip, trying to identify just what it was that made him feel, occasionally, so peculiarly uncomfortable.

THE COMPANIONS had discovered that there were thirty-two permanent staff at the Institute of Peaceful Oceanographic Research; twenty-six men and six women. But that didn't include the enigmatic director himself.

Despite his initial reservations, Ryan had been happy enough to allow his group to split up and explore on their own, even permitting Dean to go for a boat trip out onto the crystal waters. Nobody had made even a passing suggestion about handing in their powerful array of blasters, far superior to anything they saw around the institute. So everyone walked around fully armed.

By the third day everyone felt a little more relaxed.

By the fifth day, only Ryan and J.B. still wore their pistols.

If they were going to be treacherously attacked, there'd been too many chances.

So, by the fifth day, every member of Ryan's group had their own good memories.

Chapter Twelve

Dean had never seen such miraculously clean water in his entire life.

One of the younger men from the institute, Chuck Cybulski, was pulling on the oars, easing the fifteen-foot-long boat out from the quay, into the placid Lantic.

Like almost everyone in the place, Chuck wasn't particularly unfriendly. But he wasn't exactly outgoing, either. He was content to row steadily, taking them toward an outcrop about six hundred yards from the shore.

The dolphins appeared almost immediately, five of them, their bottle noses bursting from the sea in a welter of shimmery spray. Dean leaned over the side of the boat and watched, entranced by their grace and elegance. They dived under him rolling belly-up, then seemed to be taking part in a complicated dance routine, twining and curving around one another. Finally they adopted a white-boned arrowhead formation ahead of the bow of the small skiff.

"Diviner than the dolphin is nothing yet created," Chuck said. "That's what brought us all down here to work with Professor Tomwun. And that's what keeps us here, despite the problems.''

Dean glanced up from his seat in the stern. ''What sort of problems?''

The man's blue eyes blinked several times as he squinted across the sea. ''Nothing bad, kid. Just some folks around the Keys don't take to us or what we're doing here. No problem.''

Dean noticed that Chuck's eyes didn't meet his. But he was having such a good time he never thought much about it.

ON THAT SAME MORNING Mildred and J.B. had walked along the beach, out beyond the protected perimeter of the base. They strolled hand in hand, and the woman kicked off her calf-length, black leather boots, carrying them, grinning at the feel of the sand beneath her toes.

''It's like being a child again, John.''

''I wouldn't know. I don't think that I was ever much of a child.'' He smiled, briefly. ''Though there was a shit lot of sand back in Cripple Creek where I was born.''

''You're much more relaxed these days than you were when we first met.''

''You reckon?''

''Sure.''

''Then that means you're a good influence on me, Mildred, doesn't it?''

She stopped and shook her head. "I never met a man who didn't go fishing for compliments, John. Course I'm good for you. I massage your neck and shoulders, nights. What used to be spun glass is now warm molasses. You aren't so edgy. You even smile now and again. Not all that often, but more than you used to. Smile from the Armorer was like tolerance from the Moral Majority."

"What?"

"Oh, sorry. Before your time, John. They'd have been real at home here in Deathlands, most of them."

J.B. knelt, picking up fragments of broken shells and lobbing them into the lapping waves. Mildred eased herself down beside him.

"What do you make of this place, Mildred?"

"The beach?"

"No. Institute. Trained fishes. Killer whales and dolphins and all that."

"There were people doing that sort of research, way back before the holocaust and skydark," she replied.

He nodded. "Tomwun told me that, when he was giving us his big guided tour."

Mildred lay back, her hands behind her neck, staring up at the sky. Way above, her eyes caught the flicker of movement of a vast white bird, circling effortlessly on a thermal rising from the heat of the land.

"That must have a wingspan of... of fifty feet. At least." She whistled softly. "Still can't really get used to some of these amazing mutie creatures in Deathlands. Sorry, John. What was it you were saying?"

"Dark night! I don't know, Mildred. All his talk about the good work. The way they've helped species survive from the brink of extinction."

"I'm sure that's true. I remember a piece in...must've been *National Geographic*. Said several of the dolphin family were in real danger of being killed."

"Hunted like the whales."

"No."

He stopped throwing the shells and lay back, his left hand reaching for her right hand, holding it tightly. "Then what chilled them?"

"Pollution, John. Pesticides that were supposed to have been banned years before, turning up in tissue samples. Stuff like DDT and a load of poisons. Then there were the big drift nets. What were they called?"

"Don't know." His other hand was on her breast, reaching inside her shirt.

"Mmm, that's nice. Gill nets. That's what they were called. Very fine, covering thousands of square yards of ocean. Picked up everything living, regardless of whether it was any use or not."

"Even big fishes?"

Mildred raised herself up on one elbow, looking cautiously around. But they were in a quiet, natural hollow, out of sight of the institute. And the companions had already noticed that none of the occupants of the complex seemed to wander too far from its fragile security.

"They aren't fishes. You know that."

"Seems crazy. Triple-stupe. Call a dolphin an animal. Look, there's a group of them out there."

It was a school of fifteen or twenty bottlenoses, curving around one another as they played together, looking like some sort of bizarre single creature.

"Where were we?" the Armorer asked, snatching the moment to remove his glasses and fold them carefully into the safety of one of his jacket pockets.

"You were rubbing my tit, you dirty old man. And that was getting me feeling kind of hot for you. And it looks like your pants have gotten too tight for you, all of a sudden." She touched him very gently.

And their talk about nets and dolphins and the Institute of Peaceful Oceanographic Research was forgotten for the next hour or so.

MICHAEL WAS HAVING a lesson in dolphin-speak from the youngest woman on the team. Miranda Thorson was only seventeen, but Tomwun had introduced her as being the most valuable and exciting person in the place.

"Already we can understand some elements of the dolphins' speech," he'd said. "Distress and hunger. Recognition of other members of their social group. And even good old clinical lust." He waited for the expected laugh, which dutifully followed. "But listening isn't the same as talking. And that's where Miranda here comes in.''

Now the two teenagers were together in a small research tank, part of the dozens of different-sized pools that had been constructed on the oceanside of the institute.

The water was a little over four feet deep, clean and filtered, drawn in from the Lantic a few yards away. Miranda was wearing a skimpy two-piece bathing suit in white cotton. When it had been dry it had been revealing. Now that it was soaking wet, Michael was unable to ignore the fact that it had become almost transparent. It revealed the shape of the young woman's breasts, the nipples standing out like cherries in the cool water. Lower, the prominent vee of her pubic mound.

He had borrowed a pair of dark green shorts. To Michael's inordinate relief, they concealed far more than they revealed. Even so, he found himself cupping both his hands protectively over his groin.

They had two young dolphins in the pool with them.

''They aren't like most of the others I've seen out at sea, are they?''

She shook her head. ''Right. Those are mainly bottlenoses. These are smaller, black, with kind of round noses. These two are called Eighty-one and Ninety-six.''

''Why not give them real names.''

Miranda sniffed contemptuously. "Human names? Like Marsha and John? That's called anthropomorphizing, Michael, and it's not what we do here with them."

The dolphins were swimming in tight, complex patterns, the smallness of the enclosure bringing them in constant contact with the two humans. Their skins were like hard silk, brushing against Michael's legs and stomach.

"What kind are they?" he asked, hoping to deflect Miranda's disgust over his last question.

"Vaquitas."

"What?"

She spelled it for him.

"What do we do now? I can hear the weird noises they're making from above the water."

The teenager realized immediately that he'd screwed up again with Miranda.

"*Weird noises!* Just what the fuck is that supposed to mean, you stupe outlander?"

"I'm sorry. Just that—"

"The combination of clicks and whistles is unbelievably sophisticated, and I can decode it."

"I'm sure, but—"

She wasn't to be deterred. "You shit for brains! Each one has its own signature call. When they want to talk together, they'll imitate each other's trade call, like opening up a kind of line between them."

Her anger seemed to have communicated itself to the dolphins, who were circling faster, their tails breaking the surface in bursts of blinding spray.

"All right, all right, Miranda!" Michael shouted to make himself heard above the splashing water and the high-pitched sounds of the disturbed creatures.

"No." Her rage seemed to be increasing rather than diminishing, making her pretty open face contort into a malevolent, threatening mask.

Michael had already been living long enough in Deathlands to be aware of muties, creatures whose gene bank had been ravaged and spoiled by the appalling nuking of nearly a century earlier and who had developed and mutated in sometimes horrific ways. Like the monstrous snakes that had nearly sent him down into the long sleep.

Now, for the first time, it crossed his mind that Miranda Thorson could be a human mutie.

"I'm getting out," he said, moving toward the side of the tank.

"Limpdick bastard! I can speak to them. Me. Nobody else, not even Tomwun, can do that. I'll show you what I can do. This is what I'm here for. Part of the big plan!"

Michael wondered what the "big plan" could be, but it was driven from his mind.

Miranda took a deep, sucking breath, and dropped her head below the surface of the water.

For a strange, frozen moment, the two dolphins became still, floating as if they'd been plunged into suspended animation, their muzzles turning slowly toward the stooped figure of the young woman. Michael could see her mouth opening and closing and hear the muffled sounds of the mammals' clicks and whistles, a sharp burst of incomprehensible noise.

Then she straightened, her face flushed, eyes mirror-bright. "Now you'll see."

As he began to back slowly away, the pair of dolphins erupted into galvanic action, coming in at him from opposite sides of the tank, one near the surface, the other close to the bottom. Though his own reflexes were lightning-fast, Michael had no chance at all to defend himself.

Eighty-one struck him just above the ankles, knocking him completely off balance, while Ninety-six drove its blunt snout into his ribs, punching all the breath from his body.

Michael went under and stayed under, kept there by the continuing pressure exerted by the two creatures, battering at him, using their weight and power to hold him down.

For the second time in a few days Michael felt the air disappearing from his lungs, his mouth and nose flooding with cold salt water and the darkness swimming into his brain, suffocating him.

For the second time in a few days he opened his eyes to discover that he wasn't dead after all, staring up into the faces of Ryan and Krysty as he lay on his back on the sun-warmed concrete at the side of the pool. When they helped him to his feet, Michael walked unsteadily and looked at the placid, unruffled surface. The dolphins had vanished and there was no sign of Miranda.

"You look like you lost an argument with a mess of bouncers at a pesthole gaudy," Ryan said.

"Should get Mildred to check out some of those bruises. Could've cracked a rib. And get some ointment on those scratches." Krysty patted him on the shoulder. "Then you can come around to our room and tell us just what happened."

"Nothing happened. Just me being stupid. Miranda was going to show me how she can speak to those dolphins. I teased her and she—"

"Showed you," Ryan finished, shaking his head at the deep purple bruises just above the line of the shorts, some of them leaking a trickle of watery blood. "Yeah, Michael, she sure showed you."

DOC IMMEDIATELY FELL in love with Mark Tomwun's Institute of Peaceful Oceanographic Research.

For an old scientist like him, it was almost like returning to his roots. Though a lot of the laboratory equipment was crude and rudimentary, the atmosphere of research was like a breath of life to him.

For the first day Tomwun treated him like a valuable specimen that he'd just acquired. But he quickly realized that Doc knew almost nothing about dolphins. Nothing about marine biology. Nothing about mammalian nervous dysfunctions.

And so he lost interest in Doc.

But it didn't much worry Doc. He said to Ryan that it was liberating to be able to walk around and watch other people at work in the range of labs.

"I do believe that I could watch others at work for the duration of the livelong day and never find myself bored for even a single moment."

All of the friends had been given the complete run of the whole complex, with no doors locked against them, except for a couple of windowless buildings that stood separate from the rest, adjoining the quay.

They were kept closed. Mark Tomwun explained that they held highly delicate equipment, much of it dating from way back before the apocalypse.

"Balances. Hydrographic scales. Dilithium crystals. Very susceptible to damp and salt. Some comp processors that we haven't quite managed to set to functioning yet. I'm sure that you understand."

But by the fifth day, Doc started to have the odd feeling that some things were being kept secret. Every time he walked into any of the labs, or wandered along, cane tapping on the sand-strewed stones, he was beginning to have the strange feeling that he was being watched.

"Persecution complex, Theo," he said sternly to himself. "I'm not mad, they truly are out to get me." He paused. "Was that the way the old joke went? I disremember. Best that I don't tell Cawdor. I rather think that the dear fellow suspects I'm already a few sandwiches short of a full picnic. A letter or two shy of a complete keyboard.''

He spun, like a skater pirouetting, and caught a glimpse of the pale blur of a face, visible for a moment behind a twitched blind.

"There," he said, nodding to himself. "I'm certainly not mad. Not even when the wind is northeasterly and a hawk is a handsaw. A fellow of infinite jest. I knew him, Emily. Oh, sweet Lord! Emily, my dearest wife, if only..." Great gobbets of tears coursed down Doc's chin, through the silvered stubble that clung stubbornly to the seams and wrinkles in his neck.

He wasn't even conscious that he was still walking, now picking his way in silence through banks of soft, drifted sand, past the fringes of the gently lapping sea.

"All a dream. I'm always dreaming. All I have to do is to dream. To dream a little dream. Last night I had the...sweet dream strangest baby. I must keep my dreams as clean as silver. Clean dreams.''

His lips moved, but the words were washed away in the mild Florida westerly wind. Doc fumbled for his blue swallow's-eye kerchief and dabbed at his bloodshot eyes, drying his wrinkled cheeks.

"Upon my soul. This weeping dew that rectifies all wrongs doth wash away my oft-remembered woes."

Doc tripped and nearly fell, the lion-headed sword stick dropping from his fingers as he stumbled to his knees. The shock of it brought him lurching back to something approaching normal sense again.

"Where am I going? Where have I come from?" He stood and brushed sand from his pants. He picked up the cane, smiling. "The two greatest questions of all mankind. Where do you come from and where do you go? Cotton-eyed Joe. Now what in perdition did I stumble and fall over?"

He realized that he was on a long-abandoned path that wound its way between a lichen-striped dry dock and a tank filled with peculiarly murky water, leading him to the rear of the two locked buildings.

The ones that Professor Tomwun had said were filled with delicate research material.

Doc reached out the toe of one cracked knee boot and pushed at the protruding edge of whatever it was that had tripped him up. He paused and glanced behind him, then the other way. But that part of the institute was deserted and silent.

"What have we here? Upon my soul, it seems to be some sort of packing material. Property of the United States Navy. Fissionable. What can that mean?"

More of it was visible, the stenciled lettering faded with age, but still legible.

"Bantam Contact Missile," he read.

The jagged piece of desiccated wood held no more information, beyond the beginning of a series of letters and numbers.

None of it made any sense to Doc Tanner. He kicked sand over the rubbish and began to walk quietly back to his friends.

"Must be careful where I step," he warned himself. "Or I'll trip over...over whatever it was. By the three Kennedys, but my memory is really worsening." Doc began to whistle.

Chapter Thirteen

"Used to be a missile base here, you know."

Mark Tomwun was giving a small, candle-lit dinner party on the evening of their sixth day at the institute.

They ate at a long, linen-draped table in a narrow vaulted room off the professor's main quarters. A couple of the younger women acted as waitresses for the meal, cooked in the well-equipped kitchens of the institute.

The ocean provided virtually all of the food, starting with sand crabs. The meat had been mixed with herbs and butter, then replaced in the shells. Next came some freshwater trout, baked en croute with sweet potatoes and black-eyed peas, served with saffron rice. To accompany it, Tomwun offered a range of home-brewed beers and even a couple of halfway decent wines, a strong red and a delicate blush.

"Missile base?" J.B. repeated. "Didn't know they had anything this far south, down the Keys."

"Indeed. More of this adequate pink wine, Krysty? No? Very well."

"Where do you get your provisions from?" Ryan wiped his chin where a streak of peppery sauce had dribbled off his spoon.

"Most from Father Neptune."

"Sure. Father Neptune doesn't have cows or a bakery or a vegetable garden or a brewery."

Tomwun leaned back in his chair and laughed. "Right on, Ryan. Out of sight, my friend. No, of course you are correct. We do grow a few herbs and basic items ourselves, but the Keys can be a merciless place in winter storms. To support ourselves we trade where we can. Both with the fishermen who live a little farther north and with settlements and small villes up on the mainland of what was Florida."

"Missiles?" Doc said, musing. "I do not quite remember why, but I feel sure that this rings a tiny tintinnabulation in the distant belfries of my memory."

Ryan had traveled long enough and far enough with Doc to know that his mental stability was, to put it mildly, variable. But that didn't mean that you automatically ignored everything that the old man said.

"You seen something, Doc?" he asked.

"I have been most places and seen most things, my dear companion of a thousand stirring adventures." He frowned slightly. "I have been most things and seen most places. Perdition take it! Anyway, I am afraid that I have lost track of the major elements of this conversation, though I am certain that I would agree with everything that the last speaker said."

Krysty happened to be watching Mark Tomwun at that moment, and she was surprised to see his body visibly relax, as if something that had been said had touched a raw nerve and had then passed away again.

But everyone was distracted by the doors opening and the two young women wheeling in a cart that positively groaned under the weight of food.

One of them was Miranda Thorson, who studiously avoided catching Michael's eye.

Tomwun spotted this and called to her. "Miranda, my dear sprite."

"What?" she asked sullenly.

"I heard all about your accident with our second-youngest guest in the speaking pool."

"He shitted me off."

"I didn't," the teenager protested. "I was interested in what you were doing, but you set the dolphins on me and I could've drowned."

Tomwun rapped the table with the bowl of his spoon. "Enough, children. Enough."

"Deserved it," Miranda insisted. "Anyway, you said that if any of them—"

Tomwun was on his feet, his finger pointing like an accusing angel. "I said that was enough, Miranda." The anger in his voice shut her mouth like a steel trap. "We will kiss and make up."

"Who will?" Michael asked.

"You and dear Miranda. Now, in front of this company, if you please." There was icy vanadium steel in the man's voice, insisting on being obeyed.

Michael pushed back his chair and stood, his body tense. The young woman left the trolley and walked slowly, hands at her sides, fingers clenched, to stop a couple of paces away from him.

"Now," Tomwun said, a smile on his face.

Stiffly, as though they were both strapped into exoskeletons, Michael and Miranda embraced, offering cold kisses onto each other's cheeks.

Mildred leaned across the table and whispered to Doc. "'We have done deeds of charity, made peace of enmity, fair love of hate.'"

Doc nodded, recognizing the quotation. "And look what happened to Richard the Third, huh?"

Miranda had returned quickly to the food cart, her face flushed. Tomwun applauded her. "Good, my dear. Now, let us offer our guests the selection of fruits of the sea. Mostly saltwater, of course, but a few from the fresh rivers and pools to the north of us."

He addressed the older woman. "Juliet. Perhaps you might take us on a conducted tour of the dishes?"

Holding a long spoon, the gray-haired woman pointed to each brimming dish. Some were plainly boiled, some curried, some fried and some baked.

"Lamprey. Skate. Lake sturgeon. Longnose gar. Herring. Different kinds of herring there, all mixed and mashed. Trout. Pickerel. Common carp. Bluehead chub. Taillight shiner. Blacktail redhorse."

"You're making some of these names up," Krysty challenged. "I never heard of some of them."

"Juliet. A little information about... well, about the blacktail redhorse, if you please."

Juliet turned and smiled at the flame-haired woman sitting at the table. "Sure," she said. "*Moxostoma poecilurum*. Family of *Catostomidae*. Means suckers. Spawns in April or May over shallow shoals of fine gravel, where there's a fast-flowing current. They have, typically, a slender caudal peduncle and are found in creeks and narrow rivers from—"

Krysty held up a hand. "Thanks. Sorry I even questioned you. Thanks. Believe you now."

The woman rattled off the names of several more fish before Tomwun stopped her. "I think our guests have enough information to enable them to choose a few delicacies to tempt their palates, Juliet. You may go now. We'll help ourselves."

It was all good.

Mildred sighed and pushed back her plate. "It seems a pity, but I don't think I can eat any more. Professor Tomwun?"

"Dr. Wyeth? At your service."

"Your work is concentrated on cetaceans?"

"That genus represents a rather more broad church, I think, than interest us. It is very much the family of *Delphinidae*. Ocean dolphins and their brothers the whales. They are the *Odontocetes*, in that they all have teeth. To distinguish them from the related *Mysticeti*, who have plates of horny baleen to filter water and food into their mouths." He saw Dean Cawdor yawn. "Quite right, young fellow. This is a dinner, not a school lesson. And I am just a damned bore when I clamber aboard my own hobbyhorse. Or hobby-dolphin, perhaps.''

''No. It's real interesting, Professor. Honest. Just I'm sort of tired. You look after them real well, the dolphins you work on. Don't you?''

''Work *with*,'' Tomwun corrected. ''And very soon we shall begin to show you many of the details of what we are doing here and what we are hoping to achieve.''

''What sort of fish is this?'' the boy asked, holding up a piece on his spoon.

Miranda and Juliet had come back in to begin clearing away some of the dishes before bringing in the dessert. The younger woman moved toward Dean. ''Show me,'' she demanded.

''It tasted like real crap.''

''Dean,'' Ryan warned. ''The food's been terrific. Some of the best fish I ever ate.''

''Bet you didn't have any of this.'' The flesh was textured and dark brown, with a kind of rind of greasy fat. Held aloft on the spoon it exuded an unpleasant smell.

Miranda peered at it. ''I know what this is,'' she said, sounding a little shocked, half turning to face Mark Tomwun. ''They were told not to serve—''

For the second time during the meal he silenced her. ''I see what's happened.'' His voice was gentle, but Krysty could hear the faint tremor of rage that seethed just a little way below the surface.

J.B. leaned forward, the yellow light of the candles dancing off the lenses of his spectacles. "Just what *has* happened?"

"Mistake, Mr. Dix."

For a few long moments nobody spoke. Miranda had backed off from the table, edging toward the door, with Juliet shuffling along beside her. Both disappeared silently through the double swing doors.

"Wouldn't by any chance be a haunch of one of your pet dolphins, would it, Professor?" Ryan looked at his son. "Lay it down, boy."

"Yes, all right. Absolutely correct. It was number Thirty-six if my memory serves me well. One of our earlier subjects. If 'subjects' is the right word. Passed over from this world to the next only a day ago. As you know, protein isn't easy to come by to feed the others."

"How come we're eating it?"

"Because it was a mistake, Dean," the scientist insisted. The rimless glasses hid his eyes from them. "It was not supposed to be served as part of this meal. Just ground up for food for the rest of the—"

"Subjects," Michael finished.

"Precisely."

Chapter Fourteen

The Trader used to say that the only possible way to use a knife effectively was to go in point first. "Gets there quickest and sharpest."

Ryan's attacker was so confident in his superior speed and strength, combined with a total surprise, that he tried to carry out the killing in silence. He locked a wiry forearm around the throat of the one-eyed man, cutting off air and choking back any possible cry for help.

But, even as the knife came back for the butchering blow to the heart, Ryan was reacting, his own razored reflexes slipping him instantly into combat mode.

There was the immediate realization that he was about to be stabbed. If he tried to pull away forward, then the arm tight across his throat would hold him still, making him, literally, a sitting target.

Digging his feet into the treacherous, shifting sand, Ryan powered himself backward.

Twisting as he moved, his right arm cut behind him to parry the blow that he knew would be on its way, feeling the jarring of flesh against flesh. His left hand, fingers stiffened, lunged toward the invisible face of his attacker, stabbing at the eyes, coming close enough to make the assailant flinch.

The grip on his neck loosened and he wrenched himself clear, rolling forward and sideways, finishing up on the edge of the sea with water splashing at his ankles.

The shadowy figure recovered more quickly than Ryan had expected, giving him no time to draw the panga from its soft leather sheath, rushing in at him, the moonlight glinting on the cold steel of the knife. It was held low, point up, the way an experienced fighter would use it for the upward cut into the less-protected groin and lower belly. An amateur would hold the blade high, point down. The tip would skate across the overlapping ribs, protecting the internal organs from serious damage.

Ryan dodged again, hands out to try to fend off the darting lunges of the knife, backing away until he was nearly knee-deep in the Lantic.

At least he could now see who he was up against.

The man was about five foot six, nearly nine inches shorter than Ryan. He had a muscular build, with broad shoulders, tapering to a slender waist and slim hips. His long hair was as black as a raven's wing, tied back with a strip of light-colored cloth. His eyes were narrow, his cheekbones heavy, his mouth a slit of murderous hatred.

Ryan guessed that the attacker was probably an Indian, maybe a Seminole. But none of that information was worth a flying fart in a thunderstorm. All that mattered was that he was out to kill him, the point of the knife flickering in and out toward Ryan's stomach, forcing him deeper and deeper into the cool, sucking surf.

There was no chance to snatch a nanosecond and grab the hilt of the panga.

The sea was now riding at Ryan's waist, the swell making it hard to keep his balance. But it was more difficult for the shorter man.

The moment came.

The Indian stopped to gather breath and wait out a larger than average wave.

Ryan drew the eighteen-inch blade from his belt and tightened his fingers around the water-slick hilt. "Right, you back-creeping son of a bitch," he growled.

Now all the advantages rested with him—height, power and the extra foot of steel in his hand.

The Seminole started to shuffle sideways, parallel to the beach, the moon shining in the blank eyes.

Ryan had the ace on the line now, content to wait and patiently close in. He'd already checked along the line of the land to make sure that his attacker didn't have any reinforcements rushing to his rescue.

"You deserved death," the Indian hissed. "You and every one of you."

Ryan was puzzled by that, but he wasn't about to stop and engage his putative murderer in a discussion of combative philosophy.

He'd already figured that the shorter man now had only one slender chance of winning the fight. So, when the move came, Ryan was ready for it.

The Seminole whipped his arm back and hurled the broad-bladed knife at the face of the one-eyed man who was coming at him out of the sea.

A tiny spray of sparks was generated as Ryan met it with the side of the panga. The knife sang over the waves and splashed into the water, forty yards behind them. Inevitably Ryan had closed his eye at the last moment.

Now he opened it again and his opponent had gone.

"Fireblast!"

The wiry Indian had doubled his chances. If the knife had struck its target, then Ryan would probably be dead. Or badly wounded. If it missed, he had a second or so to dive beneath the dark, impenetrable water and try to swim as far as possible from him before breaking surface again.

"Which way?" Ryan said to the waves that rolled inexorably around him.

The man could easily have a second knife, could be coming straight at Ryan, under the mirrored surface of the Lantic.

Just for a handful of heartbeats, Ryan felt the fluttering approach of panic.

Once he had visited, twenty years ago now, a frontier gaudy that had both electric power and a working antique vid player. There'd been a scratched copy of some predark film about a great white shark that came up and swallowed a naked girl, swimming in the sea at dead of night.

It had always impressed Ryan, touching some primitive and atavistic terror.

Mildred had recently said that ninety percent of all shark attacks took place in less than five feet of water. Ryan didn't know if it was true or not, but he knew that he felt as exposed as a dog turd on a wedding dress.

The one place he guessed the Seminole wouldn't be trying for was back to the beach. He'd be too visible too soon if he swam that way.

Moving a little faster than he really intended, Ryan stumbled on the shifting shingle as he ran for the land, battling against water that seemed to have a thousand hands, all tugging at him to stop his reaching safety.

Panting, he finally made it to the dry sand, holding the panga out in front of him like a religious icon, shaking his wet hair from his face.

But the Indian seemed to have totally disappeared into the night.

Ryan waited and watched.

Unless he'd drowned, the man was going to have to come up for air in the next ten or fifteen seconds, thirty seconds at the very outside.

Ryan bit his lip, cursing his decision to walk out without wearing a blaster on his hip. If he'd been carrying his trusty 9 mm SIG-Sauer, there was enough moonlight for him to be certain of picking off the escaping Indian. At that range he could have put a single round through either eye.

"There."

A dark head cautiously broke the surface, fifty or sixty yards off, turning toward the beach. The Indian saw Ryan standing and watching him, helpless to do anything to stop him from swimming away to safety.

It crossed Ryan's mind to follow the Seminole along the shoreline, forcing him to stay out in the Lantic. But if the man was strong enough in the water he could lure Ryan so far away from the relative security of the institute that he could find himself blundering into an ambush.

The Indian yelled something to Ryan, the words vanishing into the night. But his gesture, with a middle finger raised, was unmistakable.

There was no profit in entering into a slanging match of insults with someone beyond the power of harming, so Ryan spun on his heel and began to walk toward the distant light of the buildings.

Then he heard a strange sound, the clicking of dolphins, clear in the stillness, followed by a yell of shock and pain from the swimmer.

There were a half dozen of the creatures, circling the Seminole, as though they were a pack of wolves driving a recalcitrant buffalo. The sea was whipped up by their tails as they closed in on the helpless man, butting him and pushing him toward the shoreline.

Ryan blinked. He'd sheathed the panga, but now he drew it once more in a whisper of sound.

"I'll be..."

It was done with unbelievable speed and efficiency, almost as if the graceful mammals had been specifically trained to perform the capture.

"Hey, help me!"

"Fuck you!"

"Please. They're goin' to drown me."

"I don't think so."

"Help!"

"I don't reckon to help a piss-yellow bastard who was going to stab me in the back."

Now he was barely waist deep, spinning around and around to try to push off the dolphins as they nudged him farther into the shallows. He might as well have tried to harness a war wag with a length of wet string.

Ryan waited patiently, glancing behind to make sure they were still alone.

Now they were less than ten yards apart.

"Let me go, mister."

"Why?"

"I haven't seen you before. You mebbe outlander? Not from white-coat place?"

"What difference does that make?"

The dolphins were now lying in a patient semicircle a few feet from their captive, closing off any hope of escape toward the open sea. Their whistling and clicking had ceased, and they were quite silent.

The Seminole shook his head wearily. "You right. Don't make no difference."

Ryan was taken by surprise when the man suddenly came splashing out of the water toward him, fingers clawing in an attack of hopeless fury.

It was so hopeless that it nearly worked.

The panga wasn't a weapon designed for close-quarter subtle fighting. It was a long, broad hacking blade, for swinging rather than thrusting.

But the point was sharp enough as Ryan jabbed it out to check the attacker, feeling it slice in at the side of the ribs, drawing a fountain of warm blood.

The Indian staggered, but still tried to twist away and run up the sloping beach toward the possible safety of the line of brush and palm trees.

Ryan was after him, not intending to allow a second chance of escape.

It was all over very quickly.

Just as Ryan swung the panga around in a hissing arc, the Seminole half stumbled, then straightened in a clumsy, skipping sort of jump. He glanced over his shoulder into the eye of his grim-faced nemesis.

The slicing blow had been aimed at the man's nape, below the bobbing ponytail. But it hit home under the left ear, the edge hacking between the jaws, splintering teeth and shredding the ligament at the root of the tongue. Ryan had put so much power into it that the whole lower jaw was completely severed, falling away to the left, hanging on by a few shreds of skin and gristle on the right side.

The doomed man tried to scream, but his mouth and throat filled with hot, bubbling blood. It was one of the most ghastly sights that Ryan had ever seen, and he held back, unable for a moment to strike the final, merciful blow.

Ryan stopped, holding the panga at his side, staring at the macabre spectacle. Dying, the man was running in small circles, his feet kicking up a pattering spray of moist sand. He was close to the high-water mark, and the rippled tide was washing away each footstep within seconds of its being made.

As though he'd just received some supernatural call, the Indian stopped circling and ran arrow-straight into the Lantic. As soon as he was waist deep he plunged forward and disappeared into the darkness.

This time he didn't reappear, though Ryan waited several minutes to be sure.

Chapter Fifteen

Tomwun was extremely concerned to hear about the murderous attack.

"I must confess that there are times when my philanthropic views on my fellow man become more than a little jaundiced. We have done everything we can to try to help the Seminole. They sail all the way from the swamps and bayous of the Mississippi delta, and we trade with them. Then they come sneaking along in the darkness and attempt foul murder."

Ryan had stopped off to tell Krysty about the attack and the death, asking her to pass the news on to the others in their own rooms while he went to Tomwun's quarters.

The professor was reading through an old illustrated book on oceanic mammals, still wearing his white lab coat.

The image, for a moment, made Ryan think about the odd and brief conversation he'd had with the Indian. He'd been asked if he was an outlander or whether he came from the "white-coat place."

Ryan had accepted a small glass of a sweet, fiery liqueur from Tomwun.

"I hope you appreciate it, my dear Cawdor. It is an old, old vintage offered to me, oddly enough, by one of those selfsame Seminole rogues who said he found it in the ruins of a house near a park in Miami."

"It's good."

Tomwun nodded. "Indeed it *is* good. The label revealed that it was called Benedictine. Another glass?"

"No. Thanks, but no."

"When it's gone, Ryan, it's gone. I seriously doubt that there is another bottle left in all of Deathlands. Perhaps in all of the terra cognita. The known world." He poured himself another measure, gesturing to Ryan's glass. "You certain? Take what comes, when it comes. That has always been my motto. If I found someone who had the Latin, I would have it worked into a sampler, or limned into a coat of arms."

"You get attacked very often by Indians?"

"No. These waters are not much traveled. Both the Gulf of Mexico to the west and the ocean to the east of us are dangerous to the unwary. Even before the nuclear holocaust devastated the planet there were frequent hurricanes and inexplicable vanishings from the maritime ledgers. Since then, there have also been undersea quakes and giant tsunamis and boiling eruptions of mud. Volcanoes, ten thousand feet deep. Parlous places and parlous times. But there is likewise a wind on the heath, friend Cawdor. Who would wish to die?"

The liqueur seemed to have raced to the scientist's head, and he lay back and smiled at the ceiling.

"I'm going to my room," Ryan announced. "See you in the morning."

"You know that there is a myth that dolphins were once humanoid and dwelled with mankind in great cities? The rumored lost continent of Atlantis."

"Yeah. So I heard. You believe that?"

The blurred haziness vanished and keen eyes turned to Ryan. "Of course I do. Of course. Now, you must get you back to your room. I'll send out a search party upon the morrow of the morning." He stood and clasped Ryan by the hand with a surprisingly hard grip. "Now nobles all, come let's away, to try the fortunes of some happier day."

Ryan wondered if the man was triple-mad.

TWO EVENINGS after the death of the marauding Seminole, Mark Tomwun threw a beach party.

"To remove the sour and bitter taste of what happened here recently," he said.

There were four large bonfires, crackling and flaming, sending fountains of red and orange sparks two hundred feet into the night air. The workers in the institute had also built a grand barbecue, cooking on iron grids over a trench of glowing coals. The mixed smell of wood, fish and meat swamped the senses.

The produce from Florida and Louisiana was in evidence—spareribs of pork, and an endless array of chicken wings and legs; beef and horsemeat, ground up into circular patties, bringing a gasp of delight from Mildred.

"My sweet Lord!" she exclaimed. "Real burgers. Best food I've seen since you dragged me awake into this godforsaken place. I'll have a double cheese-and-chickenburger with all of the trimmings. But go easy on the relish. Brings me out in a rash."

Dean stuffed himself with charbroiled swordfish steaks and fried potatoes, topping the whole thing off with a foaming beaker of ice-cold orange-flavored milk. He grinned happily across at his father. "This is a triple-gross food-out, Dad. I reckon... Oh, I don't—"

The boy's face, ruddy in the reflected flames of the fire, suddenly paled and he staggered a few steps into the shadows of a nearby palm, stooped over and puked up the entire meal.

Krysty was at his shoulder. "Want to go back to your room and lie down awhile?"

"No. I think.... All that food's come back looking just like it did when I ate it first. Hardly seems to have been changed inside me. Makes me feel hungry all over again."

A couple of minutes later, he was tucking into a plate loaded with swordfish steaks and fried potatoes, gulping down another mug of the orange milk drink.

"I'm getting too old for all this," Krysty said to Ryan.

"Want to go somewhere quiet?"

She nodded. "Why not?"

Krysty led Ryan by the hand into a patch of deep shadow beneath the tumbled ruins of some profoundly old concrete building. She sat and tugged him down beside her. "How much longer, lover?"

"To stay here?"

"Yeah."

"Don't know."

"You like it?"

"Seen lots worse. What do you think about it, Krysty?"

Her face was almost invisible in the velvet darkness. "Still got a feeling I don't understand. Like looking at a handsome man, but seeing a grinning skull under the skin. I can't explain it. And there's not any hard evidence for feeling that way. They've all been kind to us."

"Tomwun's promised us a fishing expedition tomorrow that we'll remember all our lives."

"Yeah." She lay back, looking at the stars. "Listen, lover. If there was intelligent life up there in the stars, and they developed a really powerful sort of telescope, they could look down here and eventually see the nuking of dark night."

"No. Why eventually? Why not now? Even if they could see this far."

Krysty sat up again, elbows on knees, chin in her hands. "All to do with the speed of light, lover. Uncle Tyas McCann explained it to me once, back in Harmony. It would take about a hundred and fifty

years before images from Earth reached them out
there. That's what he said.''

''Who cares?''

There was a note of chilling bitterness that struck
home in Krysty's heart. During the time she'd been
with Ryan Cawdor, she'd got to know his many
moods. In the early days there'd been a paralyzing
cold at the core of her soul, the product of the endless period surviving the Deathlands, alone. Sure he'd
had J.B., the Trader and the crews of the war wags,
but he'd generally slept and woken alone.

Now he was happier. No, that would never quite be
the right word for Ryan. Perhaps ''contented'' came
closer to the kernel of it.

But she still had a bleak terror, something that
came crawling, unbidden, into her mind at three in
the morning. That time when small babies wake and
cry out. When breath is slowest and the elderly and
infirm let slip their frail hold on life.

The fear that one day she'd wake up and find him
gone.

The fear that the specters that still haunted the distant corridors of his memory would one day come
cheeping and muttering out of the gray shadows and
take him away from her.

''I care. I care about you, Dean and the others. You
telling me you don't care, Ryan?''

He didn't answer, and Krysty felt something hor-
ribly close to panic.

Away on the horizon she saw a streak of purple lightning as yet another chunk of deep-space detritus met its final rendezvous with its home planet.

"Ryan?" she persisted.

"Sorry. I was a thousand miles behind." The warmth had come back into his voice and she relaxed a little. "Course I care. Be deader than a felled tree if I didn't. But there's just times I wonder about it."

"What, lover?"

He laughed and stood. "Come on." He offered her a hand to rise, pretending to let her fall backward, then saving her at the last moment.

"Think Dean'll have puked and eaten again by the time we get back there?"

"Doc told me that some old ville...Rome...used to have rooms where you used to go to upchuck during a meal. Not after. Right in the middle. Then you'd be like Dean and go and stuff yourself again."

Krysty pulled a face. "Looks like some of the olden times weren't really any better than the now times."

"Who knows? All we know about the past is only a small bite out of what it must've been like. Anyway, I feel tired. Ready for bed."

"Me, too."

"Get ourselves ready for this fishing expedition that Professor Tomwun claims is going to be so memorable."

They walked together, feet sliding through the soft sand, toward the distant block of buildings.

Unseen by Ryan and Krysty, a young bottlenose dolphin tracked them, parallel to the beach.

Chapter Sixteen

"I'm beginning to find all this endless meteorological perfection just a little tedious," Doc complained. "My heart weeps for a November morning in Vermont, with drizzling rain and clouds that cling dripping to the topmost branches of the dank conifers." He laughed, showing his perfect teeth. "Well, perhaps I can wait until tomorrow for that."

Michael was standing by him in the doorway of their building, staring out over the strip of scrub, past the beach toward the dock.

"Should be pushing off straight after we've had breakfast," he commented.

"You coming in the big boat with us?" Mildred asked, appearing behind him.

He hesitated. "Miranda asked me if I wanted to go along with her in the small outrigger."

J.B. laughed. "Outrigger. Getting very nautical all of a sudden, Michael."

"Watch she doesn't try and push you over the side and hold you under!" Dean cackled with laughter, poking the teenager in the ribs and scampering past him into the bright morning sunshine.

Ryan and Krysty joined the others. "Haven't been fishing for sport in a long, long while." He grinned. "Most times I fished for food I wasn't that great at it."

"I have the happiest memories of trolling the wild white rivers of Oregon with my dear wife, Emily," Doc said. "Camping beneath the stars and eating over an open fire." He hesitated. "Truth to tell, Emily was not the finest of ourdoorswomen and found an iron skillet over a beech fire was not conducive to producing a *cordon bleu* repast."

"Burned offering, huh, Doc?"

"I could not have put it better myself, Mildred."

"Here they come," Krysty announced, as the fishing party approached, led by Tomwun.

He waved a hand and hallooed a greeting. "It's such a perfect day, my friends. Let us get afloat. To the boats, to the boats!" He pointed the way with a long steel-pointed gaff.

There were eight or nine members of the institute with him, all wearing casual clothes. Miranda Thorson had on the skimpiest pair of shorts that Ryan had ever seen. From the front they looked like a tiny kerchief and from the back there was just a narrow strip of material that almost vanished into the cleft between her buttocks. She and Michael walked close together, apart from the rest of the party.

"WHERE DO YOU GET the gas from?" J.B. had jammed his fedora low on his head to avoid the risk of losing it over the side of the speeding boat.

Tomwun was at the helm, standing up, the wind peeling his grin of delight even wider. A white bone foamed under the prow of the eighteen-footer, their wake lengthening behind them toward the distant blur of the institute.

"Trade for it, John. Like everything else."

The Armorer glanced across at Ryan, who was sitting on the starboard side between Krysty and his son. They'd talked briefly the previous night about this "trading," trying to work out just what it was that Tomwun had to offer that was so valuable to the inhabitants of the scattered villes to the north.

And nobody had been able to come up with a satisfactory answer to the question.

The rattle of the engine, combined with the rushing wind and the kick of the boat against the choppy swell, made conversation impossible, and J.B. didn't bother to pursue the subject of the trading.

The little outrigger, propelled by a square of stained and patched canvas, was bowling along a quarter mile away from them, tacking away from land. The young woman was at the tiller, with Michael barely visible, scuttling about, hauling on sheets and trying to avoid the swinging boom.

"Good clean air," said Thorund, one of the older men from the institute. He had a long, thin face, rather like a bewildered sheep, with a short-cropped thatch of thinning hair. His eyes were a piercing blue.

"Not so clean as when we started off first thing this morning." Mildred sniffed, head on one side. "Sulfur. You smell it, John?"

"What?" He leaned closer to her. "Can't hear you over the engine noise."

"Said I could smell sulfur."

The Armorer dutifully took in several lungfuls of air. "Yeah. Something..."

"Like eggy farts," Dean squeaked. "Comin' from over that way."

They all followed the eager, pointing finger, toward the north and east.

"Cloud there," Krysty said. "Right down near the surface of the Lantic."

"Yellow cloud," Ryan agreed, moving carefully toward the stern of the boat, attracting the attention of Tomwun. "Look over that way. Cloud."

The professor nodded, the sunlight flashing off his spectacles. "We get plenty of them, Ryan. There are still all manner of undersea explosions and movements of the tectonic plates. Don't worry about the scientific details. All seismological. Bit beyond you, I expect."

"Like a volcano?" Ryan shouted, steadying himself with a hand on the smaller man's shoulder.

"Possibly. No danger."

"What if we get closer to it?"

"What?" Tomwun threw Ryan a slightly blank look of vague amusement. "You want us to go closer to it?"

"No. What if we do?"

"Ah, reading you scale ten now. Well, it would be a little like standing on top of a volcano as the vent blows and the magma strikes the fan."

"I seen eruptions." Now Ryan could catch the smell of sulfur more strongly.

"Indeed?"

"Yeah."

"Yet you've lived to tell about it? So it obviously isn't too fearful."

But he adjusted the boat's course slightly closer to land, easing back on the throttle to slow its progress, keeping it at a safe distance from the menacing cloud.

THEY RAN INTO A SCHOOL of striped mullet. The two boats seemed to be almost floating in a torrent of the silvery fish. Lines were obsolete and everyone lent a hand in scooping them out by the dozen in the long-handled nets. A cascade of flailing, gasping mullet covered the bottom boards of the small vessel.

"They're like crazed," Chuck Cybulski shouted, struggling to heft a loaded net over the side, grinning at Dean as the boy slithered across the mound of dying fish to help him with the catch.

The torrent of blue-striped fish was racing all around them, seeming to be heading in a southerly direction.

"Think there's some sharks after them?" Michael called from the outrigger a few yards away from the main party. "Or a great whale?"

With the engine stopped, conversation was easier, and Tomwun answered him.

"I can assure you, categorically, that there are neither dangerous sharks nor any threatening whales in this sector of the ocean."

"How do you know?" Doc asked curiously. "How can you be so dogmatic about that?"

"I know, therefore I know. Surely as a man of science you're familiar with Lobkowitz's First Principle of Certainty, Tanner?"

"I can't say that I'm familiar either with the gentleman, or with his work."

"He's probably one of the newer fellows, Doc," Mildred said.

"Perhaps, perhaps."

The surging flood of mullet ceased as suddenly as it had started.

There had been a noisy flock of black-headed gulls following the shoal of fish, screaming and diving, every bird emerging every time with a struggling, blue-green striped mullet clamped in its orange beak.

Now they too had disappeared. For a few minutes they'd been visible and audible, pursing the fish. Then, almost as though they'd been swallowed by an invisible shroud, the whole flock had vanished.

"There was a great stillness that lay between heaven and earth," Doc intoned. "I rather suspect that someone must have opened the seventh seal and let loose the dogs of war and cried out for havoc and . . . Upon my soul, but I fear that I have again lost the thread of what I was saying."

"It is quiet," Thorund agreed, ignoring Doc's mumbling. "Where are the escorting dolphins, Professor?"

"Escorting?" Ryan repeated. "I haven't spotted any dolphins escorting us."

"You wouldn't," Miranda called. "Not unless they want you to see them."

"But you knew they were here?"

"Course."

"So, where are they now?"

She looked at Tomwun, as though she were waiting for permission to answer the question. When he showed no reaction, she shook her head. "Don't know. I picked up interest, fear and quick-move talk. Then nothing. If I had my equipment here, I could monitor them, even if they're miles away from us."

"'Where' isn't the question," Tomwun said quietly. "Why is much more the point."

"They're amazingly sensitive to all sorts of natural phenomena," Cybulski added.

Mildred had been sitting with her boots among the megacull of fish, her right hand trailing idly over the side of the boat. She suddenly pulled it out. "Mary and Joseph!"

"What?" Tomwun snapped.

"The water's fucking—pardon my language, but—it's really hot."

"Wow!" Dean had dabbled his fingers in the ocean. "Like boiling soup, Dad."

"Fish soup," J.B. said so quietly that only Ryan and Mildred heard him.

"And I can smell sulfur again." Krysty leaned over and stared down into the deeps around them, shading her eyes to try to pierce the mirrored surface.

"Bubbles!" Miranda's voice would have fractured sec steel at eight hundred paces.

Tomwun spun like a stoned dervish and tried to get the outboard engine started, winding the strip of cord and jerking at it. A sputtering cough, and then nothing. He tried a second time with an equal lack of success. His glasses hung crooked, and his eyes were open so wide that blank white showed all around the irises.

"It's really starting to bubble," Michael said, staring into the sea in utter bewilderment.

Ryan knelt, put his hand into the water and jerked it out again. "Fireblast!" The temperature was rising fast to boiling point.

A moment later they heard a roaring sound and the air was filled with the noxious stench of sulfur. The boat lurched and tipped, and Ryan was was thrown violently over the side into the frothing scum of the ocean.

Chapter Seventeen

There had once been a long conversation, stretching out over several evening camps, about the nature of death and near-death experiences, conversation that sometimes veered toward argument; argument that sometimes flirted with the skirts of bitter violence.

Ryan remembered that Hunaker, the green-haired, bisexual driver of War Wag One, had gone after Loz, the cook, with a lean-bladed flensing knife. Trader had stopped her by cracking the butt of his beloved, battered Armalite against the side of her skull, laying her out flat and cold.

The point that had produced such bitter anger was whether your whole life really did flash by you at the moment of your death.

Loz had insisted that he'd met a gaudy once who'd nearly died when a bondage game with a john went wrong. She swore that she saw every single second of her thirteen years as the rope tightened inexorably around her throat.

Hun had suggested that she was overloaded on jolt at the time.

Ryan had been surprised that almost all of the crew had some story or other. About hearing their long-dead mother speak to them as they were about to set their foot on an implode gren, or seeing themselves as little babies in a dream and the next day they were nearly fragged in a mutie raid.

Ryan himself had been finger-width close to death on a number of occasions.

One fine summer's day, when he'd been just eighteen, he'd been walking across a flower-decked meadow in New England, without a care in the world. He'd spent a few days working for a farmer, and enjoying the farmer's daughter in the dark of night. Now he was on his way, seeking fresh fields and adventures new, chewing on a tender stalk of green grass.

The very next splinter of recorded time saw him flat on his back in the dirt, staring up at the sky, with no sense at all of what could have happened. There had been no sound and no feeling of any impact.

The bullet had struck him just above the right ear, glancing off at an angle into a shrub oak by a nearby stream. His luck was that the murderous farmer owned only an antique smoothbore black-powder musket, and was using it at extreme range, actually firing from the bedroom window of his weeping thirty-year-old daughter.

But Ryan was definitely certain that nothing in his past life had flashed before him at that moment.

ALL HE REMEMBERED as he was sucked deep under the surface, was the foul stink of chemicals and the intolerable heat of the Lantic Ocean. His hand had reached out for balance, toward Krysty and their fingers had brushed.

Now it was dark.

Despite the monstrous horror of his predicament, Ryan managed to hang on to some shreds of sense. He realized that there must have been a gigantic underwater explosion, probably volcanic in origin: the pale yellow cloud in the distance, the clogging stink of sulfur, the fleeing shoal of striped mullet, the unnatural stillness of the moment, then the heat and the bubbling.

Knowing what was killing him didn't seem that much of a consolation.

His legs kicked and his fingers clawed at the water. The eruption had brought up so much primeval mud from the bottom of the ocean that it had turned day into pitchy night, making it almost impossible to distinguish up from down.

Ryan's ears were filled with a dull roaring, like being directly inside a revving war wag engine. And there was enormous pressure all around him, mocking his feeble efforts to try to swim to safety. It was a similar sensation to being tumbled over some roaring rapids.

Ryan had the illusion that the temperature of the sea was slightly cooler. But the buffeting was worse, and the rumbling seemed louder. All his senses were starting to slip uncontrollably away from him.

His skin was tender, feeling loose on his body, and both his good eye and the raw puckered socket were stinging, as if someone had sprayed acid in them. And his breath was rapidly vanishing from his lungs.

Ryan probably slipped from consciousness, though he had no sentient awareness of any change. The darkness and the suffocating oppression didn't alter at all.

But suddenly he was breathing, air that was as thick as oatmeal and flavored with a rich gruel of ancient stenches.

The one-eyed man drew a great roaring gasp of it into his chest, arms flung high toward the ochre sky.

Though he'd just hovered on the brink of the drowning abyss, his fighting reflexes quickly reasserted themselves. He sank again for a moment, swallowing a sickening gulp of foul salt water. Then his legs kicked and his arms flailed and he was swimming once more, trying to direct himself away from what seemed the core of a massive undersea explosion.

The ocean was in turmoil.

The eruption had somehow affected the weather, and the fine morning had gone, replaced by leaden clouds and crackling bolts of purple lightning that tore the sky apart. The waves all around him were massive, gray-green mountains that fell roiling into the next swell, white-topped and menacing.

Ryan kept finding himself in the trough, unable to see more than a few yards in any direction, unable to see what had happened to the two boats. Worse, unable to see in what direction the land might lie.

He could make out where the center of the disturbance lay—about a hundred yards ahead of him, where a column of steam, smoke and liquid mud was hurled into the air, tinted a dark yellow-orange color.

Ryan's luck lay in the eruption hurling him away from its murderous center, where he would have either drowned or been boiled alive. But his predicament was still extremely hazardous, seemingly alone in the lethal wilderness of ocean.

The weight of his clothes, boots and the SIG-Sauer on his hip were all uniting to try to drag him down. But he knew enough about survival in Deathlands to shrink from abandoning anything until he absolutely had to.

The first priority for Ryan was to try to establish his bearings.

He had drifted a little farther from the danger zone, with the water around him only a few degrees above blood heat. Timing his effort, he swam into the next rolling wave, seizing the moment to try to look around him. But the acidic filth in the sea hurt his good eye as he blinked it open, making it impossible to make out anything beyond a vertiginous blur.

Ryan rubbed at it with his fingers, repeating the maneuver with the next roller but one, struggling to hold himself at its apogee long enough to see what was going on.

It was partly successful, but still intensely dispiriting for him. The gigantic pillar of debris and steam had blotted out everything in one direction, concealing a full quarter of the Lantic from his gaze.

The rest of the horizon offered no hope at all. It wasn't possible to see any clear distance because of the force and height of the waves. At that first glimpse Ryan could see no sight of the Keys. But he knew that the strip of beach couldn't be that far off. His last visual memory before going over the side of the boat had been of the land, to the left, no more than six or seven hundred yards away.

But in what direction?

Another particularly large comber came toward him, lifting him with immeasurable power, carrying him higher than before, allowing him a better view of his drowning world.

Ryan had seen enough this time to allow him a total awareness of what faced him.

At the edges of the boiling eruption he had glimpsed the two boats. They were a full half mile away from him, just tiny specks of light against the darkness of the biblical catastrophe. It was difficult to judge, but it looked to Ryan as if they were heading away from him, back to safety.

In his heart he couldn't blame them.

After he'd gone over, the chances of his surviving would have seemed a deal less than a million to one against. And he would now be an invisible speck in the vastness, effectively out of any hope of being spotted.

To his friends, Ryan had no doubt at all that he would be stone dead. If that was the blackest side, there was also a glimmering of light.

And hope.

He had seen land, an indistinct strip of whiteness off behind him, the sight snatched away again as he plunged into the valley between the rolling waves.

Distance was difficult, but it looked like his memory of around the half-mile mark was close enough.

All he had to do now was swim to safety.

IT WAS HARD, grindingly tough, plowing stubbornly through the Lantic, out of sight of his destination for most of the time. There were several occasions when Ryan realized he was swimming slightly off course, angling away from the enticing beach, fooled by the swirling currents and the tumbling swell.

Three or four times he trod water, trying to look behind him, in case the miracle had happened and the boats were, after all, coming to search for him.

But now they were out of sight.

The other thing that Ryan looked for was some marine life, with the profound hope that he saw nothing. Michael's experience with the mutie snake and his own, some time ago, with a great white, had put him off aquatic encounters for life.

If anything had enabled Ryan to reach the shore quicker, it would have been a dark fin cutting through the water in his general direction.

THE LAST FEW MINUTES were the longest.

The waves were gentler, helping to roll Ryan toward the gently sloping beach. But he was getting close to the limit of exhaustion.

As he allowed his feet to trail, the boots feeling like leaden weights, Ryan finally touched bottom, swimming a few more ponderous strokes, until he could stand, waist deep. Even then he still stumbled and fell twice clambering onto the soft, sloping sandy beach.

Once he was clear of the water he sat down, taking the chance to look all around. Out at sea the smoke and steam had almost vanished. There was no boat to be seen. Behind him were palms and, behind that, he guessed there would be the remains of the ancient highway.

The one thing he didn't know was how far up the coast the current had carried him.

But for now all he wanted to do was lie down and rest.

Chapter Eighteen

Ryan blinked and opened his eye. The sun was overhead, blazing down from a pink-tinged sky. The dark clouds of the storm that had blown up during the undersea eruption had drifted away.

He had an acute sense of time and figured that he'd been crashed out for around ninety minutes. His body ached, and the skin across his forehead felt tender and tight. His clothes had begun to dry on him. The panga was still on one hip, the blaster on the other.

The Lantic stretched out to the east as far as he could see, untouched and untroubled, and totally devoid of any sort of life.

He stood, wincing at the muscular pains that lanced through his thighs and shoulders. There was a still a squidging wetness in his socks, and his mane of black hair was damp at his nape.

The institute lay to the south, to his right as he faced the sea. Far off to the north was the mainland of old Florida. The best guess that Ryan could muster put him about five or six miles from home.

"First things first," he said. "Best strike inland and find out if the old Highway One is still there."

His right hand stung, and he saw that he'd scratched it on some coral while fumbling ashore. A narrow thread of blood oozed from it, and as a precaution, Ryan sucked hard at it, spitting crimson into the white sand.

He plodded through the ubiquitous palms, past a line of dried brush and came to what might once have been a picnic area. The rotted remains of benches and tables stood gaunt on the cracked concrete. A square building, roof long fallen, still showed faded signs that read Men and Women.

Ryan walked to the structure to look at a metal-framed board, which he guessed had probably once held a detailed map for travelers. Now there was only a small section of colored paper inside the broken glass. Less than three inches long by one inch high, it held the runic message You Are Here.

"Where?" Ryan asked.

THE FOUR-LANE HIGHWAY WAS only a few yards inland from the rest area. The median divider had rusted through and been distorted by earth movements into a corrugated ribbon. The actual pavement was also badly scarred and furrowed, showing breaks and long gaps.

Something moved in among some stunted bushes on the far side of the blacktop, and Ryan reached for the butt of the SIG-Sauer. But the rustling ceased.

As he started walking south, he saw a tumbled road sign. Wind and sand had scoured it clean, but someone had used it to daub graffiti in yellow paint. "The simplicity of bigotry" was all it said. It had been tagged with capital letters: BB. Ryan read it twice, then shook his head and carried on.

Ahead of him was the ruin of what had once been a tourist eatery.

The idea of vacations and tourism was something that had always fascinated Ryan, and he had relished several talks with Krysty about the concept.

That someone would work for a whole year until their backs broke or their brains fried, so that they could go somewhere different, just for a couple of weeks, and lie on a beach or climb a mountain or ride a white-knuckle funfair, seemed the height of madness.

"Why not do what they wanted more often?" Ryan would ask.

"The work ethos. That's what Peter Maritza used to quote when I was a little girl. Used to tell me that work was a blessing to the soul and character of the person who did the working. How it bred diligence and self-respect. Said a man without work simply wasn't a man at all."

The idea was so ridiculous that it used to break them both up. In Deathlands it was very fundamental. You worked and you got to eat. Unless you happened to be a powerful baron, in which case you persuaded others to work for you, so that you got to eat. That was all there was. Work equaled food. You got the food so you stopped working until you needed to eat again.

Ryan stood a few paces off from the tumbledown building and stared at it. There were plenty of regions in Deathlands where you'd step triple-careful around old places. But the Keys seemed to be almost devoid of human life. If you didn't count the occasional murderous Indian.

The sign along the front had been sealed in clear plastic and had survived nearly a hundred years of storms. It wasn't easy to read it, but it was possible—Mom's Place was the name.

Oddly Ryan had eaten in a dozen eateries called Mom's Place, and they had been universally terrible.

He wondered whether this one might have been any different, before skydark.

One window was unbroken and carried the symbol of Coca-Cola on it. Ryan knew that it had been the drink that everyone wanted back then. He'd only ever sampled it once. The Trader had found a case hidden in the corner of a cellar of an isolated house near the ville of Crested Butte. The crews of both war wags had gathered around for a ceremonial opening and tasting.

Most of them had liked it, though one or two had thought that it was too fizzy for them to really enjoy.

Ryan glanced around, then pushed open the front door. What remained of the front door. The bottom half had been kicked in and the top part was broken, hanging crookedly by a squeaking hinge.

It was slightly cooler inside, with that flat, damp smell of all long-empty buildings. Ryan wondered why it was that they all seemed to carry the faint scent of stale urine. There was a three-legged chair propped up in one corner, and two tables in a flowered Formica pattern.

A mark on the floor showed where a counter had stood alongside a hole in the wall that probably led through to the kitchen. A board was nailed to the wall opposite the entrance, carrying what had been the last menu that Mom's Place ever served.

Ryan stepped closer, aware of broken splinters of glass crunching under his heels. The light was good, daggering through the open spaces between the roof joists. He read, "All entrées include soup du jour and dinner roll as well as numerous visits to the salad bar."

Added immediately beneath that was: "And choice of desserts, as well as free refills of coffee."

It was an odd feeling, reading a menu from nearly a hundred years ago, offering meals that had last been eaten in the quiet days before the holocaust brought megadeath.

Some of the details had been erased by the worn finger of time, but Ryan could still make out all of the basic ingredients of Mom's Special: Boneless breast of chicken smothered in chunky peanut butter with tender young grapefruit slices, baked in bubbling brown sugar. Served with choice of potato or rice, with our own creamy blueberry and brandy sauce.

Ryan found it hard to imagine just how horrendous it must have been. But the idea of food made him realize that he was beginning to feel a little hungry. They had taken packed meals aboard the boats, ready for the fishing expedition.

But that was then.

This was now.

"I'll have the Special with baked potato, but hold the grapefruit, hold the chicken and for God's sake hold all of that fucking sauce!"

A MILE SOUTH the road disappeared. It had been extended over one of the numerous gaps between the islands on a causeway, but that was long gone, leaving the exposed stumps of the supporting pillars like a scattering of rotten teeth in the gaping mouth of a corpse. It meant an expanse of ocean, with the Lantic and the Gulf of Mexico mixing freely in a turbulent tide race.

Ryan measured it with his eye, figuring it was no more than one hundred and fifty yards across. But it didn't look the easiest of swims. He had partly recovered from his long ordeal, but he knew from experience that fatigue could fool you, make you think that you were free of its insidious tendrils so that you took dangerous risks, finding out too late that it was still alive and well and living in all of your muscles.

The rip of water looked ferocious, particularly where it raged around the concrete supports to the long-lost highway. Ryan could see dark, oily holes and swirling pools that waited to suck down anyone stupid enough to try to swim through. He decided to try to find some way to avoid taking the plunge.

AFTER THE HEAT of the early afternoon, the water struck cold as Ryan walked down the sloping expanse of beach.

It had taken him over an hour of arduous exploration before he found a length of driftwood that he judged was large enough to help him through the raging sea. It was part of the scarred trunk of an aspen that must have been carried a vast distance down onto the littered shore of the Keys.

Ryan dragged it behind him, panting and sweating with the effort. He stopped to rest for a quarter hour before attempting the hazardous crossing.

He hooked one arm over the slippery length of wood, kicking out to propel himself in roughly the right direction. His plan had been to try to work his way out to sea, into the Gulf, bypassing the worst of the maelstrom.

But the current sucked him into the narrow channel between the two small islands, buffeting him from side to side with white-crested waves breaking over him. If it hadn't been for the support of the chunk of aspen, Ryan could easily have been drowned trying to make the crossing.

As quickly as he was pulled into the whirling heart of the tide race, he came shooting out the other side into much calmer water.

The only slight risk was that the movement of the sea might pluck him off to the west, carrying him right out into the Gulf of Mexico.

But by kicking hard, using his free hand to steer, Ryan was able to work his course toward the southerly key, pushing away the log and hauling himself out over a low concrete piling onto dry sand.

If his guess was correct, he should soon be passing the section of the Keys where the redoubt lay hidden. From there it was only a short distance back to the institute.

THE HIGHWAY HAD DROPPED to two lanes at that point, but it had also been destroyed by quake action, turned into a jagged strip of unwalkable tarmac and dirt.

Ryan picked his way clear, sticking closer to the rugged shoreline, where, ten minutes later, he found the wrecked boat and the corpses.

Chapter Nineteen

Ryan's first glimpse of the wreckage was through some dried sagebrush. For a moment he perceived it as the ruins of some shanty dwelling. Then he saw the clear line of a keel, jutting out of the dunes.

And his heart sank.

He'd been certain that he'd spotted both of the boats from the institute flying away southward, safe beyond the devastation of the massive underwater eruption. Now it looked as though he'd been wrong.

As Ryan drew closer to the wrecked vessel, he realized that his initial suspicion had been false. This was a bigger boat than either of the other two, different in many ways.

From what remained of it, Ryan could see that it looked like a oceangoing fishing boat, at least thirty feet long. It was very old, clinker-built, from varnished strips of oak. The superstructure had been painted a dark green and it had once carried two masts, though both were broken off only a foot or so above the decking. There was also a battered brass propeller, though an initial glance didn't reveal whether it had been powered or not. There was a name printed on the side, in florid yellow lettering, ornamented with tiny red flowers. A single word. A name. *Leander.*

There was no clue as to where the vessel had come from.

Ryan paused and stared at it. The port side loomed over him. What was interesting was what must have caused the wreck. There were two holes in the wooden hull, both about five feet across, showing white splintered oak at the edges.

It was obvious that there had been twin explosions, blasting the vessel's flank, probably resulting in its destruction within minutes. The captain had, perhaps, driven the *Leander* ashore to try to save lives.

As the one-eyed man walked slowly around the smashed boat, he saw that the captain, if that had been his plan, had failed.

There were five corpses.

Three lay side by side, with the ominous look of being the victims of a planned execution. A fourth dangled head-down over the starboard side of the the wrecked boat. The fifth lay sprawled near some stunted mimosa bushes, as though death had caught him trying to escape.

Flies in their hundreds buzzed angrily away as Ryan stepped closer, disturbing their feasting.

It was obvious that death had come to that place within the past two or three days. In high temperatures the human body deteriorated at an alarming rate. Ryan couldn't tell if the five corpses had been white or Indian or what. Because all five of them were now a somber black. In raiding the bodies for meat, the variety of carrion scavengers had torn off most of the clothes, so at least Ryan was able to tell that three of the dead had been male and two of them female. From their sizes, it looked as though one male and one female had been young. Perhaps under ten years of age.

The eyes had gone completely and all of the soft tissues, mouth, nose, tongue and genitals. It was probably birds that had ripped open the stomachs of four of the five, spilling the intestines in great yellow-gray loops all over the sandy earth. The fifth one, who looked as if he might have been running away, had fallen facedown. His stomach had swollen, giving him a grotesque appearance of posthumous pregnancy.

From the crusted and blackened rags that remained, Ryan suspected that they might have been local fishermen, wearing cotton pants and shirts. All were barefoot.

Despite the strips of flesh that had been peeled away from the skulls, it wasn't hard to determine the manner of their passing.

The three in a row, including the children, all had neat bullet holes in the centers of their foreheads, possibly 9 mm rounds. The backs of their heads had been blown away, leaving small fragments of bone stuck in the wooden planking of the boat.

It had been a deliberate execution.

The man who hung from the deck had three bullet holes that Ryan could see, though there might have been more. A tight grouping was in the upper chest, any one of which would have been fatal.

The last man, arms ahead of him like a diver striving to enter deep water, had been hit at least seven or eight times. Ryan didn't bother counting the bullet holes.

There wasn't any point.

RYAN MOVED SOUTH, leaving the stinking corpses to the blowflies and the night crabs. In another forty-eight hours there wouldn't be a lot left to show that five human beings had gone into the long darkness there.

But the wrecked boat would stay for many months. Probably for years.

The boat was a puzzle that Ryan pondered as he walked steadily along the endless beach, parallel to the impassable stretch of bleached highway. Two large holes had been blasted into its sides.

Below the surface.

That was the real enigma wrapped up in the bigger mystery of the killings.

The only things that could have done that sort of damage were either grens of some kind, or mines using plas-ex. Or possibly land-to-sea missiles. However, the latter wasn't really feasible. And if they were mines, how had they been planted? Or had they been carried and somehow placed against the sides of the boat?

Suddenly, out of the corner of his eye, Ryan caught a flicker of movement out at sea, the dorsal fin and tail of what looked like a dolphin. Then he spotted two or three of them, their long noses protruding from the water as though they were watching him. They were less than fifty yards away from the beach.

One of the creatures dived, and Ryan could see its wake as it raced south at high speed.

Almost as if it were carrying a message.

IT WASN'T FAR OFF EVENING by the time he recognized that he was close to the institute. The currents had carried him a deal farther to the north than he'd suspected.

The two dolphins had kept pace with him for the remainder of the afternoon, eventually being rejoined by a third creature. Ryan had no way of knowing whether it was the same one that had sped away south earlier.

He saw half a dozen figures walking toward him through the waist-high scrub, led by the stocky Chuck Cybulski, carrying what looked like a rebuilt Browning rifle. J.B. was second in line, and he waved a casual hand to Ryan as they drew closer.

"Thought you'd gone mermaiding, friend," he called.

"Thought that myself. Everyone else make it back safe?"

"Sure. The eruption sort of helped to blow us out of the triple-red zone. Krysty wanted to circle back, but Tomwun said there was no point. Have to admit it looked that way to me. Still, good to see you again, Ryan." He grasped the one-eyed man's hand in his own and gave it a firm shake.

MARK TOMWUN LED the group that was waiting for them when they made their way through the gloaming to the group of buildings. The sun was a glowing ember on the horizon, casting its bloody light across everyone standing there.

"My dear Ryan, this is such a wonderful triumph of the will, is it not?"

"Guess it is."

He was touched at Dean's struggle not to betray any emotion and act like a man. "Hi, Dad. Thought you were going to be...be late for supper." But there was a tremble in the voice and a suspicious glistening at the corners of his eyes.

"Good swim?" Michael asked, shaking his hand.

"My father always swore that I'd likely die in hot water." Ryan grinned. "Nearly got it right today."

Mildred said nothing, simply hugging him so hard he felt his ribs creaking.

Doc inclined his head toward Ryan. "I have always insisted that you were born to be hanged, my dear fellow. Welcome home."

"Thank, Doc."

Krysty was last.

"Bastard," she whispered. Her mouth was soft against his, her fingers gripping him by the back of the neck. As she pressed against him, Ryan could feel the tension trembling through her entire body. "You bastard, lover."

"I'm here now."

"Sure. What would I have done if..."

He kissed Krysty very gently, holding her tight. "Sorry."

Ryan eased his way out of Tomwun's offer for a meal to celebrate his safe return, explaining, truthfully, that he was very tired from his ordeal and that he wanted only to go straight to bed and sleep the clock around, which wasn't true.

"DEAN?"

"Yeah, Dad?"

"Go take a walk outside, will you?"

The boy's face fell. "Why? What is there that you don't want me to know about?"

Ryan ruffled his hair affectionately. "Not that, son. Not at all. Just that I don't want there to be any pairs of big ears hanging around outside the windows."

"Oh, sure." The boy's face brightened again. Watching him from across the room, Krysty felt a small pang of emotion at how like Ryan the boy was.

"No secrets from you, Dean. But I want to feel secure. Just sort of go outside and walk around for a couple of minutes."

"Take a piss?"

"If you like. Yeah. Then come back inside."

The boy darted out, leaving behind him a silence that was broken by J.B. "Something while you were away from us, Ryan?"

"Yeah. Wait until the kid's back, then I'll talk about it. Mebbe nothing. Don't know."

IT TOOK LESS THAN twenty minutes to run quickly through what had happened to him after being flung from the boat, concentrating on the wrecked vessel and the five corpses.

Mildred spoke first. "You say the ship was blown up by a mine or by some kind of a rocket?"

"Not necessarily. I'm saying that two explosions, external, had ripped her hull apart. And that someone had massacred the crew. Question of who?"

"Tomwun?" Dean asked, his voice sliding uncontrollably up the register. "He's a good sort of dude, Dad. Looks after all the dolphins, doesn't he?"

Ryan shrugged. "I wish I knew. He's been nothing but friendly to us. No sort of threats. But..."

Mildred was sitting at the table, her chin in her hands. "Used to have a saying that there's no such thing as a free lunch. If there's something that doesn't set right here in the institute, then the question you have to take on board is where do we fit in? What does Tomwun want from us?"

They talked for another hour or more, but ended up going around in circles, unable to reach any kind of clear conclusion. In the end they all went off to their beds.

Ryan found sleep difficult.

Chapter Twenty

When he checked his wrist chron, Ryan found that it was only a few minutes after two in the morning.

The slight movement was enough to bring Krysty awake. "All right, lover?"

"Sleeping badly."

"Bad dreams?"

"Can't remember. Just that I keep finding myself walking along a dark corridor with no doors and no windows. Figure it's a kind of drowning dream."

"Probably. Want me to give you a massage? Try and help you relax?"

Ryan swung his legs over the side of the bed. "Might walk a while. Often helps."

"Long as you don't get some crazed killer coming after you with a knife."

"Sure. Fancy a walk, lover?"

Krysty nodded. "Why not?"

"I'll get dressed."

"Go barefoot?"

"Glass and shit out around the buildings. Better get your boots on."

"Wait for me."

Filtered moonlight angled through the smeared window of their bedroom. Ryan watched as Krysty jumped from under the sheets, wincing as her feet touched the cold floor. She pulled on a shirt and a pair of navy pants, then tugged on the boots that she'd been wearing the first time Ryan Cawdor saw her. They'd been through fire, ice and water, but they still looked good.

There were chiseled silver points on the toes, which turned the boots into lethal weapons. The dark blue leather was ornamented with silver, spread-wing falcons. In the stacked heels Krysty was only an inch below Ryan's six-foot-two.

"Ready," she said.

THEY MOVED QUICKLY off the concrete paths onto the soft, soundless sand.

Ryan took the lead, walking away from the main buildings of the institute toward the distant glitter of the Lantic.

"We looking for anything special, lover?" Krysty spread her arms and sucked in a great breath of the night air. "Gaia! That's so good and fresh."

"Anywhere special?"

"No. Anything special."

"If there's a secret here that we ought to know about, then it's linked to the sea. To the dolphins. That's what Tomwun is all about."

Krysty took his arm as they picked their way carefully over a patch of rough ground, with some ancient foundations sticking up through the scrubby grass. "I've been thinking about it since we got here. I keep having a feeling that not everything's right. But... I can't really explain it."

"But it's bad."

"Yeah."

They stopped in a patch of shadow at the side of the communal dining room, watching as a white-coated figure shimmered toward the laboratories, walking from the direction of the quay.

The light wasn't good enough to make out who it was.

"Why're we hiding, lover?" Krysty whispered. "We aren't doing anything wrong, are we?"

"Not yet."

THEY DIDN'T SEE anyone else, and there were no lamps burning in the group of buildings near the dock area. Ryan walked past them, pausing on the edge of the quay, one foot resting on a huge rusting iron ring that looked as though it dated back two or three hundred years.

"Mebbe we ought to get ourselves a boat. Or a ship. Don't know the difference between them. Boat's bigger, but when does it turn into a ship?"

Krysty joined him, staring down into the dark, lapping water. "The same time that the magic princess's royal coach turns into a pumpkin?"

"Funny. I was thinking if we had a big enough boat...or ship, then we could all live on board it. Go where we wanted. When we wanted. Could be a good life.''

"Mebbe. I was born on land and I've lived on land. I like being by the sea, Ryan, but I'm really not all that sure about the idea of living on it.''

"Keep out of trouble.''

She punched him lightly on the arm. "Sure. Like you did today, lover.''

The shadow of the quay spread over the black water twenty feet below them. Ryan thought he saw something break the surface for a moment, then disappear with scarcely a ripple. But it wasn't possible to be sure.

"WHAT'S IN HERE?" Krysty shaded the glass with her hand, trying to peer slantwise into the building.

It was rectangular, jutting out right to the end of one of the number of smaller docks. Ryan pressed his ear to the double door. "I can hear the sound of splashing. Think there's some sort of a tank inside. Must be the place where Tomwun does some of his secret experiments. He said that they did a lot of work with living creatures.''

"There's a lock on the door.''

It was an old-fashioned brass padlock, its exterior stained with a layer of green verdigris. Ryan shook it, but it was enormously heavy.

"Could break a window,'' Krysty suggested.

"Don't want them knowing we've been doing us some poking around,'' Ryan said, looking at the

ground behind him. "Reckon it's worth a try using... Ah, there." He picked up a large stone, about
the size of a house brick.

"You can't smash the lock with that."

"Not aiming to." He drew the panga from its
sheath and handed it to Krysty. "Put the point there,
just against the top of the lock. Mind your fingers."

"No, *you* mind my fingers, Ryan." She turned her
head away as he hefted the stone and brought it down
in a short, chopping blow against the hilt of the long-
bladed cleaver.

They heard a muffled, metallic click, and the padlock sprang open.

"You got skills I never knew about, Ryan," Krysty
said admiringly.

"One of the things that Trader taught me. Ways of
doing it right."

Krysty gave him back the panga. Ryan checked the
needled tip, making sure that the impact hadn't damaged it, then sheathed the weapon. He carefully lifted
the lock out of the iron hasp and pushed at the door.

It swung silently open and they were inside.

The heavy smell of the sea was overlaid with the
odor of stale fish. The splashing sound that Ryan had
heard from outside had utterly ceased.

"Things are goin' on in here," Krysty whispered,
standing so close that her hip was against his.

"Bad?"

"Not good."

It took a little time for Ryan's eye to get used to the pitchy darkness. The only illumination came from a row of rectangular skylights set at angles in the sloping roof. There were two windows, both of them shuttered on the inside.

His mind flicked for a moment to Jak Lauren, the young albino boy who'd ridden with them for so long and who now ran a small holding in the Southwest with his wife and child. Jak had poor vision in bright light, but in the gloom he had eyes like a soaring hawk.

"There's tanks. Look a bit like cages. Small." Krysty took a cautious couple of steps farther into the building. "Got things in them."

Now he was beginning to perceive the interior. The roof was iron, with long girders spanning and supporting it. At its highest it looked to be close to twenty feet. The length of the building was well over a hundred feet, and its width about forty feet. A number of fragile catwalks stretched out over the sheen of water.

"I reckon we could risk the lights. Might be a bit of leakage around the shutters."

"How about the windows in the roof? Shine right out through them?"

Ryan considered that. "Be at an angle. Think it's a chance worth the taking."

"Where's the control switch?"

"One by the door as we came in."

Krysty walked over, her heels ringing faintly on the slabs of damp stone. "There's about five different switches, Ryan."

"We don't want too much light. Just try one of them. See what happens. Turn it off quick if it's not the right one."

He heard the click of the switch, but nothing seemed to happen. Then Ryan looked behind him and saw a pale halo of gold around the edge of the door frame.

"Off," he said. "It's turned on a lamp outside the main entrance."

At a second click the light vanished. The next one put on a string of bulbs that ringed the walls a little above head height. They were obviously only intended to provide background illumination, but they were sufficient for what Ryan and Krysty needed. Also, there was less chance of their being spotted from the main section of the institute.

Ryan leaned on the cold metal rail that ran around the building, protecting from an accidental fall into the water, and stared down.

It was a bizarre sight, unlike anything else that they'd been allowed to see anywhere else in the complex. All the other laboratories that Tomwun had permitted them to visit had been places of light and space, and the dolphins that they'd seen had all been free-swimming and had given every appearance of being perfectly contented.

Here there were a dozen or more pens, none of them looking bigger than ten feet square. Each held a single dolphin, and every one of the dolphins had its head craned awkwardly upward, straining to look at the two humans.

"What the fuck is going on here, Krysty?"

"Those pens got iron bars and there's wires running to some of them. Like they've been giving electric shocks to them. This is double-sicko, lover."

The stillness was unnerving.

Ryan walked along the side of the internal quay, looking at the shelves of equipment that lined the walls. There were rows of strange harnesses made of rubber, leather and steel chains. On the edge of what had once been Canon City, Colorado, he'd once visited a high-jack gaudy that specialized in what they called "Sadie-Maisie" sex. The sluts carried whips and wore high-heeled boots, and the johns got their kicks from being tied up, beaten and humiliated. Most of the bedrooms carried their specialized equipment. Ryan thought that the stuff on the shelves looked remarkably like that bondage gear.

"What's that down there, Ryan?" Krysty's voice seemed to disturb the dolphins, and several of them started to move their tails back and forth in a strange rhythmic movement.

"Where?"

"End. There's some blasters and spear guns. Something like that. Can't make out the details."

"I'll take a look."

The long shed seemed increasingly like the abode of some demonic torturer.

The row of low-wattage bulbs didn't give quite enough light to examine the shelves and closets in detail, but Ryan could still see enough. More than enough.

There were spears, some of them with ferociously barbed points, most handmade, but a few with the patina of original age. And harpoons. Ryan recalled the appalling time he'd spent on board a whaling ship and the way the harpoons had torn the life from the hearts of the great cetaceans. Some of these ten-foot spears had cavities in their hollow heads, designed to carry explosive charges to quicken the destruction.

The strange, clumsy harnesses suddenly began to make a horrific sense to Ryan. At the far end, against the blank seaward wall, were a number of hand-built grens and mines, shaped to fit snugly into the leather and chain rigs.

"Bastard," Ryan breathed.

"What's there?"

"That ship I found, with its ass blown apart. And the shot bodies."

Krysty moved along the catwalk, heads and eyes following her. "You think it was done from here?"

"Sure of it. The dolphins are trained . . . Fireblast! There's some kind of electric cattle prod here . . Trained to carry the mines like missiles. No wonder Tomwun kept this shithole place locked tight."

Right on cue the door was flung open and every one of the lights flared into dazzling life. There stood Mark Tomwun and five of his men, all holding rifles.

"Oh, dear," the scientist said. "What a very great pity, Ryan."

Chapter Twenty-One

Krysty had her own Smith Ryan Wesson Model 640 in its holster, the double-action, 5-shot .38-caliber blaster with the stubby two-inch barrel.

Her hand hovered over the butt, her eyes turned toward Ryan, waiting for the tiniest clue from him that would lead her to draw and start shooting.

Ryan rested his fingers lightly on his 9 mm SIG-Sauer, weighing up the situation, considering the odds, a phrase of the Trader drumming in his mind. "First five seconds give you your best chance. After that the odds go downhill faster than a brake-failed war wag."

The six men were holding their blasters at the hip, pointing vaguely toward himself and Krysty. Not even the most skillful shootist was going to be very accurate firing a rifle from the hip. The range was only about twenty yards, but Ryan still figured that the dice lay for himself and Krysty if they decided to draw their handguns and start shooting.

The other factor that he took into consideration was the way that Tomwun had been treating them since they'd first arrived at the institute—with soft hands, rather than with a metaled fist. And it would have been easy to have stormed into the shed and started blasting at them.

If that was what he intended.

The scales tipped slightly in the one direction.

"Think we'd better do some talking, Tomwun," Ryan said, though his hand never moved from the blaster.

"Perhaps."

"Take them out, Professor," said a tall, skinny man on the right of the group. Ryan knew him slightly. His name was Jerry Knight and he seemed to work mainly in the technical side of the operation, maintaining the power source.

"Perhaps not, Jerry."

"They saw all this."

"Perhaps. But..."

Ryan sensed what was coming, reading it in the man's tense posture, the knuckle whitening inside the trigger guard of the old M-16.

He spoke to Krysty, his lips barely moving, his voice pitched so low that nobody else would have heard it above the background noise of the small waves.

"Draw when I do, but don't fire. Think we can avoid a bloodbath here."

"No, Jerry," Tomwun said, also realizing, too late, that events had moved beyond his control.

"Fuckheads!" The word was screamed out, echoing around and around in the metal-roofed building, overlaid by the deafening crack of the rifle being fired.

The bullet was low, to the left, missing Ryan by a good yard, punching a hole in the wall and howling off into the surrounding blackness.

The built-in baffle silencer on Ryan's handgun no longer worked with the same efficiency that it once had, and he'd never been able to pick up a viable replacement for it. But it still dulled the thunder of the powerful SIG-Sauer as it slid from the holster into Ryan's hand.

The single shot was all that was needed.

Despite the speed of the draw, Ryan's aim was impeccable, picking the safest target, like any ice-heart killer would, which was the upper part of the chest. A narrow miss would still mean a hit on a vulnerable part of the body. Amateurs would try for a flashy head shot, with a far greater margin for a potentially lethal miss.

The full-metal-jacket round hit Knight smack through the sterno-clavicular joint at the top of the breastbone, drilling through the right lung as it started to distort and rotate, chipping the edge of the spine and exiting through the right shoulder blade in a welter of blood and fragments of shattered bone.

The force of the impact spun Knight, the rifle clattering from his hands. He staggered into the man immediately behind him, who was gaping in shock as his face and chest were splattered with warm crimson.

Professor Tomwun had also dropped his gun, his hands flying to his mouth. He lurched sideways, eyes closed, beginning to vomit uncontrollably.

"Nobody else do anything triple-stupe!" Ryan's voice snapped commandingly in the stillness.

Knight was out of the reckoning, even though he was still on his feet.

He tottered to the right, hands waving to the private beat of a silent drummer, blood fountaining from the exit wound in his back. His feet gave the illusion of moving more slowly than the rest of his body, as though he were wading through a deepening pool of molasses. His mouth sagged open, already brimming with a scarlet froth, and his eyes were staring sightlessly at the roof.

"Go down easy," Krysty whispered at Ryan's side, her own blaster covering the other five demoralized members of the watching group.

Before anyone could react, the dying man took half a dozen quick, dancing steps farther to his right, and folded neatly over the iron rail into one of the pens below, landing with a hollow splash.

"Get him out!" someone bellowed, certainly not Mark Tomwun, who was now crouched on his hands and knees, preoccupied with vomiting.

Ryan moved sideways and peered over the rail.

It was a hideous sight.

Knight had fallen between two of the cages, his head and shoulders drooping into one, his legs and lower torso landing in the other.

One of the dolphins had seized the skull of the dying man between its jaws and was frantically tugging it back and forth, trying to separate it from the upper body. There was the clearly audible crunching of bone, and more blood spurted from the severed carotid artery. In the other cage was a bottlenose, but it looked like it had suffered some kind of accident. The end part of its upper and lower jaws was missing, giving it a macabre, porcine appearance. It had bitten down on Jerry Knight's left foot, tearing it away at the ankle joint. Rising up on its powerful tail, it rotated at great speed, flourishing the severed foot, still in its neat black shoe.

The dolphins in the other constricting pens were going triple-crazy, whistling and clicking in a frenzy of noise, adding to the bedlam by thrashing their tails against the surface of the water.

Despite his ghastly and terminal wounds, Knight was still alive.

His dying screams were barely audible above the cacophony of sounds, but his arms were still flailing from side to side, fingers grasping convulsively at the bars of the cages.

"Save him. Oh, save him, Professor!"

The desperate shout from one of the rifle-toting men didn't seem to reach Tomwun, who was still retching onto the stones in front of his dead-white face. He didn't even look up at the disturbance and screaming.

Ryan leveled the SIG-Sauer and squeezed the trigger once more, aiming carefully for Knight's exposed nape, avoiding the dolphin. The body immediately went limp, though the death did nothing to calm the feeding frenzy of the creatures in their cramped, foaming pens.

"Professor, they're eating poor Jerry, tearing him limb from limb."

At last Tomwun seemed to recover his senses. He pulled himself to his feet, avoiding the pool of puke, swallowed hard and looked around him with a ragged semblance of his former dignity. "Use the shocker," he said.

"On all of them?" asked the oldest man in the group.

"Yes!"

Ryan watched, still holding the SIG-Sauer, though all thought of anyone doing any shooting seemed to be long gone. The man ran to a big control board bristling with levers, gauges, dials and colored buttons.

He reached for a large red lever, glancing once over his shoulder as though he wanted confirmation from Tomwun. But the professor was standing on the brink of the quay, leaning on the rail, staring at the devouring of his erstwhile colleague. Sensing the delay, he looked behind him.

"Do it, man!" he screamed in a ragged, out-of-control voice.

The lever was rammed down, and there was a tremendous crackling of electricity. The lights in the laboratory building flickered and dimmed, as if they were about to plunge everyone into total blackness.

Ryan saw a ghostly blue light dancing along the iron bars of the cages, hissing below the water.

The galvanic shock was powerful enough to stun every one of the dolphins, sending them into a stiffened stillness, floating belly-up in each tank.

"You've murdered them, you red-eyed bastard," Krysty raged, turning toward Tomwun, her index finger tight on the narrow trigger of the Smith & Wesson.

"No. They will recover very quickly, Krysty. No permanent harm is done to them. Believe me."

"I wouldn't believe you if you told me that shit floated and gold sinks," she snarled, trembling with the bitterness of her own furious anger.

"You murdered Jerry Knight. Shot him down in cold blood, Ryan."

"You got a fucking poor memory for a white-coat scientist, Tomwun."

"What?"

Ryan gestured to the hole in the wall of the building, behind him. "Think that was made by someone spitting a chew of tobacco? You stupe!" The one-eyed man was unable to conceal the contempt he felt for the man. "He shot at me, Tomwun. Nobody, I mean nobody, in all Deathlands does that and gets away with it."

Now the SIG-Sauer was pointing at the professor's face, drilling a laser-line between his eyes. Tomwun was slowly recovering a little of his self-control, and he shook his head. "There'll be no more shooting here tonight. You have my word on that."

"Worth as much as a baron's charity." He spit down into the water. "You said we should talk, Tomwun. Well, I tell you that I don't see much we got to discuss."

"Oh, but you are wrong. There is much. I was wrong to conceal some things from you, but I felt you might be shocked." He looked at Krysty. "I am truly sorry."

For several long beats of the heart nobody moved or spoke. In one of the pens there was a coughing noise and a single slapping splash.

"Coming around," Tomwun said. "Quickly. Get poor Knight's bedraggled body away before they start devouring it again. Come on, quickly."

Ryan nodded to Krysty, and they both holstered their blasters. While the professor watched, tapping his fingers on the rail, his assistants clambered nervously down the old iron ladders and, after an edgy, bungled struggle, emerged back onto the quay with the limp, savaged, bloodless corpse, laying it dripping on the stones.

"I'm going back to our rooms, now," Ryan said. "Give you the benefit. Just for the time being."

"We can talk in the morning. There are things that you don't know and don't understand." Tomwun was crying as he stared down at the remains of Jerry Knight. "In the morning."

Ryan nodded, reaching out to take Krysty's hand. "In the morning."

Chapter Twenty-Two

Krysty convinced Ryan that it was better to wake the others early the next day, rather than drag them all from sleep when they got back to their quarters. But the two of them were still fully awake well after midnight, lying in their bed and talking over what had happened in the quayside shed.

There was no possible argument that Professor Mark Tomwun wasn't anything like the gentle and caring ecologist that he'd portrayed himself. And the Institute of Peaceful Oceanographic Research wasn't what was described in its title.

Particularly there was overwhelming evidence that it wasn't at all peaceful.

"You think that he's just another megalomaniac baron on the make?"

"No. Not really. I mean... Fireblast! I don't know. He seems a real weird contradiction, doesn't he?"

They were lying pressed against each other, like two spoons snug in a drawer. Krysty had her arm across his chest, holding him close.

"I don't pick up any clear vibes from him," she said. "Lots of men and women, you can *see* them. Sort of see the real person under the mask. Some of the time I like Tomwun and some of the time... It's as though he's two completely different people, living inside the same skin.''

"Bombs and mines and dead people scattered on a beach... And electric shock treatment to condition those poor bastard fish to obey him."

"They aren't fish, lover," she corrected. "Mammals. Cetaceans. Not fish."

Ryan didn't reply. He had either fallen asleep, or he was giving a convincing impression of someone who was.

BREAKFAST WAS unusually massive, even by the generous standards of the institute. But, by the time it arrived, carried by two taciturn young men called McBride and Colquhoun, who shared the given name of Bob, Ryan and Krysty had recounted their adventures of the night before and the marvelous meal took on the appearance of a feeble bribe.

Despite the serious reservations that they'd all been discussing, the food was so excellent that everyone stuffed themselves: chilled fruit juices, orange, pineapple, grapefruit, mango and lime, and some others that none of them even knew the names of; dishes of cereals, both hot and cold, with either milk or cream, and honey or syrup; a platter with a rainbow assortment of fish laid all around it, alternating slices of red salmon and silver trout with pale swordfish and the coarser fillets of what could have been shark.

To Dean's delight, there was also a huge fry-up in a variety of chrome-plated dishes: golden eggs, fried and scrambled, and strips of crispy back bacon, with tomatoes and link sausages. Michael took two enormous steaks, each as big as a man's clenched fist, placing a fried egg on top of each, then scooping up four ladles of hash browns, finishing it with a side dish of grits and strips of deep-fried chicken breast.

"Perhaps they could butcher a steer or two for you, for later," Doc suggested.

"If we're going to leave, then I need to get my boiler well-fired, the youth replied.

"Does the professor know that you're going away from here?" asked one of the Bobs.

Ryan jumped in quickly, sensing the potential difficulty. "Not yet. Michael meant leaving for a trip down the coast for the day by boat. Thought it might make up for the disaster we had the other day."

Michael mouthed "Sorry" to Ryan, unseen by the two institute men. "Sure," he said. "Miranda mentioned it."

The other Bob was passing around a woven basket filled with a variety of breads. "Remember you all got a meeting with Professor Tomwun after this meal."

"We remember." Ryan helped himself to a warm sweet roll and spread it liberally with butter and raspberry jelly. "How could we forget?"

THEY HUNG AROUND, waiting for Tomwun to send the word that he was ready to meet with them. Dean played jacks with some tiny pink shells. Mildred was suffering from a mild migraine and had gone back to bed to rest. J.B. was stripping his Uzi, reassembling it in his lap without even looking at what his hands were doing. Ryan simply sat on a molded plastic chair, picking at a sliver of rough skin at the edge of a thumbnail. It was a habit that never failed to annoy Krysty.

"Stop doing that, lover. It drives me mad." She leaned against the side of the door, staring out across the complex toward the distant glitter of the Lantic.

"Sorry."

Michael had wandered over the section of the institute where Miranda worked on communication with the dolphins, but he was still within shouting distance.

Doc paced slowly up and down the sand in front of their quarters. His hands were folded behind his back, his eyes hooded, looking inward. The big Le Mat swung at his hip in time with his walking.

One of the Bobs, Colquhoun was Ryan's guess, was walking swiftly toward them from the direction of Tomwun's own personal quarters.

When he joined the companions he addressed his remarks directly to Ryan Cawdor, ignoring the rest of the group.

"He's ready for you."

"We're ready for him, too," Krysty said, moving down onto the area of trampled sand.

"Not you. Not any of you except for Ryan Cawdor. Just one-to-one. Professor said."

"We are his creatures and needs must obey," Mildred said, standing in the doorway. "Y'all come back soon, Ryan, y'hear what I say?"

He nodded. "Be back soon." He made a circle between thumb and forefinger and smiled at them all. "Be seeing you."

IT WAS A SHOCK to see Mark Tomwun. He looked like he hadn't slept a wink overnight, his face lined, gray beneath the eyes, and a faint stubble blurred the angles of his jaw.

"Come in, come in." He beckoned to Ryan from a long sofa, covered in faded maroon silk. "Have you eaten? Yes, of course you have. I remember now."

The door closed behind Ryan as he walked into the room, picking a high-backed, plain chair.

Tomwun nodded approvingly. "Good choice, Ryan. Not long after I came down to the Keys one of the local fishermen told me he'd found a house on a very isolated island. Several miles off the coast, in fact. This was before the locals began . . . But I run before my horse to market. Said there was some furniture I might like. Mostly rusting chrome and rotted leather. Rubbish. High-tech kitsch when it was new and simply moldering dreck now. But that chair was the jewel in the tiara. It's a genuine Shaker piece."

The man had been babbling, the words tumbling over each other in their eagerness to escape from his mouth. Ryan nodded, unsure what was going on. The only certainty was that the other man was possessed by nerves.

"Yes. Shaker work. Would be worth a fortune to the right collector." He paused and laughed, a high-pitched, fractured sound. "If there were still any collectors left in Deathlands, of course. But there aren't any, of course. Must stop saying that. Of course I must."

"Can we cut out this crap?"

Tomwun laughed again, rubbing his hands together as if he'd been trying to dry them on a damp towel. "Why not? About last night, Ryan..."

"Let me go first. We've all talked this through, and we've decided that we're leaving."

"When?"

"Soon as I walk out of here."

"But let me—"

"No. I found a wrecked boat up the coast a ways, when I got thrown overboard by that undersea eruption. The bottom was blown out of it and there were some rotting corpses. All been shot."

Tomwun jumped to his feet. "We were not responsible for the shootings. I swear to you on my mother's grave."

"But the sinking?"

"Ah, that was... Before you run away, I think—"

"Walking, not running. I don't run away from places, Tomwun. I walk."

Which wasn't strictly true.

There'd been plenty of times that Ryan had run for his life. The Trader used to joke that the only steps you took, when faced by a triple-red danger, were fucking long ones.

"Please, please. I understand that you... I should have been honest."

"Generally best."

Once again, Ryan was conscious that the slightly sententious statement wasn't strictly true.

"The death of poor Knight. Nobody blames you, Ryan, for what happened last night."

Ryan shrugged, aware that the vaunted Shaker chair was agonizingly uncomfortable. "Makes no odds what you or anyone thinks about it. Man tried to chill me. I chilled him. End of the story."

"It's only been in the past year or so that we have fitted out that laboratory. Until then it was pure research, trying to understand our fellow creatures. Then we started trying to train the dolphins to help us against danger."

"Danger?"

"Pirates."

"Pirates? Guys in a ship with eye patches and parrots and the bones-and-skull flag?"

Tomwun managed a feeble smile that failed to cling to his lips. "I understand your reaction, Ryan. The old pirates from children's tales were kindly and gentle compared to these bloodthirsty bastards."

"Go on."

"They are led by a half-breed called Red Jack Yoville. If you ever have the misfortune to meet him, you'll understand the reason for his name. Perhaps a hundred or more in his gang, but they raid the Keys in small groups. Rarely get together in force. Yet. Go up the delta and into the bayous. Where they sail, there is rape and fire and death. And they intend to destroy us here."

"Why?"

"I once read that a mountain climber was asked the same question. Why he risked his life, scaling the tallest peaks. He replied it was simply because the mountains were there. For Yoville the same applies. We are in his way. On what he believes is his demesne. So, to try to save ourselves we are training the dolphins to carry weapons for us and to attack humans, things that are quite contrary to all my beliefs and to all their ways of living."

"Always knew you scientists were proud of your work," Ryan said. He stood. "Sorry about the threat. Your fight. Nothing to do with us. We leave."

"They'll kill us."

"Mebbe. How about those poor dead folks on the wrecked boat I saw?"

"Accident. We thought they were with Yoville. One of his vessels had been seen. They were Seminole fishermen. Two of our dolphins carried the charges. By the time we realized our error, it was too late."

"For the dolphins, as well?" Ryan grinned mirthlessly. "Your fellow creatures? That what you just called them."

Tomwun looked down at the floor and said nothing.

Ryan walked to the door. "So long."

"I'll die."

"We all do, Tomwun."

"The pirates shot those people."

"After you'd wrecked their ship so they were fucking helpless victims." He turned and took a couple of steps toward Tomwun, who cowered against the wall, his hands covering his face.

"No. I won't hit you. Nothing personal in this. I won't bring my friends into something that's not our fight."

As he stepped out into the dazzling sunlight, Ryan heard the man start to cry.

Chapter Twenty-Three

Ryan had half expected the scientists to make some sort of attempt to stop them from leaving the compound, but everyone from the institute seemed to have vanished. Doors were closed and blinds drawn down across most of the windows. As they readied themselves for their departure, checking weapons and taking some food and drink, he told the others a little about Tomwun's plea for help.

Dean and Michael were the only ones to raise any sort of objection.

"We could chill these pirates, Dad. Couldn't we?"

"I agree with Dean. They might make some mistakes along the line. Who doesn't? But they don't seem to be truly evil people here, Ryan."

"I'm not too strong on what's evil and what isn't. Lot depends on circumstances. That doesn't matter."

"It should matter," the ex-monk replied. "We fight against evil or we become a part of that same evil."

"Claptrap and cant, my boy," Doc boomed. "You'll be telling me next some arrant nonsense about success being the only failure and that failure isn't really any sort of success. Ryan is right. Life is survival. We know enough about this so-called self-styled scientist to be absolutely sure that his favorite color isn't as pure white as a Montana snowfall. Nor, however, is it the black of a mole's rectal orifice.''

Michael looked bewildered. ''Thought you might have sided with me, Doc. You of all people.''

The old man patted him on the shoulder. ''Expect the worst and you'll rarely be disappointed.'' He looked around. ''I shall miss the food, the hot water and the softness of the mattress. Still, we shall go some more a-roving, shall we not, my brothers and sisters?''

''Yeah,'' Ryan said. ''We shall go right now. I'll take point. J.B., take the rearguard.''

THERE WAS THE FAINT, allusive scent of sulfur carried across the Keys by a mild westerly.

''Another quake or volcano or something,'' Mildred said. ''Doesn't show in the sky. There isn't a single cloud anywhere in sight, is there?''

The sky was an unsullied blue.

As they left the Mark Tomwun Institute of Peaceful Oceanographic Research, not a face showed at any of the buildings.

Ryan figured that they would easily get back to the ruins of the underwater redoubt before dark, though a small part of him felt a prickle of fear at the thought of plunging into the cold gloom, with the massive coils of the mutie sea snake waiting among the slick caverns.

If Michael shared that horror, he certainly wasn't showing it.

Though Ryan kept them mainly to the folded ribbon of the old blacktop, he kept sprinting to one side or the other, particularly at the point where the Key was so narrow that you could almost have thrown a stone from the shore of the Gulf clear across into the Lantic.

Dean followed the older boy, engaging in a mock battle with him, using a couple of lengths of driftwood, each about the size of a two-handed sword. Michael's reflexes were so uncannily fast that he could have beaten Dean within seconds, but he deliberately slowed himself down, allowing the eleven-year-old to occasionally score a glancing hit.

Krysty had broken from their extended skirmish line, joining Ryan at the front, Linking her arm in his, whistling under her breath.

"Hope we don't get attacked by Tomwun's pirates," he said. "Caught cold if we do."

"Worried, lover?"

"Not really. Sunshine and fresh air. Once we get through that dark-blasted tunnel into the gateway and make the jump, I'll be pleased."

"That was the nearest we've had to a vacation since ... Oh, I can't even remember."

"Yeah. Good to relax a little. Apart from having to chill the Indian and then that guy in the shed last night. Only two dead in all those days. Close to a vacation."

Krysty shook her head. "You know what I mean, lover. Least we could sleep all night without any clothes on and not expect to find a stickie trying to rip our faces away."

"Sure. But the way things turned out, it was like we'd been eating this wonderful apple and then, eighteen bites in, you find you've got half a maggot between your teeth. The institute was kind of like that."

"You got a great way with words, lover." She squeezed his hand. "I know what you mean."

As they moved slowly northward, they didn't see much wildlife—a few orange-capped gulls, circling far out to their right, toward the east, and unidentifiable furry creature, around three feet long, with a prominent jaw and a small horn in its forehead that had scampered across the blacktop in front of them and vanished into some scrub.

All the dolphins were still there.

Oddly there were several species, keeping station with them a hundred yards out in the ocean. Ryan had been long enough in the institute to recognize the main types.

Several of the most common were bottlenoses, their smooth glistening bodies appearing and disappearing in complex, sinuous patterns. There was a pair of spotted dolphins, with their beautiful white-on-black patterns, and one each of the rarer species, the small franciscana dolphin with its long snout, a round-nosed black vaquita and a humpback dolphin, looking just as though they were a trio of mer-children at play.

"Look," Mildred said. "That's a killer whale out there, isn't it?"

"Yeah," the Armorer agreed. "Hey, it's the same one from Tomwun's place."

"How do you know that?" Ryan shaded his eye from the bright sunlight that came lancing off the rolling swell. "All look the same."

"No. One that they called Lorca."

"Orca, surely," Doc interrupted. "Lorca is a long-dead poet."

J.B. took off his fedora and rubbed at his forehead. "Could be you're right, Doc. But I recognize that big double notch out of the dorsal fin."

"Why's Tomwun sent his army of spies after us?" Krysty stared at the gamboling array of the lithe and beautiful creatures. "Protect us?"

"They saved me from the snake." Michael's face was set like stone. "Don't any of you ever forget that I'd have been dead if it hadn't been for them. Not one of you could have rescued me, could you?"

"Fair comment," Ryan agreed. "But they can't speak to us and we can't speak to them, so let's keep moving."

THEY WERE more than halfway toward the buried redoubt, making good time.

"Is it my ancient imagination, or can I catch the scent of wood smoke?"

Ryan stopped, glancing behind him. Doc was standing still, head back, sniffing the air.

"I can smell it, too, Dad."

Now that it was drawn to his attention, Ryan realized that he'd subconsciously noticed it several seconds ago. There was a momentary anger at his own carelessness, strolling along with Krysty as though they didn't have a worry in the world, forgetting in the sunshine that they were still very much in Deathlands.

"Coming from ahead, to the left. Just about make a faint haze, beyond those three palm trees." J.B. pointed with the muzzle of the Uzi.

Now Ryan could see it, a ghosting of white, drifting innocuously into the sky behind a ridge. There was also the top of a building just visible.

"Could be fishermen," Mildred said, her own doubts riding across her voice, "couldn't it?"

Ryan didn't bother to answer her.

"Wait here. J.B., let's you and me go and have a look at what's down there."

They moved quickly forward, stooping slightly to keep as low as possible. Ryan had his SIG-Sauer drawn and ready, while the Armorer gripped his Uzi.

"Pirates," J.B. whispered in what was more a statement than a question.

"Likely," Ryan replied.

Now they were off the road, in among some windblasted junipers, following the line of an old track toward the Gulf of Mexico. The smell of the smoke was stronger, overlaid with the flavor of roasting meat.

Through a dip in the land they could suddenly glimpse a short stretch of the beach. Two boats were drawn up above the tide line. Both were twenty-footers, with furled sails, both had auxiliary motors bolted to their sterns and they were being guarded by a tall black with a blaster slung across one shoulder.

"Yeah, pirates," Ryan hissed.

They were lying on the crest of the ridge, flattened in the spear grass to avoid being silhouetted against the skyline. They passed forward the last few feet, peering cautiously down.

It was obvious that the site had once been a small trailer park, with a few clapboard cottages on two sides. The roofless hulks of the buildings looked as though the first strong wind would blow them clear across the Keys, yet they had obviously survived there for a hundred years of hurricanes and storms.

Scattered around were the rusting hulks of thirty or more trailer units, mostly windowless and many of them also doorless. They'd settled on their hubs, rotting fragments of old tires still visible on a few of the wheels.

Ryan saw two fires. Both had iron tripods suspended over them, holding black caldrons. What was infinitely more interesting was the group of men—and women, he noticed—who were standing or sitting around the dancing flames. A quick count produced nine.

Every one of them wasn't just armed, but somewhat overarmed. They all had at least two handblasters, either in belts or in crossed shoulder holsters. Three piles of various rifles stood neatly by the side of one of the fires. Bandoliers of ammo lay in the sand, and Ryan could also see a mixture of long and short knives sheathed on every hip.

Fishermen they weren't.

He glanced sideways at J.B. "Tomwun was telling the truth."

"His worst nightmare," the Armorer agreed.

"Back to the others. Cut across to the eastern side of the Key and stick to the beach for a half mile or so north. Should be safely past them by then."

"Yeah."

Like all good plans, it was a good plan.

Like a lot of good plans, it was ruined by a stroke of unforeseen bad luck.

As Ryan and J.B. started to wriggle back down the slope to rejoin the others, they were confronted by a fat mulatto woman, rising from behind one of the junipers, still hoisting her panties from answering a call of nature.

"Who fuck're you?" she asked, her brutish face reflecting a mixture of anger and growing suspicion.

She was just too far away from them to be taken out with silent steel.

So Ryan shot her.

Chapter Twenty-Four

The range was around fifty feet, but for a haunting moment Ryan thought that he must have missed.

The woman was wearing a shirt made from strips of rag loosely sewn together, and there was no sign that the 9 mm bullet had found its target. She stood still, her eyes open, starting to point an accusing finger at the two strangers, her mouth open to yell a warning, a warning that the barely muffled bark of the SIG-Sauer had now rendered superfluous.

"Again," J.B. urged, also thinking the unthinkable, that Ryan Cawdor had missed one of the easiest shots he'd ever had in his life.

While they both stared, aware of the loud burst of alarmed shouting from just over the brow of the low hill, the woman went down. Her feet didn't move. There was no staggering. She was like a balloon when all the air is suddenly released.

The life departed in a great rush, accompanied only by a mournful sigh, more of resigned sorrow than pain or terror. The woman slumped to the sand, lying completely still, resembling a bundle of old clothes fallen from the back of a cart. A trickle of urine darkened the sand between her spread thighs.

Ryan could see Krysty and the others, alerted by the noise of the shot, standing and staring in their direction, waiting to know what had happened and what to do.

"Run or fight?" J.B. asked, cutting instantly to the heart of the business.

They were slightly outnumbered, and certainly outgunned in terms of quantities of blasters. But they probably had the better weapons and the combat skill to make them count.

If Ryan had known in advance that there might be a major confrontation, then he would have arranged to ambush the pirates from hiding, shot as many down as possible in cold blood. Since the redoubt was close at hand it wouldn't even matter if some of them escaped. But enough of them would be down to enable Ryan's group to reach safety.

Now things were different.

If they tried to move quickly up the coast, the pirates could outflank them in their boats or hold them up long enough for reinforcements to arrive, which led to a single, inevitable course of action.

All of these calculations took Ryan less than two and a half seconds.

"Fight," he said, turning immediately and climbing on hands and knees to the crest of the rise, looking down into a scene of considerable confusion. The men and women of the pirate gang were scrambling around the fire, grabbing for their rifles and snatching up the belts of ammunition. Their heads kept looking up toward the sound of the gun.

It was longish range to hope for an ace on the line with a handblaster, but Ryan leveled the SIG-Sauer and opened fire on the enemy camp.

J.B. was instantly at his side, the Uzi set on semiautomatic, pouring short bursts of lead into the pirates.

Behind him, Ryan was aware that Krysty was leading the dash toward him, his rifle in her right hand. Dean and Michael were together at her heels, Mildred close behind. Doc was last, his ancient knee boots slipping and sliding in the sand, cursing like a trooper as he struggled to unholster the Le Mat while on the run.

Within seconds the area around the fires was deserted, the survivors of the raiders having darted into the cover of the ruined buildings and the sagging remains of the trailers, leaving one certainly dead and two seriously wounded.

The corpse was facedown in the smaller of the fires, flames licking at her greasy hair, igniting her ragged clothes. The skin around her face and breasts was already blistering and beginning to char and darken. Ryan wasn't sure whether he or J.B. had put her down.

One man, who seemed to have lost a hand, was rolling on the ground, knees drawn up to his chest, screaming out in agony from a bullet that had angled sideways through his stomach. Ryan was certain that he was definitely a victim of the SIG-Sauer's power and accuracy.

The third was a younger man with very long, straw-colored, straggling hair that covered his face. A triple burst from the Uzi had stitched along his spine and he was trying to crawl to safety, his paralyzed legs dragging uselessly behind him through the trampled sand.

Michael flung himself flat alongside Ryan, staring down toward the sea. "You going to shoot those two?" He pointed at the injured pair.

Ryan was genuinely surprised. "Why?"

"Put them out of their misery, of course."

"But I never put them in their misery in the first place, Michael."

Now there was sporadic resistance from below them, bullets kicking into the top of the dune within a few feet of Ryan and the others.

"Heads down," he warned unnecessarily.

"How many there?" Krysty asked.

"About six or seven. We spotted one farther over, out of sight, by two boats. Could be more. We never saw that fireblasted woman until she came out of the bushes. Hadn't been for her we could have moved quietly on past and gotten free away."

Krysty had given him the Steyr SSG-70 rifle, and he had the walnut stock pressed into his shoulder. As often before, there was the momentary awareness of his luck that his brother Harvey had destroyed the sight in his left eye, not his right. It meant he could still fire a standard bolt-action rifle.

J.B. called out a warning to all of them. "Don't waste bullets from up here. Only blaster that's much use is Ryan's. Rest of us save lead."

"Haven't you forgotten something, John?" Mildred asked, wiping sand from her face and hands.

"Oh, yeah. I reckon you might do something with that .38 if you see a chance."

The killing ground that lay below them, like a map of an urban wasteland, offered limitless hiding places for the survivors of the pirate gang. They'd be able to scuttle from bungalow to trailer unit, dodging through long grass and bush, gradually working their way to the beach.

"They're going to get away from us," J.B. called. "You can pick them off from the headland behind us if they try to take to the boats."

Ryan didn't answer, waiting for a moment, breath held, finger taking up the first pressure of the trigger of the 10-round hunting rifle, waiting and watching. One of the gang was hiding at the corner of a weather-stained Airstream unit. Already he'd made two linking runs, each one moving him a few yards closer to the beach and the boats. Now, Ryan knew, he would very soon have to make a third move.

And when he did, the crack of the rifle found an echo in a faint cry from below as the man toppled backward, drilled through the forehead.

A slender woman with a long single-shot home-built musket at her shoulder stepped from cover, screaming incoherent abuse toward the top of the ridge.

Mildred whispered softly, "Yes," then steadied the Czech ZKR 551 revolver and put a Smith & Wesson .38 round through the center of the young woman's nose. She kicked over onto her back, arms and legs flailing in the spasmodic finality of dying.

"Shit a brick, Mildred!" Dean exclaimed, almost dropping his own heavy Browning automatic. "That was the best shot I ever saw."

"Worst," she grunted somewhat irritably. "I was aiming at her mouth."

The shooting slackened and there were no further attempts from the men and women in the trailer park to work their way to the sea.

"Mist out at sea," Krysty said. "Thickening and moving this way."

"And I can taste that stinking farty smell again." Dean wrinkled his nose in disgust. "That mean there's another of those eruptions?"

"Could be, son."

They all watched as the hazy gray cloud darkened and adopted a more solid form, drifting in from the west, shutting down the horizon.

"Be here in fifteen...twenty minutes." J.B. glanced at Ryan. "Taken out four of them. We could go and skirmish after the rest."

It was tempting. "Best enemy was a dead enemy" was what a child learned in Deathlands at his mother's knee, and it was one of the greatest of all truths.

But the old trailer park could be a death trap. The surviving pirates could hide in a hundred different places and wait. Chances were they'd be able to chill at least one of their attackers. It could be done, but it would take too much time and a lot of slow care.

"Move around so we can cover the part of the beach where they've got their boats hidden," Ryan said. "Give them a hard time of it, getting off."

"They won't move until they think the fog's enough to hide them." The Armorer pushed back his fedora. "They can see it coming, just like we can."

"Once they're off the beach we can think about moving." Ryan glanced at the sky. "Clouding over. Could be a storm."

"Are we still entertaining the concept of traveling north toward the redoubt?" Doc had just holstered his Le Mat, realizing that there would be no likely call for it in this particular firefight.

"Why not?"

"I am certain that I spotted some other small vessels. Unless, of course, they were more of our friendly dolphins."

"Where?"

"To the right of the fog, as we watch it moving toward us now."

"That's north," Mildred said. "If Doc's right, then we could get cut off that way. The mist might bring them into the shore and that would place them pretty damned close to where the gateway is hidden.''

Michael's dark eyes had widened. ''Think I saw them, too, Doc. Four or five. I didn't say anything, because I couldn't be that sure. Didn't want to risk looking stupid if I was wrong. You know what I mean?''

Doc nodded. ''Indeed I do, my boy. Fortunately, when you survive beneath below...what's the...? Beyond. Survive beyond a certain age, then looking stupid becomes a congenital aspect of personality.''

Ryan sucked at his teeth, considering the new developments. He had to assume that Michael and Doc were right. Odds then made it likely the newcomers would be pirates. The survivors below them would probably escape with the fog sweeping over the Gulf like a sentient giant.

It didn't leave them much choice.

''We'll go back south. To the institute.''

Chapter Twenty-Five

Ryan was in a furious temper. He'd been to see Tomwun as soon as they trudged back through the security gate of the Institute of Peaceful Oceanographic Research. The scientist had been out in the Lantic with three or four of his senior assistants, setting free a young killer whale that they'd rescued after it had been found with the broken shaft of a harpoon through one eye socket.

It was late afternoon before the boat chugged into the harbor and the bespectacled figure of Tomwun climbed the iron ladder. He'd been unable to conceal his surprise at seeing Ryan and the others back on the dock.

He'd deliberately snubbed them, throwing over his shoulder the suggestion that Ryan should go and meet him at his quarters in an hour.

It took all of Krysty's powers of persuasion to stop Ryan from going immediately to the quay and stealing a boat at gunpoint, then circling wide out to the east until they reached the point where they could land and cut straight across the narrow band of islands to the redoubt.

"Snot-sucking son of a bitch thinks he can treat me like that! Fireblast, Krysty!"

"Easy, lover." She put her arms around him, holding him tight, feeling the brittle tenseness slowly melting away. "Life's too short for this." She used all of the skills that her mother, Sonja, had taught her, calming the angry man. "Better?"

"Yeah." He smiled. "Yeah, better."

WHEN TOMWUN EVENTUALLY appeared, he made no apology for keeping Ryan waiting, nor did he seem all that interested, or concerned, to hear about the fire-fight only a few miles north of the institute. He had poured himself a large beaker of grapefruit juice and sipped slowly at it while Ryan gave him a sketchy description of what had happened.

"Less than a dozen. And you were responsible for killing several of them?"

"Yeah. Probably three down."

"Then the fog came?"

Ryan suddenly realized that what had appeared at first to be disinterest was now, more obviously, something that was completely different.

Disbelief.

"The fog came," he repeated.

Tomwun drained his drink and leaned back, his chair creaking. "Convenient."

When Ryan had been a younger man, his temper had been legendary—fierce, ever ready to flame, sometimes slipping from the bonds of his control.

Often to the pain and misery of others. Occasionally to himself.

It had been the Trader who'd gradually persuaded him that his blinding rage would, eventually, only hurt that one person. Himself. And, since then, Ryan had tried—really tried—to control that blood-eyed anger.

But now he could feel the long scar down his right cheek beginning to twitch and burn. He took a deep breath and lifted his hand to touch the gouged cicatrix that sliced across his face from his good eye to the corner of his mouth.

"What's the matter with you, Cawdor? Just commented that the fog was convenient for your story." Tomwun shrugged, hands spread like a merchant in a pesthole low-jack store offering a customer a dubious bargain.

Ryan was across the room and leaning over the leather-topped desk before Tomwun could even blink. He grabbed him by the collar and hauled him to his feet, heaving him up so that their faces were only inches apart.

"What did you—" the scientist began. But Ryan tightened his grip and the words were choked off.

"You gutless little bastard! You torture those dolphins so that they'll go kill for you. Try and enlist us on your side as hired guns. Then when we run into those same pirates, you sit there, smug as a gaudy whoremaster, and make it fucking obvious you don't even believe me."

Tomwun was fumbling for a small automatic pistol tucked into his belt. But Ryan slapped him hard across the face with his free hand, stopping the movement. A bright worm of blood crawled from the man's nose, across his lips, staining the bared teeth. Drops of it pattering onto the white coat and onto the pile of papers on the desk.

Now Ryan was experiencing that frightening exhilaration that went with brutish power. The taste of Tomwun's fear was in his nostrils, rank and heavy, bringing a buzz with it that was almost sexual in its delight.

"Please..." The word was muffled with blood. Tomwun's eyes, red-rimmed, protruded from their sockets as though they were on stalks. His tongue, blackening, lapped at the air between lips that were turning a cyanotic blue.

"You piece of..." Ryan pushed him disgustedly down into his seat, which tilted right back so that Tomwun's feet pointed for a moment at the ceiling.

"Blood of the Martyrs, Cawdor. You might have killed me. Might have throttled me."

"If I'd wanted to chill you, then you'd be on the last train by now. Just that you touched me on a sore kind of place. Place that doesn't like being called a liar." Tomwun didn't speak, massaging his bruised neck. "You understand what I'm saying?" The scientist nodded, his eyes down on the golden edge to the leather top of his desk. "Didn't hear you, Tomwun.

I asked whether you understood why I was a little angry.''

"Sure. I understand.''

"Fine. Now that's out of the bastard way we can get to talking about what happened. What might happen. And what's best to do about it.''

IT WAS FULL DARK. A fine rich clam chowder had been served in their quarters by the two Bobs. It was almost as though they'd never left the institute, as though there'd never been the run-in with the pirates and the murderous exchange of fire.

The thick soup was followed by a huge bowl of pasta, liberally larded with shrimps, prawns, mussels and delicious shredded crab meat.

Tomwun, now far more eager to make amends, had also sent over three bottles of a better-than-adequate pink wine that Mildred described as being an acceptable substitute for a white zinfandel from before skydark.

Ryan had called everyone together straight after his stormy meeting with the professor and run quickly through what the two men had discussed.

And what had been agreed.

It didn't take long.

"We stay another five days. If there's an attack during that time, then we'll do what we can to side with the people here. If the pirates don't come, then we'll carry out a single recce on the fifth day. Then, if there's still no sign of any threat, Tomwun lends us a boat and a pilot and we get taken back north by sea to the redoubt.''

Everyone was broadly happy with that.

With the possible exception of Michael.

He slowly got up and walked around the room, standing and staring blankly out of the rectangular window that faced the Lantic.

Ryan watched him, seeing from the young man's body language that there was going to be an argument. He was unable to guess on what grounds, though Michael had been spending a deal of time with Miranda from the institute.

It crossed his mind how much the teenager had changed since he'd first been plucked from the life-long security of the monastic retreat of Nil-Vanity. Then he'd been withdrawn and shy, often hardly speaking. He'd been a barefoot innocent in so many ways, out of the real world for virtually his entire life, wearing his long brown robe, with its thick knotted cord.

Physically he'd hardly altered at all. He was still in terrific shape, still with the fastest reflexes that Ryan Cawdor had ever seen in a human being. Then he'd also carried a pair of slim daggers, the only weapons he would permit himself.

Time in Deathlands had wrought its changes.

Michael shifted at the window, half turning as though he were finally going to speak, then changing his mind yet again and gazing out once more at the blank reflection of the night in the smeared glass.

Instead of the brown robe and the naked feet, Michael Brother was now an elegant figure, dressed in black from top to toe. The only touches of color were the copper rivets and silver thread in his black jeans.

The other major change in his appearance was holstered at his left hip, a small, powerful revolver, with an impressive name—the .38-caliber, center-fire, 6-round Texas Longhorn Border Special.

"Spit it out, Michael," Ryan said, impatient to clear the air from whatever was bothering the teenager.

"Five days?"

"Yeah."

"Only five days?"

"You never had trouble with your hearing before, Michael. Must be all that time with your head underwater with Miranda. We go in five days."

"Doesn't seem long enough to me."

"No?"

The youth's dark eyes narrowed in anger. "No, it doesn't, Ryan. Why five days?"

"Why not?"

"Why not ten?"

"Why not fifty?" J.B. asked. "Or why not a hundred, Michael?"

"Five isn't long."

Ryan got up and walked over to confront him. "We saw the pirates. Tomwun obviously thinks that an attack of some kind is imminent. I reckon the odds are that he's right. And we might have helped to provoke that by our ambush this afternoon. Made them tri-ple-crazy.''

The teenager grabbed at the opportunity. ''Then, if it's our fault we must have a definite sort of an obligation to remain here and help.''

''I only said it *might* have helped, Michael. All you can do is the best you can. We'll give them five days. Take their side if... What was his name? Yeah, Red Jack Yoville and his gang come down on us.''

''Like the wolf on the fold,'' Doc said in one of his mysterious and inexplicable interruptions. ''Though I rather doubt that his cohorts will be gleaming in scarlet and gold. Scarlet? Yet, Red Jack might be scarlet. What of Scarlett? Frankly I don't give a damn.''

''Thanks for that useful thought, Doc.'' Ryan stared into the boy's face. ''I'm not going to make you do something you don't want to do, Michael. Not the way we work. You've ridden with us long enough to know that, haven't you?''

''Yeah, sure.''

''So. The rest of us are going to be here up to five days. Then we're going back to the redoubt and we're going to take another jump. You come with us, and that's fine with me. Fine with us all, I reckon. But if you want to stay behind then, that's your decision, Michael.''

''I hear you, Ryan.''

''You want time to think about it?''

The teenager nodded. "Guess I do. Guess I'm seeing things clearer all of a sudden."

Ryan turned back to face the others, sitting amid the remains of their meal. "That's it, then."

Chapter Twenty-Six

The first day passed by in a haze of bright sunshine and soaring temperatures.

Ryan and J.B. took the opportunity to walk around the complex with Tomwun and a couple of his senior aides, trying to find all of the potentially strong and weak points of the defensive perimeter.

After an hour they stood together not far from the long building where some of the dolphins were still kept in the cramped confinement of their little cages.

"Well?" Tomwun asked, taking off his glasses and wiping away the tiny windblown speckles of salt.

"Impossible," Ryan said, looking sideways at the Armorer, who gave a barely perceptible nod of agreement.

"Why?"

"Land and water."

"What's that mean, Cawdor?"

J.B. answered the scientist's question, stooping and drawing a rough plan of the whole region in the soft, smooth sand at his feet.

"None of the Keys are more than three or four miles across. Most of them a lot less." He used the small piece of driftwood to give an overall sketch of the area. "Redoubt, here. Mainland up there where we saw the boats. And here's the institute." He scraped out a square. "The Key's only three-quarters of a mile wide here. Pirates can easily come down the east or the west side. The Gulf or the Lantic. Gives them the option of landing north or south of us. Means they've got every card in the fire-dark pack to play against us. Any and every direction. See what I mean?"

Tomwun nodded slowly. "Of course. Forgive me, Mr. Dix, but this is all as plain as the nose on my face. The problem is obvious. Is there a solution?"

Ryan took the piece of sun-bleached wood from his old friend. "No such thing as a solution. Depends. They come in with three hundred men, eight war wags and a half a dozen land-to-land missiles, and they win. No solution. They come in with two men, on foot, armed with two bows and four arrows, and there's an easy, ace on the line solution. Reality lies between."

One of the scientists, his graying hair cut savagely back so that it showed the suntanned scalp beneath, shook his head. Ryan thought that his name was Lee Burroughs and that he had something to do with the communications project of which Miranda Thorson was a part.

"Reality is in the mind of the thinker. The practical man must take his reality and extrapolate it into the real world. Tell us your reality. Mr. Cawdor."

Thorund, another of the older men, pointed at J.B.'s rough plan, where the wind was already beginning to shift the grains of sand and blur the outlines.

"We know this. Tell us what we don't know."

Ryan turned on him, feeling a brief flurry of the same old anger. "Don't fuck with us! There isn't a lot we can do. Just be ready. Place some guards, in pairs, on twenty-four-hour watch. Here... and here. Two more here, above the beach." He made small holes in the sand to indicate where he wanted them situated. "Tell them that if they sleep or if they're careless, then we can all end up dead."

"I'll tell them," Tomwun promised.

"Make sure that everyone is armed if you've got enough blasters and ammo. Any spare guns, keep them central, where they can be reached easily." J.B. looked at Ryan. "That's all we can do and say now?" He paused. "Oh, and you can mebbe have boats ready to run for it at the last. Think that's really all, Ryan?"

"Yeah. That's all."

AFTER SUPPER it was such a beautiful night that everyone sat outside on the porch of the frame building that housed their living quarters.

Across the way, near the main gates of the institute, there were pools of vivid light, with more lamps now situated near the potential danger areas of the beach and the docks. All of them were attracting great swirling clouds of tiny midges.

Outside one of the other buildings, someone was playing a violin. A strange and haunting sound from the far, far-off past of the country.

"That's beautiful," Krysty said. "Gaia, that brings tears to my eyes."

Michael stood, stretching himself until the powerful muscles in his back and shoulders creaked. "Think I'll take a walk before bed."

"Don't go beyond the defensive perimeter we've established," Ryan warned. "In fact, I think I'd keep well clear of it, Michael, in case some trigger-blind white coat gets nervous and tries to put you away."

"Sure." Waving his hand with a casual gesture, he stepped off the porch and disappeared, walking briskly toward the part of the complex where some of the main dolphin research was carried out by one of the groups of scientists.

Dean grinned and spit out into the blackness. "Off to see his slut."

"Dean!" Krysty exclaimed.

"What?" he asked, hearing the note of anger in the red-haired woman's voice. "What'd I say?"

"You know damned well. There's no excuse for calling someone a slut."

"What if they are?" Ryan said, halfheartedly taking his son's part.

"Don't try and turn this into a joke, Ryan." Her eyes were narrow slits of fiery emerald. "It's about respect, and he's old enough to know how to show it."

"Hear, hear," Mildred applauded.

"Anyway." Krysty wasn't finished yet. "How do you know where he's going? You mean he's sneaking away to go and meet up with that little Miranda?"

"Sure. Can't keep away from her," Dean sniggered. "Bee and a pot of honey."

Doc also stood, his knee joints cracking like musket shots.

"I believe that I, too, shall take myself off for an evening's constitutional."

"Can I go?" Dean asked, leaping up like an eager puppy. "Can I, Dad?"

"No."

"Why not?"

"Reason we're here is because there seems a good chance that this Red Jack Yoville and his chillers could be coming this way real soon. They won't send us a messenger to say when they're going to attack us. Could be tonight. Early morning. Tomorrow. Could even be never."

"So, it's probably safe, Dad?"

Ryan shook his head. "No such thing as 'probably safe,' Dean. Either it's completely safe, or more likely, it's not safe at all. Sorry."

The boy sat down again, shoulders slumped. Mildred and J.B. exchanged a glance and rose together.

"Early night, I think," the Armorer said.

"Sure," Ryan looked at Krysty. "Might be we won't be too late, either."

Doc WALKED through the institute compound, the soft sand silencing the tapping ferrule of his sword stick. Somewhere he could hear the violin playing, but now it sounded hard and discordant to his ears. Every now and then he skirted the golden lakes of spilled light.

It was a beautiful night, with the sky like an inverted cloak scattered with diamonds. He stopped and looked up at them, finding that his eyes were suddenly brimming with tears.

"Oh, my dearest dove. My darling of love and comfort. Oh, my Emily."

He tried to calculate how long it had been since he had last seen his wife and held her tightly in his arms. But the confusion of the two chron jumps had addled his brain and he swiftly lost count. All he knew was that it had been an infinitely painful time of not being together.

His feet led him in the tracks of Michael Brother, following the teenager toward the section of the institute where Miranda was doing her work on speaking to the dolphins. It was no great surprise to the old man to realize where Michael was heading. Like Dean, he'd spotted the growing passion of the ex-monk for the attractive young woman.

The door was half-open and he paused outside it, squinting through the gap into the brightly lighted interior. He'd been there several times, finding himself fascinated by the experiments in communication, so he was familiar with the building and its number of small tanks.

At first he couldn't see Michael, though he could catch the faint sound of conversation. Then he saw the flicker of shadowy movement against a white-washed wall.

The young man was sitting in the far corner, feet dangling into the shallow pen. Doc could just see that Miranda was standing in the water, leaning her elbows on the edge, close by Michael.

There was a narrow chipboard passage down one side, with a couple of makeshift offices. Once there, Doc would be close enough to hear without being seen.

The idea of eavesdropping brought a malicious glint to his rheumy eyes and he tiptoed out of sight, creeping along until he was within eight feet of the couple. The faint slapping of water helped to cover the creaking sound of his cautious progress.

Now the voices were more distinct, though he still couldn't quite catch every word.

Miranda was speaking.

"... your own mind, Mike."

"I do."

"Not the way it seems to us."

"Ryan's the man in charge."

"Doesn't make him some sort of god, does it?"

"No."

Doc couldn't quite catch the woman's reply, as it was drowned out by the noise of her climbing from the tank.

Michael still sounded strained and under pressure. "You say I don't owe them anything, but I'd probably have died a dozen times without being with Ryan and the others. You have to see it from my side, Miranda."

"I don't think that *you* see it from your side, Mike. How can I?"

"Can't betray them."

"Not asking you to do that."

"You are."

"No, I'm not. You know I care. I've showed you, haven't I? This afternoon when we came here and I..." To his frustration, Doc couldn't hear the rest of the sentence, as Miranda had dropped her voice to a whisper.

"Course it was good. But I did it for you, as well."

"Only when I pulled your hair to make you get down there, Mike?"

"Well..."

Miranda laughed. "Don't look so miserable. You were very good at it." Then her voice was too quiet for Doc to hear more. But she seemed to be urging Michael yet again to do something, something that he appeared to be very reluctant to do.

"No. If we fight the pirates for you and win, I couldn't go against them."

"But then that one-eyed bastard and the redhead and the shootist and all of them, they'd be a threat to the institute, wouldn't they?"

"No." Hidden behind the thin partition, Doc could almost taste the doubt in Michael's voice.

"Yes, they would. But if that happened, then you could help us against them. If you did, you and me could..." Yet again the soft voice dropped beyond a whisper. But Doc also caught the sound of a zipper sliding down and it took precious little imagination to deduce what sort of persuasion Miranda was using on the inexperienced teenager.

"Theophilus," he breathed to himself, "I believe that the time is now appropriate for you to reveal yourself from behind this arras."

With a spluttering cough he clattered along the passage, emerging once more from close to the front entrance of the building. Michael had jumped as though he'd found himself to be sitting on a red ant's nest, his hand fumbling at his groin as he tried to adjust his zipper.

Miranda had turned to see what the interruption was, her pretty face revealing her anger.

"You," she said.

"None other, my dear." He made her a low bow, so florid that his chin nearly brushed the damp concrete. "I was just passing by and saw the light and heard the voice of our young companion, Michael. Is all well, my boy?"

"Yeah, Doc. It's a real hot pipe. Good. Fine. No problem at all." The words were in such a hurry to escape from his mouth that they were tumbling over one another. He finally paused for breath. "How long have you been here, Doc?" Anxiety pushed his voice up a couple of octaves.

"Yes," Miranda said, "just how long have you been listening in on our private conversation, Doc? Bit like spying, isn't it? Lot like spying."

"Not at all, my dear young lady." He repeated the bow. "I have only this moment entered the building. But, what sort of conversation could be so secret that you needs must accuse me of being some sort of snoop? Not, I trust, some kind of guilty conscience, my dear Miranda?"

"Fuck you."

"Hey!" Michael stood. "There's no need for that, Miranda."

Doc smiled. "I can't begin to imagine why such stern anger from so pretty a face. It isn't as though this innocent maiden was attempting to suborn you from your friends and your duty, is it, Michael?"

"Sub born? Don't know what—"

"To suborn, Michael. To seek to persuade another to perform a wrongful act. I suppose that means something like, let us imagine, trying to encourage someone to betray their friends. You take my meaning, Michael."

"Yeah, Doc."

"Perhaps we could stroll together, back to our quarters, Michael."

"Sure," he replied, not meeting Miranda's scornful stare. "Feel sort of tired."

"Good night, sweet lady." Doc didn't bow this time, simply inclining his head briefly. "May choirs of angels sing thee to they rest."

"Like I said, fuck you, Doc. And fuck you, too, Mike. Fuck all of you."

AFTER MAKING SLOW and gentle love together, Ryan and Krysty fell into an easy sleep. But in the middle of the night, Ryan found himself trapped in a bizarre dream.

He was swimming deep beneath the ocean, in water so crystal clear that it was possible to see for miles. Also, he could breathe under the water, as though he had gills like a fish.

There was a large white chair, crusted with coral and lumps of rose quartz. In it, beckoning Ryan toward him with his battered Armalite, was the Trader.

Before he could swim closer, Ryan woke up.

It took him some time before he slipped again into sleep.

Chapter Twenty-Seven

It had been snowing for nearly three days, banking up against the walls of the line shack that had been home to Abe for the past week.

He had hoped to reach the coast before the great blizzard came swooping down from the Cascade Mountains to the east, but the pewter-colored clouds were too fast and too close for him. For a few hours the wind had shifted direction to the west, bringing the bitter taste of salt onto Abe's lips, offering the brief expectation of making it down to the gray Pacific Ocean. It couldn't be more than twenty or thirty miles away, down through a series of mazelike valleys.

It wasn't a part of the world that Abe knew. There was a vague memory of riding there, years ago, in War Wag One at the Trader's shoulder. But he couldn't pin any fast details to the blurred recollection. There had been a city on the coast that he thought had been called Seattle, which had been an endlessly rambling series of ruins.

It was Abe's hunt for the Trader that had brought him this far north.

Following rumor, myth, legend and gossip, the trail led him ever farther into that bleak and lonely country beyond the frontiers of what had been old California. The trail was already marked with graves and with a number of corpses, some of them the responsibility of a darkened figure carrying a battered Armalite, a stooped and gray shadow with the remnants of a hacking cough who was always moving on.

For Abe the chimera was always around the next corner in the trail. He'd been in a ville only a month before, a week before . . .

"Yesterday, and he left a brace of sec men kicking in their own blood and guts. Baron put a jack price on the stranger's grizzled head, but there was no rush to join the posse to try and hunt him down."

Abe had been so close, but there had been an earthfall that had blocked off one of the high trails, forcing him to detour thirty miles to the east before he could pick up again on the tracks of the man who might be the Trader.

And now it was the snow.

"Fucking snow!" Abe spit, carefully picking crystals of frozen snot from his drooping mustache, flicking them at the clay-lined log walls of the small cabin.

The bitter cold had worked its way into some of his old wounds, and Abe had more old wounds than any other ten men put together. Scars teased their way across his body, some of them seaming through the taut flesh of his face. The broken and badly set bones in his arms and legs ached, as did the numerous injuries to muscles, tendons and ligaments.

He hated winter, hated snow in the mountains.

And here he was, condemned to spend time in an isolated hut in the high country, at the heart of one of the worst blizzards that he'd ever seen.

"Fuck it," he said, leaning back, his bare feet pushed toward the flickering flames of the tiny fire that he'd just lighted. There was a temptation to pile on the precious kindling and bank up the hacked and broken branches and logs that Abe had found heaped out back of the cabin.

Abe wasn't that worried for his own survival. He knew enough to be sure that he could make it for several more days yet. There was snow to quench his thirst. Enough wood to keep a fire going for a while yet. That and the roof and walls would shelter him from the worst of the gale. And he had strips of jerky in his pack. Not that exciting, but it would keep body and soul together.

"Fuck you, Trader. Fuck everyone," he raged in a querulous bellow of anger.

HE FREQUENTLY SLIPPED AWAY into the nebulous world of half sleeping, half waking, and the hours slithered by almost without Abe noticing them passing.

Once he thought he heard someone banging on the door of the cabin, rattling the great bar of wood that acted as a security bolt. By the time he'd got up and grabbed his stainless-steel Colt Python, the noise had ceased. But when he checked carefully Abe found that there were deep gouges in the outside of the door that hadn't been there before, and the thick snow was trampled with what he knew were the tracks of a bear.

A large bear.

The only window in the hut was high on the eastern side, near the level of the dipping roof, and it was normally well above the reach of any normal predator. But the fresh snow had piled up against the walls and frozen, creating an easily scalable drift.

Abe had been intending to go out and shift it away, but the wind was howling, and the glowing embers of his fire were far more attractive. But he did take the basic precaution of checking that the small iron catch on the inside of the square window was safely locked.

He was confident that it would be a remarkable animal that managed to get in through there.

HE WAS WHEELING HIGH over cold gray waters, the white crests of the waves like spilled stitches on a vast tapestry. Canvas crackled around him, and his fingernails were raw and broken with the effort of hanging on to the shrouds. His feet hung over a singing space and his eyes were wide with terror.

The wind was pressing against him like a living weight, its breath hot in . . .

Breath hot . . .

Hot?

Outside the cabin there was a full moon, its sharp-edged brightness flooding into the line shack through the glass of the single small window, through the jagged, splintered glass of the single small, *broken* window.

Abe was lying flat on his back, legs straight, arms at his sides, under the double layer of his quilted sleeping bag. He was pinned onto the narrow frame by the heavy weight that lay sprawled on top of him.

The breath that feathered against his stubbled chin was hot and rancid, like the sweetness of decayed and rotted meat in a forest glade.

His eyes blinked open, staring in unbelieving horror into the yellow slitted eyes of a big cat. It was lying full-length, its face within inches of his. Abe felt a momentary looseness of his bowels, but he fought against messing himself.

The jaws of the creature gaped open as it yawned, showing canine teeth that were at least six inches long, slightly curved. Abe was aware that the animal was purring contentedly, the vibration making his own body tremble.

Now he had an idea of what had broken into the cabin during the night. It looked like some sort of cougar, with fur the color of fresh cream.

But it was far bigger than any comparable creature that Abe had ever seen. Its head and front paws were on his shoulders, but its haunches seemed to be hung over the bottom end of the bed, making it around eight to ten feet long.

Abe's manly effort not to lose control over his bodily functions came to nothing when the big cougar opened its mouth wider and pushed out its tongue, starting to run it caressingly over his face.

"Oh, fuck," Abe breathed, not sure whether the words had stayed within his brain or whether they might have whispered out into the cold room.

The purring became louder, and the stink of the mutie animal's vile breath made him want to vomit, knowing that to give in to that temptation would be the same as swallowing the muzzle of his blaster and pulling the trigger.

Moving with an infinite slowness, Abe wriggled his right hand, trying to free it from the constrictions of the sleeping bag. His Colt Python was just under the bed, about level with his head.

On the right side.

Because he remembered putting it there. He always put it there.

The cougar had stopped licking his face, as though it sensed that he was moving. The purring had changed its note, somehow seeming much more threatening.

Abe lay as still as death, trying to count his heartbeats. But they were coming so fast he kept losing track of them. He waited until he reckoned there'd been around a thousand, then he tried to free his right arm again.

This time there was no mistake. The animal growled threateningly.

Abe felt an overwhelming temptation to try to smile placatingly at the huge creature, show those implacable yellow eyes that he meant it no harm. But he knew someone had told him that predators regarded a smile as a threatening gesture. Could've been J.B. told him that. Baring the teeth was a double-aggressive thing to do.

Or was it the other way? Was it a submissive gesture to show you weren't a threat?

One paw, as large as Abe's head, lifted and he watched, paralyzed, as the razored claws unsheathed, touching him on the side of the face as delicately as embroidery needles, piercing his skin. Four tiny threads of blood ran warmly down his cheek.

But his arm was free.

He moved his fingers along the dusty, splintered floor, glacier slow, feeling for the familiar chill of the metal against his hand.

Now the cougar was growling deep in its chest, making the cold air in the cabin vibrate with its intensity. A hot, ferocious, jungle sound.

Abe was suddenly aware of the smell of his own body. Sweat, shit and fear.

There.

The butt slipped into his hand, his palm slick with perspiration. He started to lift the gun an inch at a time.

Now the massive paw settled against his throat, touching the throbbing pulse of his jugular, as tender as the embrace of a familiar lover.

By moving his head a fraction to the right, straining his eyes, Abe could now see the silver moonlight off the polished cylinder of the revolver.

There was only going to be one chance.

Even if he got everything right, there was a better than even chance that the cougar would still erupt into violence and rip his head from his body.

"One chance is better than no fucking chance." His lips moved slightly, and the great amber orbs turned impassively toward his mouth.

The Colt was lifting, almost without his control, like some miraculous levitation. The tip of the four-inch muzzle brushed the bristling albino fur and moved behind the pricked ear with the motionless cougar, touching it.

Abe tried to brace his wrist, difficult in his clumsy, frozen position, then pulled the trigger.

The small line shack was filled with noise, movement and terror.

The .357 roared, kicking against Abe's hand. The cougar gave a cry of rage and pain that literally deafened the man. It swung its paw in a vicious, scything blow that would have shredded the flesh from his face.

But Abe wasn't there anymore.

Bracing his legs and pushing upward, the movement combined with the effects of the bullet in the head to send the mutie animal sideways off the narrow bed.

Abe rolled across the wooden floor, gripping the butt of the Colt, coming up from a crouch, facing the horror on the far side of the room.

It was standing stiff-legged, fur bristling along its spine, making it look twice its gigantic size. There was a little blood darkening the milky fur, leaking from a black wound near its left ear. Its mouth was open, and sticky threads of saliva dangled from the curved fangs. The muscles in his haunches were twitching as though it were gathering itself for a spring.

Abe looked into the slit eyes and saw his death reflected there.

The Colt Python held six Magnum rounds. One gone. Five rounds to go.

Abe brought the gun up and held it as steady as he could, supporting his right wrist with his left hand. His breath was flooding the room, like mist from a faulty geyser, and he could hear his heart pounding.

He knew better than to pour the bullets out in a volley. The kick of the blaster would destroy his aim. So it was careful, measured shooting.

The first bullet hit the cougar somewhere behind its shoulder, ripping through the muscle and angling sideways so it burst from its flanks, near the fifth rib, in a welter of dark spray. The impact made it stagger, but it was still on its feet, turning its head to snap angrily at the fresh wound.

Abe was losing his fight against stark paralyzing terror, and the third bullet missed completely, missed at a range of less than ten feet. But the noise made the animal shake its head, taking a careful step toward the crouching man, its long tail swinging to and fro across the floor.

"Fuck you," the man whispered.

The fourth round hit the cat in the shoulder, knocking it off its feet, sending it rolling on its side, one front paw dangling uselessly. Its growling had risen to a bedlam of noise, high and shrill, like a panicked woman's scream.

"Teach you to..." Abe started, struggling to regain a few shreds of self-control and confidence. Then the cougar battled itself upright again. "Oh, shit!"

A fifth bullet drilled it smack between the eyes, finally putting it down in a big way.

Its legs kicked and thrashed, knocking the bed into matchwood. A spray of urine voided in a glittering arc, splashing off the ceiling.

And it was still.

Abe finally regained his courage and crawled over, putting the barrel of the Colt Python between the bloodied jaws, firing the sixth and last round to blow away a chunk of the animal's skull, splattering brains on the far wall of the cabin.

Abe went and slid across the security bolt, walked into the freezing night and puked in the fresh, bright snow.

The cougar meat made good eating for several days.

Chapter Twenty-Eight

At Ryan's request Professor Tomwun had sent out recce parties, going by boat, keeping well offshore, using a couple of pairs of field glasses to scan the beaches.

They went both north and south, ranging as far as the sun-dried remains of Key West and up to Key Largo, in sight of the nuke-blasted mainland. Ryan had made it clear that he also wanted them to cut through between some of the island, past the tumbled bridges and causeways, checking both the Lantic and Gulf for some sign of Yoville and his pirate gang.

During the second day back at the institute, Ryan sat and waited for a positive sighting. But the boats came chugging back to the docks, again and again, with no sign of any danger.

Tomwun brought a bottle of a dry white wine that he said had come from France in Europe well over a hundred years earlier. But there was no label on it and everyone wrinkled up their noses, complaining it tasted dry and bitter.

"It's *supposed* to be dry," the scientist said. "It's called a dry wine. I read old books about it. French wines were called 'dry' back then."

Only Doc was prepared to try to savor it, but even he eventually pulled a face. "My heartfelt apologies, my dear fellow, but I rather think that this particular wine has failed to travel well, through either time or space."

Tomwun had snatched up the dark green bottle, stalking off with it, back toward his own quarters.

Dean spit in the sand. "Why can't we just get a high rush out of here, Dad?"

"Because we said we'd stay five days."

"What if there's no sign of the sea killers?" Krysty asked. "What then?"

Ryan shrugged. "News so far today has been no news. See if the last patrols bring in anything."

"If they don't?"

Ryan half smiled. "Then you and I might go out on a boat tomorrow."

But the final reports finished up just as negative as the first ones had been. There wasn't the least trace of Yoville. No smoke, no cooking fires, no other vessels.

Nothing.

THE BOAT WAS CALLED *Damfino*. It was made from some sort of plastic and painted a dark greenish blue. The small engine on its stern showed signs of having been repaired and rebuilt a number a times over the years since its keel was first laid down in a place called New Haven.

The kitchens of the institute provided Ryan and Krysty with a good packed meal, though it was becoming noticeable that the quality of the food had been deteriorating since their first arrival there. It was something that Ryan put down to the presence in the area of the pirates.

There was also five bottles of clean spring water and a couple of rods, though neither of them had much intention of doing any fishing.

Ryan packed the Steyr rifle carefully into the boat. He was wearing the SIG-Sauer, and his coat pockets carried a couple of spare 15-round mags for the handblaster. Krysty's Smith & Wesson double-action M-640 was holstered on her hip.

The weather had turned colder, with bunches of pink-gray clouds scurrying south on the back of the chilly winds. The surface of the sea was like processed slate, with patches of white horses showing farther out beyond the shoals.

But Thorund, who claimed to be something of an authority on local weather conditions, told them that the sun would soon be breaking through and the late morning and afternoon would be fine and warm.

Dean had pressed his father to be allowed to go out with them on the boat, but Ryan had told him to stay at the institute and keep his eyes open for trouble. The idea that there was some sort of responsibility in such a mission satisfied the boy, and when he went down to the quay with the others to wave them off, he was smiling broadly.

"Bring us back some mackerel," Doc shouted. "Or a saddle of fine mutton with caper sauce."

"Watch the sun side of the horizon," J.B. called. "Danger side."

Mildred was standing close to the Armorer, and she gave Ryan and Krysty the thumbs-up. "Watch out that he doesn't run out of gas," she warned, grinning.

Michael stood silent, hands in pockets, scowling out to sea.

Ryan gunned the engine and steered the craft away from the institute's dock and along the narrow inlet that would lead them quickly out into the Lantic. He caught a glimpse of Mark Tomwun, leaning on an iron fence at the side of one of the laboratory buildings. Neither man waved to the other.

"Which way?" Krysty asked, lying back in the bow, the fresh breeze tugging at the flaming strands of hair. "North or south, lover?"

"South, I think. Thorund said that the good weather would come from the south."

The engine chugged along, pushing them out from the land at a steady five knots. They had a spare can of gas in the bottom of the boat as well as a mast that could be jury-rigged and a pair of oars as a final precaution.

"Think the pirates are coming?"

Ryan shook his head. "Can't hardly hear you above the engine and the waves. Did you say that you figured that the pirates were coming?"

"No. I asked if *you* thought they were coming. Should've seen some sign of them by now."

"Don't know. When we saw them and chilled a few, I guessed they'd come after us. Mebbe they got some bigger, safer fish to fry."

RYAN HAD INTENDED to make a decent easting to keep well away from land, but the wind was stronger and the waves bigger, splashing over the bow and soaking Krysty, forcing him back in toward the Keys.

"Company," Krysty called.

Ryan reached automatically for the SSG-70 hunting rifle, its walnut stock already dappled with spots of salt water. Then he saw where she was looking. A few points off the port bow, a lean gray shape rose and fell, keeping station with the boat, occasionally lifting its smooth, intelligent head as though making sure they were still there.

"Don't know its name, do you?" Ryan shouted.

"No. Odds on that it's one of Tomwun's pets. Keeping a tracker on us."

"Yeah." He took his hand off the narrow tiller and waved at the cetacean. He wasn't surprised when it seemed to nod back at him, mouth opening in what looked like a human grin.

THORUND PROVED to have been a good forecaster. The skies cleared as though someone had reached down and pulled across a curtain of brightest blue. The sun had a hint of a pink-purple corona around it, which in Deathlands was normally a sign of some kind of residual nuke-activity out in space.

A part of the Totality Concept had been to flood the airless dark beyond Earth's atmosphere with innumerable missiles and spy satts, all of them powered to greater or less degree by nuclear energy.

So, during the long years of the nuke winter, these mechanical creations, and their Eastern counterparts, began to malfunction, slipping into crazy orbits. Most descended back to their home planet within the first ten years, causing further damage to the decimated population and to the blasted land. But even now, a century later, an occasional chunk of deep-space debris would slither wearily down toward its base and burn up as it came through the upper layers of the atmosphere.

Ryan had eased back on the throttle, cruising inside a long shoal that was breaking up the long Lantic swell. The dolphin was still with them. It was almost as if it occasionally got bored and started to entertain itself, speeding up and diving under their keel at the last moment, then swimming around and around the boat, faster and faster, on one magical occasion actually jumping right over it, splattering Krysty with a dazzling rainbow of salt spray.

"Gaia!" she gasped. "That was pretty triple-amazing, lover. First time I've had a fish fly over me."

"Amphibious mammal, lover," Ryan corrected, grinning broadly. "Not a fish. Remember?"

She dipped a hand in the warm waves and splashed him. "Nobody loves a smart-ass, Ryan."

"TIME FOR SOME LUNCH." Ryan throttled back until the propeller was barely revolving, angling in toward a narrow stretch of white beach, shielded at north and south by rolling sand dunes. The key itself was cut off at both ends by fallen bridges and looked totally barren.

"Can we go ashore, lover?"

Ryan glanced around, but there was absolutely no sign of life. "Why?"

"If you want the details, then it's because I need to take a dump. All right?"

He grinned. "Do it over the side of the boat. Ocean's big enough to cope with a little contamination."

"Not when there's some land just fifty yards away. Either you steer us in, Ryan, or I'll dive straight into the water and swim right in."

The dolphin was close on the seaward side, almost motionless, its long nose out of the water, keeping itself upright by a swirling motion of its powerful tail.

Krysty watched it watching them. "Anyway, I couldn't just stick my ass over the side of the boat with that staring at me. Wouldn't be decent."

Ryan gunned the engine and cut it toward the strip of sloping shoreline, his eyes raking the coast for any sign of danger. But his first impression was confirmed. There were a number of seabirds, including some large pelicans, dotted along the dunes, a sure sign that there was no unusual predator in the area.

"You coming out?" she asked as the bottom of the boat whispered onto the soft sand.

"Why not? Could eat the food while we're here. I'll drag the anchor up the beach a ways."

She swung her long legs over and walked through the shallow water, her boots leaving deep impressions. "I'm going that way," she said, pointing to the south. "Soon as I've finished I'll come back. Where're you going?"

"Just up the top there to have a look over the other side. Make sure there isn't any pirate camp."

Krysty waved a hand and set off along the beach, pausing to pick up a beautiful whorled shell, its interior glistening like a moonstone. She held it to her ear, shook her head, then lobbed it into the waves where it sank without a trace.

Ryan watched her for a few seconds, experiencing one of those sudden swells of affection that all lovers feel. Then he climbed out of the boat and heaved the small iron anchor up a dozen yards, burying its flukes, kicking them into the sand to make sure they held, checking before he took out the food that the other end of the sun-faded rope was tied firmly to the bow thwart, which it was.

The dolphin had disappeared, perhaps going to Tomwun to report.

It was about a hundred paces from tide line to the crest of the dunes, but the sand was so soft and yielding that Ryan found himself going three steps up and two steps back down. By the time he got to the top, he found he was panting and sweating hard. His arrival had sent the birds wheeling into the sky, protesting noisily.

He blinked the perspiration from his good eye and laid down the food and the bottles of drinking water, straightening and looking around.

And stopped dead. "Fireblast," he whispered.

Chapter Twenty-Nine

He didn't go down to explore, choosing to wait until Krysty had made the weary climb to the top of the dunes to join him.

"What're you sitting there for?" she called from halfway up the slope.

"Got something to show you when you get right up to the top, lover."

She paused, bending over and shaking her head. "Bet you say that to all the girls. Phew, it's hot today."

"Come on. Worth the effort."

"Yeah. I bet you say *that* to all the girls, as well. I'm coming."

Panting and red-faced she finally reached where Ryan was sitting cross-legged, waiting for her.

"Now, what do— Oh, sweet honey from the rock, look at that."

Hidden from the sea on both sides of the narrow key by a bowllike depression in the land was a large two-story building.

Ryan guessed immediately that it must once have been a hotel, big houses where people stayed for a day or so while traveling across the country and paid for their beds and for their food. There were literally thousands of such ruins scattered all across Death-lands, mostly derelict, though some of the larger frontier pestholes had resurrected one or two and used them as jack gamblers or as gaudies.

What was truly bizarre about this one was that it didn't look as though it had been damaged at all. Most of the windows still stared blankly toward Ryan and Krysty, and the roof and walls looked stained by the weather, but solid.

It was certainly true that the farther you moved from cities, or from strategic military sites, the better were the chances of finding a few buildings still standing from the lost days before skydark.

"It looks perfect," Krysty said, kneeling by Ryan, her white shirt stained dark under the arms and be-neath the breasts. "We haven't tumbled into a chron spot have we? Been trawled back in time?"

"No. There's our boat behind us and the dol-phin's reappeared again."

The bottlenose was swimming up and down, very close to the beach, seeming distressed. They could actually hear its continuous stream of high-pitched clicks and whistles from where they were on the dunes.

"We going to take a look, lover?"

"Hell, yes."

SOME OF THE PLASTIC LETTERS above the main en-trance had been destroyed over the years, but there

was enough left to guess at what the name had been:
B ST ES ER F ORI D K YS.

"Best Western Florida Keys," Krysty said. "Seen a few of these hotels over Deathlands. Must've been really built to last forever."

"Amazingly well preserved. Guess it's because of being down in this sort of natural hollow. Saved it from the worst of the weather as well as keeping it out of sight of any roving fishermen passing by."

"We going to check in?"

"Take a recce around the outside first. Looks safe, but looks don't mean shit."

The glass was tinted to keep out the blinding sunlight, making it impossible to see inside the building. It made Ryan slightly uneasy, imagining half a dozen men behind each dark mirrored window, each drawing a careful, lethal bead on them with a scoped-sight rifle.

On the south side there was obvious structural damage, probably caused by a localized earth movement. A whole wing of the hotel had gone down in a heap of rubble, showing only cracked, bare walls inside.

At the back there was what had once been a tennis court, riven by a long, jagged fissure that had split the rotted net in two. There was also a swimming pool, filled only with a few inches of dark green scum and littered with fallen leaves.

The Gulf of Mexico came within a few yards of the back of the hotel, which was protected by the surrounding sand dunes and the remnants of a small stone harbor. Ryan led the way out onto the quayside, glancing back at the forbidding pile of bleached concrete behind them.

He shook his head. "Something creepy about it looking so good."

"We can go in, can't we?"

"Sure." Ryan sat down on the dock of the bay, enjoying the morning sun. Krysty sat beside him, letting her legs dangle over the side.

"Water's deep."

Ryan leaned forward, peering into the unexpectedly shadowed depths. "Yeah." He picked up a chunk of white stone the size of his fist and lobbed it between his feet. It plopped in with a surprisingly little splash, sinking down, swinging from side to side as it plunged toward the distant bottom, as if it were on a length of thin string. He followed its pale shape for what seemed an eternity before it finally vanished.

"Hasn't hit the bottom," Krysty said. "Must be hundred feet or more. That's incredibly deep for water alongside a quay like this, isn't it?"

"Yeah. Might have been some kind of grotto or canyon opened up down there."

They sat for a while longer, eating their tuna sandwiches, washed down with water. There were also some slices of pineapple wrapped up, but the heat of the day had turned them soft and unpleasantly mushy.

They followed the stone into the sea.

"IT'S LIKE SOMEONE'S cleared a path through here," Krysty observed, leading the way back toward the main entrance of the Best Western hotel.

"Animals of some sort." The undergrowth did appear to have been kept down in a straight line from the harbor to the building, but the soft blown sand didn't retain any sort of prints.

"What sort of animals come out of the sea, lover? Can't think of many in these parts."

Ryan shrugged. "Don't know. Doesn't much matter. We got enough blaster power to take out anything we might find."

The lobby smelled like a tomb—dusty and dry, overlaid with a paradoxical hint of ancient damp.

With the door open the outside wind whispered in, making the motes stir in the farthest corners with a faint crackling sound, as though the shroud of some wizard's mummified corpse were unwinding.

Ryan stared around them, getting his eye used to the gloom, seeing chairs and sofas all about the room.

"Amazing." The entrance hall was virtually untouched by the passing of the years.

Posters were still pinned to the walls, showing other Best Westerns around the country with unimaginably exotic names and locations: Golden Hills Resort, Trade Winds Courtyard, Carmel Bay View, Shore Cliff Lodge, Jesse James Inn, Heart of America Inn, Blue Water on the Ocean. Some of the pictures were faded close to invisibility.

There was a tall vending machine in one corner of the lobby, but it had been ripped open and emptied.

"Eatery here," Krysty called. The carved wooden sign said it had been called The Fisherman's Cabin.

Some of the tables had been overturned, but others still stood, waiting for diners who were a hundred years dead. Candles rose from red glass bowls, and plastic carnations stood in thin silver vases. Knives and forks and spoons had been laid out in their places, and maroon napkins still held their original, sharp folds.

"Should have brought our food in here," Ryan said. "Touch of class."

Krysty stood in the middle of the vast circular room, where a space had been left clear, showing patterned wooden tiles, overlaid with a thin covering of dust. "Dance floor, I guess. Shame there's no music. We could have shared a last waltz together."

Ryan shook his head. "Can't dance. Don't ask me. Let's recce some more."

There were several snack and soft-drink vending machines at the bottom of the stairs that led to the second floor, all raided and gutted.

On the second floor there was more evidence of either a rapid evacuation at the time of the holocaust, or of selective raiding at some later date. But some of the rooms were completely untouched, and Ryan and

Krysty went into one of them, gazing around like children in a toy store.

"People really lived like this?"

Krysty nodded. "So I heard."

"Ordinary people? Norms?"

"Yeah."

"Not barons?"

Krysty laughed, quickly checking herself at the loudness of the sound in the utter stillness. "Right, lover. Just look at the luxury of it."

"The size of those two beds. Would they have slept two in each? There's plenty of space for six in each bed."

"I reckon each bed was just for one person."

"No!" Shock registered on his face, mingled with disbelief and the suspicion that the woman was teasing him. "Could put up the whole crew of a war wag in this one room. Would have made Trader laugh to see it."

The two king-size beds stood side by side, with a painting at the head of each. One showed a vermilion marlin leaping clear of the sea, and the other a dark blue right whale with a calf, basking on the surface.

There was a kind of desk with a TV standing on it, and a round table with two padded chairs. A light hung from a chain above the table. Farther back was a huge washbasin with a speckled mirror behind it and a bathroom and crapper.

"Towels!" Krysty exclaimed. "All different sizes." She picked up one of the piles of white fluffiness. "Oh, Gaia!" The cloth disintegrated into grains of powdery dust as soon as she touched it.

"Probably the blankets and stuff are the same," Ryan warned. "They won't have lasted."

Krysty opened the drawers of the desk, pulling out a frail bag of transparent plastic. "What's this for?"

"Put over your head if you didn't have enough jack to pay the check."

"No. Says it was for laundry. Look. A postcard for the hotel. And there's a Bible in here as well."

Ryan joined her. "What's that?"

It was a card, with five little cartoon faces drawn on it: one smiling broadly, one smiling less, one not smiling at all, one frowning a bit and one really scowling. He read the line of type above the faces.

"'It will help us to provide an even better service for our guests if we know how you feel we've succeeded with you. Please tick the box beneath the faces that most corresponds to your reaction to staying with us.' Think it's probably the sort of smiling one, Krysty?"

"No. The one that's scowling a bit. Those towels just fell apart on me. And there's a massive dead spider in the tub. Sorry, but could do better."

Ryan disagreed. "When you reckon it's a hundred years since anyone checked in here, I think it's in good shape. Big smiley smile face for me."

BALCONIES IN SEVERAL of the rooms looked out over a central enclosed atrium, with games machines and a small, empty pool. There were some black-and-yellow plastic loungers and what Ryan guessed was a kind of well.

They walked along the carpeted corridors to a fire door. Ryan reached out to open it and jumped back with a loud exclamation of shock.

"What is it?" Krysty's blaster was already half-drawn from its leather holster.

"Nothing." He rubbed his fingers. "Just that I got a shot of static from the brass handle. Sorry. Let's go down and look at that courtyard."

It wasn't a well. Krysty recognized it from the flickering scraps of old vids that she'd seen. "Named after a blaster, like J.B. carries. A Jack Uzi, I think. Got filled with hot water and loads of bubbles."

Ryan peered into it suspiciously. "Don't see what that's got to do with a blaster, do you?"

Krysty didn't answer him. She turned her head, her green eyes narrowing.

"Thought I heard something, and I felt a slight draft, like a door's been opened. And…" She paused.

"What?"

"Sounds stupid, lover. I thought I heard that dolphin inside my head, trying to warn us about something."

They both stood still, weighing up the silence that washed around them.

Somewhere out in the deserted hotel they both heard the noise of a door slamming.

Chapter Thirty

The atrium of the hotel had been built with an elegantly domed glass roof, but the passing years had covered it with a delicate patina of moss and algae. The light that came through was filtered into a dark muted green, and it was like being in the depths of some primeval rain forest.

Ryan and Krysty stood together, back to back, with their handblasters drawn, looking around them.

There were at least four doors into the open space, each of them closed. What was far more threatening was the fact that the atrium was surrounded on all four sides by the blind windows of the hotel's rooms, the second story with the trim balconies. If there truly was a threat, then it could come snarling at them from literally anywhere.

"Get out of here!"

"Which way?"

"Fuck knows!"

The noise could've come from anywhere. The corridors and suites of the hotel, with their interconnecting doors and passages, made it impossible to locate precisely where the sound had originated. The only thing that was certain was that it wasn't the wind that had opened and closed the door.

Someone—or something—had entered the building.

Ryan started to move slowly toward the main accommodation wing, Krysty staying with him. "Keep watching," he said quietly.

She laughed softly. "Now I never would've thought of that, lover."

They reached the arcade comp games, standing like a row of techno-confessional booths, all with ultraviolet artwork showing scenes of urban mayhem, the colors faded to gentler tones.

Now, with a wall at his back, Ryan touched Krysty, warning her to stand still for a moment. "Listen."

"Nothing," she whispered. "Can't hear anything. Can't feel anything, either."

"Best we move. Get caught in this place and we're like hogs on ice."

They froze as another door slammed, closer, the noise echoing around and around.

"Outside," Ryan whispered. "Back the way we came, and look for a way of getting out the building again. Maze like this and we could easy get trapped."

Once they were into the corridor again, there was the satisfaction of being away from those blank, menacing windows. Now there was just a row of doors on both sides, some standing open and some still locked.

Covered by Krysty, Ryan slipped into the first open room, moving catfooted past the shrouded beds, to stand up against the closed drapes. He eased them apart at the side with the barrel of the SIG-Sauer, squinting at the sunlit expanse of tarmac that had once been the main parking lot.

He let the curtain fall shut and rejoined Krysty. "Nothing," he said.

"Nothing here, either. We going to get outside and head for the boat?"

"If it's Yoville and his gang, then they might have taken the boat. I get the feeling that whoever is in the building already knows that we're in here."

"We keep going this way, then we finish up in the eatery. Out through that into the lobby and the main doors. Or we could break a window."

Ryan shook his head. "No. Looked at the sec locks. Might be old, but they'll take some forcing. Bound to take us a minute or two and make a lot of noise. Give whatever's following us time to close in. Could put a couple of rounds through the middle of the glass and then run for it."

"Subtle, lover. Real subtle."

Ryan grinned. "You sometimes ask me why I love you," he said. "That's one of the reasons. Making a joke at a time like this. Good reason."

THE HOTEL WAS as silent as a midnight grave. The carpet muffled their boots as they stepped cautiously along, checking each open door before moving on, nearing the main doors to the Fisherman's Cabin.

The rectangular Please Wait to Be Seated sign was wedged into a chromed metal stand, just outside the entrance to the restaurant. There was a notice framed behind glass on the wall, barely readable under a veil of dead flies.

Thursdays, Fridays and Saturdays in the Lounge of the Fisherman's Cabin. Tony Cormac and his Trio with songs from the shows. Eight thru late.

A sepia photograph depicted a slender man with a heavy mustache, beaming toothfully out of the frame.

"Shame we missed his act," Krysty said. "Then again..."

"Ready to go in?" Ryan glanced back, as they both heard the repeated noise of a door swinging shut. But it was impossible to tell whether the sound came from behind or before.

"How about carrying on and around to the right? Don't like the shadows and booths and corners in that eatery."

"Me, neither. Farther on is where the whole wing's collapsed. Get caught there. Cover me."

The large room was gloomy, with enough patches of darkness to conceal a conglomerate of stickies.

Ryan crouched just inside the entrance, holding the door open a couple of inches behind him, the muzzle of his blaster weaving in his hand, like a heat-seeking missile. But he couldn't see any sign of life.

"Come in. Keep low."

Krysty was instantly flattened against the wall on the opposite side of the doors, her Smith & Wesson in her hand. She raked the room with her piercing eyes, then shook her head slowly. "Nothing in here, lover."

He pointed to the exit, tapping his chest, indicating that she was to wait while he went across first. But Krysty didn't seem to be paying him any attention, staring past him toward the far side of the restaurant. Irritated, he repeated the gesture, but now she was standing up, eyes wide.

"What are..." He turned. "Fireblast!"

The other doors were open. Standing there was one of the most bizarre creatures that Ryan Cawdor had ever seen in all his years in Deathlands.

It was around seven feet tall, with very broad shoulders, narrow stomach and muscular hips, wearing a kind of cloak of trailing rags. The brighter light from the lobby silhouetted the creature, so that Ryan couldn't make out all the details.

But he was able to see the scaled body and the web of skin between the spread fingers, the huge, goggling eyes and the crest of skin protruding along the top of its skull, like the dorsal fin of a whale, an underslung lower jaw with a row of needle-sharp teeth.

Its arms were short and stumpy, barely half the length of a human being's, ending in curved talons that looked long enough and strong enough to gut a basking shark.

One hand gripped a kind of spear that ended in three barbed prongs, the whole thing looking homemade and primitive. And very deadly.

"Gaia, it's the creature from the black lagoon!" Krysty exclaimed.

"What?"

"Old vid."

"Yeah."

The mutie saw them at the same moment and stopped, lifting the trident in a threatening gesture. Its jaws slid open and it made a weird gobbling sound, like a turkey under water. There were almost recognizable words concealed in the bubbling string of noises, but nothing that you could quite get a handle on.

Ryan and Krysty both raised their guns, hesitating for a moment before opening fire.

"It's got no sort of blaster," Krysty said. "Just that big spear."

"And the best set of teeth and claws this side of the Rockies." Ryan still waited. "Wonder if there's any more of them around the place."

There was another long stream of glottal syllables. Ryan thought he might have heard "Keep out," but he couldn't be sure.

"Go away!" he shouted. "Just fuck off and leave us be. That way you don't get hurt."

The monster let the door swing shut behind it and began an ungainly waddling walk across the restaurant floor toward them. Its hip caught a table, sending it crashing over, the candle holder breaking into shards of red glass.

"Stay back!" Ryan called, unable to keep the tension out of his voice. "Or you get to be dead."

"You go...." This time there was no mistaking the words, despite the swallowed gutturals.

The long spear was lifted, the arm flexing, ready to hurl it toward Ryan and Krysty.

The SIG-Sauer snapped once, twice.

Both shots hit the creature where its wattled throat descended into its jutting chest. It staggered backward, dropping the trident with a heavy clang, its clawed, webbed hands groping toward the double wound.

Despite its size and the horror of its appearance, there was something pathetic in the manner of its passing.

One arm swept sideways, snatching at a table-cloth, which disintegrated into dust. Off balance, the scaled mutie toppled sideways, a look of startled bewilderment in its goggling eyes, crashing onto the floor.

It raised itself on an elbow, giving out a piercing cry of distress that rang through the building, a scream that was so loud that Krysty pressed her hands against her ears to try to close it out.

"Shoot it again."

"Waste of a bullet. Done for. Look at the blood coming out of it."

The lighting in the restaurant was very poor, but Ryan had the illusion that the spreading pool of the thing's blood was a deep green color.

Now it was down on its back, legs kicking feebly as though it imagined itself in the safety of deep water. The fountaining blood had already slowed to a trickle.

"Let's get out of here," Ryan said. "Place gives me a triple ice."

"Me, too."

They ran past the dying mutie, giving it a wide berth, toward the main exit into the lobby.

Krysty was in the lead and she pushed at the swing doors, feeling the stiffness of age in the hinges, running straight into two more of the gigantic creatures.

One struck at her, missing her face by fractions of an inch, the claws ripping out a tuft of the sentient red hair. Krysty was aware of the incredible stench of fish that was seeping from their skins.

There was no time to even think about what was happening. Time only to fight and kill.

Or be killed.

She heard the boom of a handblaster, but wasn't totally sure whether it came from her Smith & Wesson .38 or from Ryan's 9 mm SIG-Sauer. Another shot. This time she felt the impact of the recoil running from wrist to elbow to shoulder. Someone or something was screaming, high and shrill.

A blow on her thigh made her totter sideways, and she fought to keep her balance, arm flailing and knocking over a showcase that had once held a fine array of scented candles to tempt the hotel's guests.

Two more shots rang out, and a body tumbled onto the thin carpet of the lobby.

One more shot, then a sudden, vibrating stillness.

"You all right?" Ryan's hand was on her arm.

"Sure. They..."

"Both chilled."

Now she was able to recover her mental and physical balance, fighting back the weakening wave of shock at the unexpected violence of the attack.

The two muties lay tangled together, one dead with half its angular skull blown away, the other dying, a bullet wound ripping away the side of its shoulder, two more dark holes gaping in its belly.

"No weapons," Krysty panted, holstering her own warm gun at her hip. "Not even a knife."

"Didn't have time to notice," Ryan replied, reloading his own blaster.

"They're both females. And I... Oh, no."

"What?" He spun, seeing immediately what had made Krysty turn away in horror.

One of the muties had been pregnant and was now, in death, beginning to evacuate the fetus. A tiny reptilian head was appearing between the naked, spread thighs, squeaking piteously.

Ryan didn't hesitate. He was still holding his blaster and he took careful aim and fired a single round, the noise echoing around the building.

"That's it," he said. "Let's go back."

Chapter Thirty-One

Trampled tracks of webbed feet led up out of the Gulf toward the abandoned Best Western, circling around the beached boat. But the small vessel didn't seem to have been touched at all.

Ryan paused and examined the spoor, shaking his head. "More than three," he said.

"More of those muties?"

"Yeah. Trail of at least six or seven of them."

"Then what are we waiting for, lover? Let's get out of this damned place."

"Sure. Looks like the muties scared our dolphin guide away. No sign of it."

Ryan tugged out the anchor and placed it in the boat. He and Krysty pushed off the beach, digging in hard. At first nothing happened.

"Tide must've dropped," he said. "Give it another go."

"Stuck fast." Krysty pushed back her hair and glanced up the slope toward the now invisible bulk of the hotel. "Company."

Three or four more of the aquamuties lurched toward them at an awkward gallop, all holding spears. They were around a hundred and fifty yards away.

"Fireblast!" Ryan pulled out the heavy automatic.

"No," Krysty said, laying her hand on his arm. "Not after that little..."

"Then we best shift this bitching boat. They get within twenty yards and they'll be fighting one another to get on the last train. Come on. One and two and *three!*"

There was a grating sound, and the boat was afloat. Krysty vaulted into it and immediately grabbed at a paddle, starting to row them away from the shore.

"They look like they'll move quicker in the sea," Ryan yelled, jumping into the stern and winding the starting cord around the top of the engine.

Now they could hear the creatures calling out, a string of noises that sounded like no language and yet was also like every language.

"Come on, you son of a bitching bastard gaudy slut shithead..."

It occurred to Krysty that she had never before heard Ryan Cawdor swear like that, which was a measure of the deathly pressure and his reaction to having to shoot the tiny mewing fetus in the hotel restaurant.

The engine on the transom in the rear of the boat shuddered and coughed, then started. A gush of blue-gray smoke rose from its copperbound side as Ryan eased open the throttle.

"They're real close," Krysty warned, her own blaster cocked and ready.

"Come on!" Ryan almost screamed with frustrated anger as the engine refused to fire properly, carrying them slowly away from land.

They were still less than fifty feet away when the nearest of the muties reached the die line, stopping there and hefting its spear like a javelin.

"Look out!"

Ryan half turned at Krysty's warning, having just enough time to fend off the clumsy weapon with the side of his forearm, despite the murderous accuracy of the throw.

Krysty fired three spaced shots into the air, just above the heads of the scaled creatures. For a moment she thought it had worked, but their hesitation was only momentary and they all slid into the water, vanishing.

"Gaia help us," she prayed, closing her eyes for a moment, holding on to the side of the boat with her left hand, then peering into the startlingly clear water beneath them.

The engine was doing better as it warmed up, but they were still a scant hundred yards from the gently sloping expanse of idyllic white sand.

"They'll get us," Ryan shouted, calmer now that the battle was inevitable. "Swim up underneath. Have to try and shoot them as they come."

"One's already out ahead of us," Krysty cried, feeling a cold thrill of fear at the hideously mutated beings that were hunting them, products of the genetic maelstrom of madness that followed the nuking of the good earth.

Something clattered on the bottom of the boat, making it rock sharply to starboard, nearly forcing Krysty to drop her Smith & Wesson over the side.

She fired a blind shot into the water, kicking up a gout of spray. Unable to see whether she'd hit anything, she knew in her heart that it had been a wasted gesture.

Ryan was standing now, one hand on the tiller, the other holding the powerful blaster, his good eye scanning the expanse of ocean all around them. He never even saw the monster that came out of the water directly behind him, one clawed hand reaching for a hold on the boat, the other snatching for the throbbing engine.

Krysty leveled the short barrel of the Smith & Wesson and fired a single shot, hardly even conscious of having taken aim, part of her fighting brain taking account of there being only one more round left in her blaster.

The bullet hit the mutie an inch below the left eye, drilling through the heavy scales on the cheek and knocking it backward into the frothing wake of the boat.

"One left!" she shouted, holding up her blaster.

Ryan nodded. He knew that Krysty didn't need telling to reload as soon as she had a moment. Or that such a moment wasn't likely to occur in the next thirty seconds or so.

Krysty saw another of the creatures swimming strongly under water, twisting and turning with the agility of a hunting seal, intending to come up alongside the stern of the boat.

"There!" she called, pointing with her blaster.

Ryan steadied himself, waiting until the ghastly head broke the surface and then put a single bullet neatly through the top of its skull, chilling it instantly.

There were now two corpses floating behind them, each with its pool of thickening blood, and there were still three muties somewhere in the depths around them.

Krysty stood and looked at the sea. But the bright sun was bouncing off the surface, blocking the sight of any movement more than twenty yards away.

It was as still as death.

"Reload," Ryan whispered. "Do it now."

She fumbled in her pants pocket and carefully took out four cartridges, sliding them one at a time into her blaster until it carried the full five rounds again. It made her feel just a little bit better.

Nothing.

A scurry of small clouds drifted lazily across the face of the sun, blanking it out for a few seconds, revealing what was happening below the surface.

"There!" Ryan's and Krysty's voices rang out simultaneously as they both spotted the trio of muties beginning their attack on the boat.

Sinuous blurs scythed toward them, spears stretched ahead like the thrusting horn of the narwhal.

It was hopeless.

Krysty saw that with a chill of utter reality. All her hopes for a future with Ryan were about to be wiped away.

They couldn't stop the muties from wrecking the boat, and in the water the creatures would simply rip them apart.

Ryan had throttled back, seeing the pointlessness of trying to flee.

Krysty gripped the butt of the Smith & Wesson, determined to try to take one of them with her.

Out of the corner of her eye the woman caught a blur of movement, something moving toward them at an unbelievable speed, cutting just below the surface.

There wasn't even time to work out what it was, with everything happening so fast.

Krysty was rocked off her feet as one of the muties lunged at the bow of the boat. But there was only one of them. A second of the creatures had been hurled high into the air in a shower of spray, while the third was screaming, waving the bloodied stump of an arm, green gore jetting from the severed limb.

Ryan registered what it was.

"Fucking dolphin," he yelled. A second later he was thrown out of the small boat into the sea.

The third mutie had come up alongside, avoiding the lethal charge of the bottlenose, lashing out at Ryan with the butt end of its spear, knocking him overboard.

Krysty half turned, seeing Ryan vanish, but for a moment she was too busy in self-preservation to even think about trying to help him.

The dolphin had spun around, driving in at the wounded mutie, clamping its long jaws on the creature's skull. Even above the shouting and the frothing of the sea, Krysty heard the dreadful sound of the top of the cranium being shoved in by the powerful teeth.

The scaled horror that had been thrown in the air had recovered and was swimming unsteadily toward the bow of the boat, where Krysty carefully put two bullets through its muscular neck.

Its arms went up, its mouth opened, and it sank gracefully and permanently below the water.

''Ryan?''

The dolphin had swum alongside and lifted its head toward her, as though it wanted to be petted or thanked for its help, which she might have done but for two factors. One was her pressing worry about what had happened to Ryan. The other was that the cetacean's jaws were clogged with glistening smears of brain tissue and tiny splinters of bone.

''Ryan!''

He couldn't hear her. He was fifteen feet deep, with the pressure of the sea against his eardrums, tangling with the huge mutie.

It was the most powerful mutie life-form that he'd ever come against. If it ever managed to get a good grip on him, Ryan knew that it would shred flesh and rend muscle away from bone. He kept kicking and moving, trying desperately to hold it away from him.

The mutie was hanging on to its ungainly spear, still seeking to stab Ryan. If it had dropped it immediately, then its vastly superior power and agility in the ocean would have brought a swift end to the fight.

Above them, Krysty was peering into the turmoil below her, totally helpless.

The dolphin was watching her. With a succession of rapid clicking sounds, it dropped back under the boat and disappeared once again.

Almost blind, Ryan was only aware of blurred movement, not realizing that the dolphin had come to his rescue. It snatched a savage bit out of the mutie's arm, severing the tendons, making it drop the trident.

But the amphibian horror wasn't done. It gave a surging kick with its webbed feet, closing on Ryan, its one good arm locking around his waist like a steel mantrap, squeezing the breath from his lungs.

Ryan had the SIG-Sauer in his right hand, and he managed, with a desperate wriggle and kick, to press the muzzle against some part of the thing's scaly skin and pull the trigger.

He knew the gun had fired, because he'd felt the jarring run clear up his arm and heard the faint tremor of sound from the explosion.

But nothing happened.

Ryan's ribs seemed about to cave in under the mutie's incredible strength, and his eye felt as though it were about to burst from its socket.

He shifted the position of the gun and fired again, knowing that if he didn't keep the barrel pressed into the flesh, the shot would be wasted.

But he had no idea in the turmoil of the fight what part of the thing's body was closest.

It didn't matter. His choices had come right down to one—pull the trigger a couple of times. If that didn't work then the options dropped right down to zero.

The SIG-Sauer kicked twice more and the creature's grip relaxed a little. Once more and the hold was gone.

Ryan thrashed his way up to the surface, narrowly avoiding cracking his head on the bottom of the boat. He sucked deep into his chest a great whoop of fresh afternoon air, blinking in the bright sunlight, staring straight into Krysty's worried face.

"You chilled it?"

"Think so. What about the others?"

"I got one and the dolphin took out the other one for us. There aren't any more, lover. It's over."

"Where's the . . . Ah, here it is."

Ryan felt it nudge him, rubbing itself against his thigh with what seemed like affection. He patted it on the side of the neck, hearing the fluting whistles and clicks as it responded to his gratitude. With Krysty's help, and pushed from below by the eager dolphin, he managed to climb wearily back into the boat.

"You all right, lover?"

He nodded. "Good as I'll be."

"We going back to the institute now?"

"Guess so." He turned toward the engine, which was still ticking over. "Not much of a day out of the war, was it? Sorry about that."

"You should never apologize, lover. You know that's a sign of weakness."

He managed a smile. "So they say."

THE TRIP BACK NORTH along the Keys was relatively uneventful. They saw no sign of any kind of threatening life. The seabirds sailed serenely by with their iron beaks sheathed. Once they saw a great whale breaching, its entire body clear of the water for a heart-stopping, magical moment.

And once they both again caught the bitter odor of sulfur, indicating further submarine quake activity somewhere beyond the horizon.

When they were within five or six miles of Tomwun's institute, their pilot dolphin went suddenly into a whirl of activity, standing on its tail, flapping its fins, staring at them as it sent out a fast string of its communication signals.

"Sorry," Ryan said, holding his hands out. "Don't understand, friend."

With an expression that somehow managed to convey an almost human contempt, the dolphin circled the boat once, then set off toward the north at great speed.

"Wonder what it was trying to tell us?" Krysty said.

Five minutes later they saw the gray blur of smoke on the horizon.

Chapter Thirty-Two

"Only a scouting party," J.B. told them.

The Armorer was lying stretched out on his bed, his Uzi on the floor by his side. Mildred sat at the table, along with Doc and Michael. Dean was outside, watching Tomwun's people finishing the job of damping down the fire in the empty building near the main entrance.

"And no casualties?"

Ryan leaned against the wall, eating a bowl of grapefruit. Krysty was sitting on the other bed in the room, picking at a dish of spiced prawns.

Mildred answered. "I helped out after the pirates had retreated." She shook her head to dislodge an importunate mosquito, the tiny beads on her braids rattling softly. "One dead. Woman. She was near the gate when they came in."

"Wounded?"

"Nobody on this side, Ryan."

"Pirates?"

Doc spoke up, eyes gleaming. "Many a scurvy knave bit the dust, Comrade Cawdor. It is a good day to die. One for all and all the people some of the time." He frowned. "I think that I have somehow mislaid my words."

Ryan put the empty bowl on the table. "Body count on their side, J.B.?"

"We brought in three corpses. Think that one more'll have bought the farm by now. Helped away by two more."

Ryan nodded. "So, they came around noon. From the far side of the island. Seven in all someone said."

"I made it eight of them, Dad," Dean said, appearing in the doorway.

"The fire out?"

"Yeah. Nothing in that old hut except some tables and shit like that."

"I counted only seven." Michael was staring at the younger boy, almost as if he were challenging him to admit he'd been wrong.

"Eight."

"Doesn't much matter, does it?" Mildred interrupted, trying to clear the air.

"Could matter," Ryan said. "You said three definites chilled. One mebbe. Two helped him away. That's six."

J.B. sat up. "And I saw a seventh, cutting through the brush back over the highway. Didn't see eight."

"There was eight!" Dean insisted.

"*Were* eight," Krysty corrected him.

"I saw the dead meat and the one with half his belly trailing around his feet. Two of them helped him away. One of the others on his own was a black, and he was the one ran off toward the highway."

The Armorer nodded. "That's right. Had a rec cap on. Tried a shot, but he was zigging and zagging like he had a rattler jammed up his ass."

Ryan looked at his son. "So, how about this other pirate you saw?"

"Yellow shirt. Tall. Blue pants. Real long knife on his belt. Can't remember what sort of blaster he was carrying. Last I saw he was down near the sea."

"Anyone else see him?" Ryan asked, looking around the room. "No?"

"There was some thick smoke in the first few minutes and a lot of panic from Tomwun's folks," J.B. said. "Not saying the kid's wrong."

"Don't call me the kid!"

"Sorry."

Dean shook his head. "Don't believe this. I'm going to go look where I saw him last." He picked up his massive Browning. "I'll show you."

He stalked out of the door.

Doc half rose, but Ryan waved him down. "Let it go, Doc," he said. "Just let it go."

"I wondered if the boy might appreciate some company. There is danger carried on the wind, is there not?"

"Sure. But still . . . Leave him be."

THEY TALKED for nearly half an hour, Ryan and Krysty recounting their adventures in the lost Best

Western, the others telling them about the sudden attack from the foraging band of pirates.

"If they are Yoville's gang," J.B. added. "Can't be certain of that."

"But it's likely. You reckon the bodies and the weapons showed that?"

The Armorer considered Ryan's question. "Yeah. Has to be. Too big a coincidence if there's some other posse of thugs around the Keys."

Krysty jumped to her feet, running toward the door. "Dean," she said over her shoulder.

Ryan was at her heels, the others close behind, everyone snatching up weapons.

"Didn't hear a thing," Ryan said.

"Nor me. Had a flash of feeling. Somewhere over by the sea. Come on."

They ran between the buildings, dodging around some of the open-air tanks, past the quay until they could see the stretch of sand and the open waters of the Lantic.

By then Ryan had established a slight lead, with Michael at his heels. But everyone was still closely bunched, Doc Tanner lumbering gamely along in the rear.

They all stopped as they came over the crest of the dunes, seeing a tall figure in a yellow shirt, with blue pants, holding a long cutlas to Dean's throat. He was dragging him backward, kicking and struggling, toward a slender canoe that was beached a few yards distant. The boy's 9 mm Browning Hi-Power lay glittering in the sand halfway between him and the nearest building.

They were about seventy yards from Ryan and the others, facing them.

"Move an' me spill little one's throat in t'sand. Stay where you is all an' me let 'im go out in t'water."

The voice was clear, ringing across the shoreline. Dean made an effort to shout something, but the pirate tightened his left arm around his throat, and the boy's desperate attempts to free himself became visibly weaker.

"Mildred," Ryan said, turning to face her, "can you take him out?"

She bit her lip, holding the target blaster loosely down at her side. "Downhill and he's right behind Dean. Could get a shot when he gets him into his boat."

"Miss him then, Ryan, and he's going to get clean away," J.B. warned.

"I know that," the one-eyed man said through gritted teeth. "But Mildred's right. Even with her skill it's a bastard tough shot. Mebbe we ought to wait and—"

"That good. You stay still and t'boy mebbe live. Me get'm in boat now."

"Blood on the Cross," Michael said. "I'll go and get him."

"You what?" Ryan said, startled, raising his voice, actually lifting the SIG-Sauer as the young man began to move swiftly toward the helpless Dean and his captor. "Come the fuck back here or..."

The sand was soft, giving a treacherous footing, but the ex-monk was running as though he were on smooth ground, jinking every few steps from side to side, drawing the Texas Longhorn Border Special from its holster and seeming to juggle with it while he was sprinting toward the pirate.

"You get t'boy dead!" the man screamed, hanging on to Dean like someone in a quicksand clinging to the last fragile branch above his head.

"Shoot him, Mildred," Ryan ordered. "Now!"

"Who?"

"Fucking pirate."

"Can't. Michael's in the way, Ryan."

"Then shoot... No..."

Already Michael was well over halfway toward the oddly frozen tableau, and they could also hear that he was singing at the top of his voice.

"'He would constant be, against all disaster...'"

"It's a hymn," Mildred said. "God save us all, but the lad's singing a hymn."

"Boy dead, fucker!"

"He's useless with that blaster," J.B. observed quietly. "Useless."

Now they all stood in silence and watched the bizarre drama being played out in front of them.

Ryan closed his eye for a moment, seeing in his mind the last act of that drama as he knew it would happen. The cutlass would be drawn across the front of his only child's throat.

Even at that most desperate moment, Ryan began to bring up his SIG-Sauer, ready to blow away the pirate who had just murdered his son.

He opened his eye onto reality, but it was a reality that made no sense.

Michael had thrown his gun away, heaving it high into the late-afternoon sky, where the setting sun caught it in an aura of crimson light. The pirate was standing stock-still, mouth open, staring up in disbelief at the spinning blaster.

He still held Dean, but the pressure around his neck had sent the boy slumping into unconsciousness, knees bent, feet dragging in the sand.

Michael was flying, performing a complicated gymnastic somersault, tucked up, spinning like a wheel right over the pirate's head. And there was the glint of silver in each of his fists.

Although Michael very rarely showed them, Ryan knew that he carried two slender daggers, one on each hip.

"By the three Kennedys," Doc whispered, standing at Ryan's elbow.

The pirate gaped at the whirling figure as it flew toward and over him. Michael did something with his hands at the moment of his closest passing, and to Ryan it seemed that he had somehow managed to reach down and gently pat the yellow-shirted pirate on both cheeks.

Then he was over him, landing effortlessly on the balls of his feet, spinning around to face the man, putting out a negligent hand to catch the falling Border Special, which dropped into his palm as if it were a gift from the gods.

"What did he . . ." Mildred began.

Then she saw. They all saw what it was that Michael had done.

He had succeeded in ramming each of his knives into the side of the man's throat, just beneath the ears, so that the hilts stood out like bolts in the neck of a monster. Each was at the center of a bright fountain of arterial blood that pattered out on both sides, pumped by his failing heart.

He dropped the cutlass, then let Dean slip from his nerveless hands.

Ryan led the rush toward the sea, still unable to believe what he'd just seen.

The man was down, his golden shirt now sodden with blood, blood that had already ceased flowing from the double mortal wounds. He was on his side, knees drawn up in a fetal position.

Dead.

Michael had his arm around Dean, supporting the boy while he recovered consciousness.

As Ryan arrived, he heard Michael talking to his son. "You were right," he said. "There were eight of them."

Chapter Thirty-Three

After talking it over with his companions, Ryan had decided that they should involve themselves in keeping watch for the attack they now knew was bound to come.

"Sea is one point. Land to north, south and west is the other three points."

J.B. was sitting wiping at the lenses of his glasses, a sure sign that he was thinking particularly deeply. "If I was Yoville, and if I had enough men and blasters, I wouldn't make the same mistake that I made yesterday, sending in too few with far too little."

Ryan nodded. "Sure. Spread yourself. I guess he might combine land and sea attacks this time."

"Night or day?" Krysty asked.

"Way it looks, Yoville could believe he has a lot more men than us. Shootists, not white-coat scientists."

"Upon my soul, Cawdor, but I will not sit idly by while you malign my profession!"

"Sorry, Doc. There's scientists and there's scientists, isn't there?"

"Apology accepted, my dear fellow."

"What was I… Yeah. Night or day? Night doesn't help him any so I figure the next move'll be an out-and-out frontal attack. Now, Yoville can get close by land without us spotting him. But at sea…that's different."

"I think that's where we can offer some positive help. Through our cetacean friends."

Nobody had heard Mark Tomwun enter the room, and every face turned to him.

"The dolphins?" Mildred shook her head. "You mean strap on some bombs and send them off to get blown up? That your idea of help, Professor?"

"I accept the blame." He bowed slightly toward the black woman. "But I can only say that a man sometimes has to do what a man has to do."

"And you're only obeying orders!" There was bitter anger in her voice. "A great American once said that the only thing that evil men need to flourish is for decent men to stand aside. Why don't you try and explain how the end always justifies the means, Tomwun? Isn't that the next line in your script?"

His face had tightened at her sudden attack. "You have no right to plead morality when you ride with a band of the worst killers in Deathlands!"

She took a half step toward him, her eyes blazing. "My father was burned to death by a bunch of red-neck racists, Tomwun. Don't you—" Mildred swallowed hard, fighting for control "—ever, ever talk to me about morality!" She turned away from him. "I'm going outside to get some fresh air. I know it's a fucking corny thing to say, but I can't stand the smell in here.''

Eventually the atmosphere cooled and it was agreed that Tomwun, helped by Miranda, would send out some of his trained dolphins to scour the coast to north and south, on both sides of the Keys, using their amazing sonic communications to check in when any seaborne attack was threatened.

Ryan and his group would lend their own combat expertise to organizing a series of patrols and sentries around the institute.

J.B. BROUGHT THE FIRST warning of action, reporting back in the middle of the following morning from the highway to the north.

"Small armored wag coming this way."

"Support?" Ryan asked.

"Nothing. Can't hold more than two or three people. Got a white sheet on it."

"What?"

"White flag."

Doc cleared his throat. "That has always been the sign, throughout history, of desiring a parley. It is called a flag of truce, you know."

"Yeah, Doc, I know. I also know that it could be a kind of trick. Take us off guard." He turned to the Armorer. "J.B., tell everyone to get on triple-red."

"Sure."

THE WAG LOOKED like it had started life as half of a
pickup truck and half of an unidentifiable green saloon. Old welds showed a vivid orange around the
body, and some rusted steel plates had been clamped
on at the front and flanks to give it some measure of
protective armor plating. A ragged white sheet fluttered from a side window.

It advanced hesitantly across the dunes, through
the scrub, finally stopping about two hundred yards
from the entrance to the institute. Blue smoke pouring noisily out of its fractured exhaust.

"Make sure the watchers around the back are
keeping their position," Ryan called, getting a wave
of response from Dean, who'd been appointed combat runner.

Tomwun had joined Ryan just inside the gate,
squinting through gaps in the wall. "What do you
think they want?"

"You guess, and it'll be as good as mine. Reckon
we'll find out soon."

A small metal flap opened on the driver's side of
the wag, and they all heard a loud, confident voice
booming out.

"I hear that Ryan Cawdor leads the defenders of
this place. True?"

The voice was rich and deep, with a hint of an accent that placed the man some ways north up the
Sippi.

Ryan leaned against the gate, making sure that he didn't expose himself to any snipers that Yoville might have concealed in the brush.

"You hear right. We met?"

"You rode with Trader. Soon as I heard about the one-eyed man being around, I guessed it was you. Met up near Norleans, five, mebbe six years back. Did us a deal over some bales of cloth and some good drinking liquor. But one of my people got greedy and there was trouble. You recall it, Cawdor?"

"Yeah. Finished with two good men getting ambushed from the bayous. Shot in the back of the head when there was supposed to be a deal."

A bellow of laughter. A hand waved, and Ryan glimpsed a flash of bright red material on the sleeve. "Deals aren't for you and me, Ryan. Deals are for the little people."

J.B. nudged Ryan. "I recall the son of a bitch now. Wasn't called Yoville then, but he wore red shirt and pants. Should've remembered that."

Ryan nodded, raising his voice again. "What do you want, Yoville?"

"Talk."

"Why?"

"Before the blasters open up. You got no chance in there, Cawdor."

"So why talk? Just come ahead."

Another laugh. "Sure. Full of tricks like that. I'll send in my right-hand man, and one other. See if you can hear some good sense. For both of us."

"Send them in."

"No tricks? We got a deal here, Cawdor? Be a blood price if you don't deal right."

"Send them in," he repeated.

"Want me to go out and try and chill that red-clothed bastard in his wag?" J.B. asked.

"No. Let's hear what they got to say. Might find out more than they intend."

Yoville was getting impatient. "Hotter than the fucking hobs of hell out here. Can I send them in?"

"Yeah. Only two." Ryan turned to the others. "Keep them covered and make sure the watch is alert on the other sides. Trust Yoville about as far as I could piss molasses."

THE SENIOR OF THE TWO emissaries was a stocky man in his mid-thirties, with slanted eyes and a totally bald head. He wore a olive green satin blouse tucked into filthy white pants. His feet were bare. He had a superb flintlock pistol, beautifully engraved, tucked into his belt. It was one of the oldest blasters that Ryan had ever seen.

His name was Kim.

The other pirate was a young woman, barely out of her teens. Her name was Meg, and she stood over six feet tall. Her eyes were so deep a brown that they verged on black. She wore a divided skirt in cerise cotton and an embroidered blouse, and like Kim, she was barefoot.

In her wide leather belt she carried a nondescript automatic that had obviously been pieced together from four or five other guns.

Meg would have been very beautiful if it hadn't been for the fact that someone had taken a broken bottle to her face with murderous effect. The first blow had circled her left eye, surrounding it with a vivid, puckered scar, while the second had removed part of the side of her nose and gouged away the corner of her mouth, giving her a permanent, twisted smile.

But her body had a lithe, feral grace that instantly attracted Ryan's passing interest. The thought crossed his mind that the young woman would be just as likely to slice off a man's genitals as to make love. She caught the expression on his face and spit in the sand at his feet.

"Easy, Meg," Kim warned. "Cap don't like us do dat sort of thing here."

"Then he can keep he cunting pity to heself. Man scarred like he should be caring."

Both of them had the same strange, lilting patois that the yellow-shirted man had used, the man whose corpse had been heaved into the surf and left for the scavengers.

It was Kim who did the talking, insisting he would speak only with Ryan Cawdor. "He t'man here say Cap Yoville. White coat just man him piss sittin' down like girly."

Mark Tomwun was extremely reluctant to leave Ryan with the two pirates, but eventually agreed to move away with Krysty and the others.

When Kim and Meg were alone with Ryan, he assumed a confidential grin. "Cap say you t'man with t'clever brain, Ryan. Say me to say him got close fifty with t'blasters."

"We got near that."

"You don't got t'war wag, Cap Cawdor."

Ryan hoped he'd concealed his shock at that. If it was true, then it was seriously bad news. The institute was moderately defensible against an attack from skirmishing guerrillas. But a war wag would wipe the walls away and chill anyone who wasn't armed with some grens or a mortar.

"We got the power to handle a wag. Anyway, I'll believe that when I see it."

Kim smiled, showing a golden tooth at the front. "Listen t'me and you don't see it. You and friends be long gone."

"Get to it, for fuck's sake," Meg snapped. "I fall into sleep while me wait."

"We give up the place to you and sacrifice Tomwun and his people and we walk free? That it?"

Kim clapped his hands. Ryan noticed he had a coiled purple dragon tattooed on the back of his right wrist.

"That it. Good an' easy, Cap Cawdor. Why we worry 'bout little white coats. Us men of blood, Cap Cawdor. You know Cap Yoville say shame to worry 'bout little others. Hey, man, they goin' t'die anyways up.''

"He could be right,' Ryan said, nodding.

"You do it?''

"Tell Yoville I'll let him know within the hour.''

Again the golden smile, and a pat on the arm, like a drinking companion. "But me say you goin' say good plan?''

"Say that.''

"Thank fuck!'' Meg spit again, narrowly missing the toes of Ryan's combat boots. "Shame me don't get way talk secret and whisper with you, Cawdor.''

It sounded somewhere between a threat and a promise, and the words sent a chill down Ryan's spine.

"Yeah, we could have made some beautiful music together, sweetheart,'' he said.

"Fuck you.''

"Now us go on back, Cap Cawdor. Safe under t'flag of truce, yeah?''

"Sure,'' Ryan replied, walking with them back to the gate, where he could see the battered armawag still waiting. There was a hand dangling from the window, holding a cigarette, the fringe of the scarlet sleeve showing bright against the dull metal.

Yoville bellowed out when he saw his people. "You agreed the deal I gave you, Cawdor?''

Both Meg and Kim faced away from the institute, toward their hidden leader. J.B., Krysty and the others stood with Tomwun, a few yards away to the right, safe behind the defensive wall.

"Like you said—deals are for the little people, Yo-ville," Ryan shouted. He drew the SIG-Sauer from its holster and put a single 9 mm round in the back of Kim's neck, dropping him like a sack of offal. The young woman was lightning quick, starting to turn, but Ryan dropped her with a second bullet through the back of her skull, blowing her face all over the sandy earth.

"My sweet Lord," Tomwun whispered.

Chapter Thirty-Four

"It was cold and calculated murder. It can only increase their anger and determination to wipe us all out to the last man and woman."

Tomwun was trembling with a potent mixture of anger and fear, his hands tangling as though they were suddenly at war with each other.

Nobody else had said anything as the bodies dropped, spurting blood into the thirsty sand. Yoville himself had made no response, except crashing the wag into gear and driving quickly off, surrounded by a drifting shroud of dust.

Ryan nodded at Tomwun, using the push-button mag release and replacing the two spent rounds.

"I hear you." Ryan slammed the blaster firmly back into its holster.

"Murder."

"You triple-stupe!" The one-eyed man spun so fast that the scientist took several stumbling steps away from him, nearly putting his foot right in the clotted puddle of blood and brains.

Without Ryan even realizing it, the SIG-Sauer was somehow in his hand again.

"No," Krysty said, her voice cutting across the tension like a straight razor.

Ryan took a slow breath and closed his eye for a moment, nodding at what had nearly happened. He reholstered the blaster for a second time.

"Tomwun," he said very gently, "I don't know how you've managed to live in Deathlands as long as you have. Yoville's coming in to try and take this place. Don't know why. Mebbe we'll never know why. Would make a good base for raiding down south to the far Indies."

"They came under a flag of truce," Doc protested. "I owe you my life, Ryan, many times over, but I must confess that I find it devilish hard to justify what you've just done. Gunned down a man and a woman in the very coldest of blood. Shot them both in the back, like an executioner."

"Doc, all of you. This isn't some fucking game of white and black and winners and losers and being caught on the wrong side. This is life for the winners and death for everyone else."

J.B. spoke up. "They have a lot more weapon power and trained chillers than we do. Now they've got two less. One of them was Yoville's second in command."

"I heard what he said. He said that we could all go free from here." Michael stared accusingly at Ryan. "Wasn't that a chance to walk free?"

"You got some excuse, Michael. Weren't born and raised in this world. Listen. Listen to me. Yoville just wanted to try it on. Try and trick us. He'd have found a way of ambushing us once we were outside the walls. And then Tomwun and Miranda and every living soul here would've got to be very dead, very quickly. Now he'll be that bit less confident. Lost two more. Played them as cards and they got taken out."

"Suppose you're wrong, Ryan? You thought about that possibility?" Mildred sighed. "I guess you have. Sorry. Stupe sort of question."

"If I'm right, we got a small chance more than we did before. If I'm wrong, then we're no worse off. Least we're still all alive."

LATE IN THE AFTERNOON three mortar shells came howling in from the north. Their dark shapes, silhouetted against a golden sky, fell in a parabolic curve from the south of the institute. One missed badly, overshooting by at least two hundred yards, exploding in the dunes with a muffled crump and an insignificant pillar of dust. The second one landed at the rear of the complex of the buildings, knocking a hole through the roof of some abandoned kitchens, and failing to detonate.

When J.B. examined it later he found that it was an old implode-gren that had wings crudely welded on to try to turn it into a shell.

The third of the missiles hit near the quayside.

Chuck Cybulski was the only person anywhere near it, walking to check on the guards who were on watch at the seaward side of the institute.

Splinters of shrapnel tore into his knees and lower legs, ripping them apart. By the time anyone got to him, he'd bled to death.

SUPPER WAS a subdued meal.

Though Ryan didn't believe that the gang of killers would attack during the hours of darkness, he wasn't prepared to risk his life on it. So sentries were posted and Miranda sent out her dolphin scouts on a nocturnal mission.

The two Bobs brought in tureens of an excellent chowder, filled with bite-size chunks of fresh and smoked fish. But the bread was stale, baked two days earlier, following on Ryan's order that all fires were to be extinguished, except those in brief and immediate use for providing a hot breakfast and a hot supper.

"Dessert's a little on the thin side tonight, as well. Oatmeal cooked in milk, then soaked in honey and quick-fried. Served with some strawberry jelly."

"Running out of eggs, as well," the other Bob added. "Wish those pirates would attack and get it over with, then we can get some decent food again."

"Could boil some fatback and a few beans, if anyone's still in need of some nourishment. Perhaps after all that killing, Mr. Cawdor? All that energy and all of that reckless bravery. Must take it out of a person."

Krysty laid her hand on Ryan's arm, feeling the muscles jumping with suppressed anger. She looked at the two young men. "I'd go now. Unless you want to find your teeth growing out of your asses. Thanks for the food."

Muttering between themselves, they left the room, closing the outer door behind them with rather more noise than was necessary. Everyone sat in silence, listening to the sound of their feet crunching away through the dry sand.

Doc broke the moment of tension, standing and picking up the metal ladle in the larger of the tureens. He took off the lid with his other hand. "Ah, that brings back so many good, good memories." He inhaled deeply, with his eyes closed. "Emily was always rather proud of the exquisite nature of her own chowder. Learned it from a spinster cousin, Harriet, who hailed from Nantucket or some such place."

"Can you help me to a serving, Doc?" Dean asked, holding out his plate.

"But of course." The chowder steamed in the cool of the evening as he ladled out a generous helping for the boy. "Dear Emily made it with fresh butter and homegrown herbs and spices." He kissed his gnarled fingers. "For that extra touch of piquancy. Oh, my dearest darling."

He sat down and began to eat, seemingly oblivious to the tears that trickled down his cheeks.

Mildred had only a small portion before pushing away her plate. She refused the oatcakes. "Just don't feel hungry, sorry." She caught Ryan's eye and smiled wryly. "Nothing personal. Truly. Just don't feel hungry. Nerves. Used to be a bit like this the night before a big shooting match. Once I reached the butts I was fine. I think...I think you did what was right, Ryan."

"Thanks, Mildred."

"Didn't like it. I remember, so long ago now, seeing a famous bit of news vid. Some policeman in Saigon who pulled out his pistol and blew away some poor bastard they'd captured. I guess the dead guy must have been what they called the Vietcong. That was different to what you did. Still..."

"Taking a life's never easy, Mildred," J.B. said quietly, laying his spoon in his empty bowl.

"I know that, John. Last few months I've seen things I'd never have... Well, enough. Time for bed." She got up from the table, walked around and stopped by Ryan's chair, bending to kiss him on the cheek. "Way to go, Ryan," she said. "Guess you did it pretty up and walking good, didn't you?"

"Tried. Good night, Mildred. Night, J.B., sleep well. Could be a bright start in the morning."

The Armorer rubbed a dribble of chowder from his chin. "If I had jack to spend, I'd lay it out on dawn tomorrow. After you put a hornet up his ass, Yoville won't be much in the mood for waiting around."

Doc also rose. "I came across a book in one of the laboratories yesterday. I shall retire and give myself the rare pleasure of reading a real book."

"What is it, Doc?" Krysty asked. "Good novel? Slim volume of verse?"

"No, no. It's called *Polydichromates in Trimolecular Halogenic Monoglutamates*. A rare pleasure."

Krysty laughed. "I read that already, Doc."

"Honestly?"

"Yes. It was the butler who did the murder. Found his prints on the dagger in the library."

Doc tutted his disapproval. "Yes, most amusing, my dear Krysty. Most amusing. You should be on the stage."

"I should?"

"Indeed. There's one leaving from the depot at seven in the morning. Be on it." He roared with laughter. "That wowed them in the vaudeville circuit when I was a lad."

"Sure. Good night, Doc."

He bowed to her. "Good night, Gracie."

"What?"

"Let it pass, my dear. Good night, gentles all. May choirs of angels...do something or other. I fear I disremember what it was."

"I'm for an early night, too, Doc." Michael stood and stretched. "G'night all."

Dean caught his father's glance. "Oh, do I have to, Dad? I'm not tired."

"Tomorrow's likely to begin quick and finish early, son. If you're going to be real useful, you need to get to bed now. Off you go."

"Sure thing. Can I stand a watch tonight, Dad?"

"No."

"Why not?"

"Because I say you need sleep, Dean. Now go on, off to bed, please."

The "please" was a rare concession, and the boy recognized it. "Sure, Dad. Good night, Krysty."

"Sleep tight, Dean."

After they were left alone, Ryan pulled out the chair next to his and rested his boots on it. He looked across at the window. With the lights on indoors, it was almost impossible to see what was going on outside. On the table, the large tureen was scraped empty, the smaller one still with a couple of inches of the chowder, congealing in the bottom. Only Michael and Dean had been much tempted by the honeyed oatcakes on the round plate.

"Going to be bad tomorrow."

Krysty looked at him, her fathomless green eyes betraying no emotion. "I know. Long odds. Backs to the sea. And if they have a war wag?"

"Well, I got an idea about that."

"Yes?"

"Going to take me a walk before I turn in, lover. Want to come?"

"No." She stood. "Got to fieldstrip my Smith & Wesson ready for tomorrow. Clean and oil it. If I got chilled because my blaster jammed, I don't think John Barrymore Dix would ever forgive me. I'll wait for you."

"Won't be long."

As HE WALKED through the cool evening with the sound of the surf a constant murmur in his ears, Ryan tried to imagine what the Trader would have done in a situation like this. He probably would have sent out a recce to find the pirates' main camp and then gone in with all blasters firing and kicked the shit out of Red Jack Yoville and his bunch of thugs.

Then again, when you had the highly trained crews of at least two combat-honed war wags, that kind of battle plan was easy to formulate and even easier to implement.

Ryan had only himself and J.B. who were really experienced. Krysty was good and Mildred was a fine shot. Doc would try and would offer to run headfirst through a brick wall if you asked him to. Dean had survived as rough an upbringing as any kid of eleven and wouldn't flinch when the shooting started. And Michael had already demonstrated his own determination to do the best that he could.

Mark Tomwun was an enigma. Ryan still couldn't decide whether the scientist was on the side of light or dark. Then again, that was true of most people.

The rest of the institute seemed to be just an average bunch of folks, which wasn't saying much when it came to an out-and-out firefight.

They had no effective transport, except for their boats with their unreliable gas engines.

"Gas?" Ryan said, punching his right fist into his left palm. He hadn't thought properly about that.

IT TOOK HIM a couple of hours to explore and then carry out the beginnings of a tactical plan, something that might work when the pirates finally arrived.

Might not.

On the way back to rejoin Krysty, Ryan found himself wandering to the glassy curtain of the ocean, among the docks and quays, seeing a light glowing in the area where most of the communication research was done.

"That you, Michael?"

"No, Ryan. That Miranda?"

"Yeah." She didn't bother to conceal her disappointment at his arrival.

"Expecting Michael?"

She sat right at the end of the wharf, feet dangling into the pen nearest to the sea.

"He comes out some nights."

"I was just going to bed. Thought I'd take a last walk this way."

"Sure."

"Mind if I join you?"

"Free country." She laughed softly. "My father's father used to say that. Said that his father's father used to say it. Kind of family joke. The old man was born in the middle of the 1900s. Free country, Ryan."

"They reckon it really was free then."

"Who knows? It's as far away as the times I read about in the Bible."

He sat down, feeling the stones still retaining a little of the warmth of the day. The steel-mesh barrier was up, offering access direct out to the Lantic.

"How old are you, Miranda? Fifteen? Twenty? Guess I'm not good at women and ages. Check that. I'm not all that good with women, period."

She smiled at him, relaxing a little, the hostility edging out of her voice. "You ride with Krysty Wroth. Seems to me that makes you like a man who knows about women. Answer to your question is that I'm seventeen. Two years younger than Michael."

Ryan read the unspoken words. "He ask you to come along with us?"

She didn't reply at first, picking up a tiny flake of concrete and flicking it into the pen below her. "Sort of," she said finally, reluctantly.

"What did you say?"

"I'd think about it."

It trembled on Ryan's lips to tell the young woman that it wasn't that simple. You didn't just get to come along on Michael Brother's say-so. If anyone made that kind of decision, then it was Ryan himself.

But there was no point in mentioning that now. Not with an attack expected in the next couple of days from a superior and murderous force. The time to tell Miranda that she might not be going with them would be when they saw who'd survived.

If anyone survived.

"Nothing from any of the dolphins?" he asked, changing the subject.

She seemed relieved. "Reason I'm out here now. Sent four out an hour ago. Still one of the previous lot not come home. Something could've happened to him."

"Tell me soon as—"

"Course. You don't need to tell me that, Ryan. Not a stupe, you know."

"I know. Sorry." He stood and stared out over the endless expanse of water. He turned away, then checked himself, looking more carefully. "Isn't..." he began.

But Miranda was already gone, slipping down into the five feet of water in the pen below with scarcely a splash, dipping her head under the surface.

Ryan watched as the dorsal fin came closer, moving fast, leaving a vee-shaped trail of phosphorescence stretching behind it, roughly north by west.

The night seemed suddenly to have gone very quiet. So quiet that he almost thought he could hear the clicks and whistles, though he knew that was impossible from where he was.

Ryan waited for the young woman to react.

Miranda's head lifted, sea water streaming down from her hair. She looked up at him, her face pale in the moonlight. "They're coming. They're on their way here."

Chapter Thirty-Five

"Say," Doc remarked. "Can you see by the early light of the dawn, that we are about to receive a number of notably uninvited visitors?"

Mildred, sitting with her back against one of the outer walls, managed a thin, nervous smile. "Just don't start on about this being the land of the brave, Doc."

"Dying's easy," Michael said, kneeling in the cool sand. "Living's hard."

"Fucking crap, Michael." J.B. spoke with unusual emotion, the rising sun glittering off the blank lenses of his glasses. "People say shit like that know nothing about death. Nothing. There's never anything easy about death. Doesn't matter how it comes."

"I didn't..." the teenager began.

J.B. wasn't done. "I'll grant you that there's ways of dying that's worse than others. A slow, bleak and lonely passing comes at the very bottom of the list. But I tell you it never, ever comes easy."

Dean had been finishing off a hasty, cold breakfast, and he scampered to join them, the heavy Browning flapping on his right hip. He half waved to his father, who was standing with Tomwun and Krysty, looking out past the main entrance.

"Hi, Dad. Anything? Hey, who dropped a real green cheesy one?"

"What? What do you mean?"

The boy wrinkled his nose. "Smells like... Oh, I know. It's that sulfur stuff."

"Right." Krysty lifted her head, the light dawn breeze tugging at the tight curls of the brilliant red. "Must be another of those undersea eruptions, somewhere not far off. Mebbe it'll blow away the pirates."

Now they could all smell it. From where they were standing, the buildings blocked off the view of the sea, off to the east. But Ryan craned up on tiptoe, seeing the ominous beginning of a dirty yellow cloud blossoming over the Lantic, starting to draw a veil across the new sun.

"Miranda," he called.

"Yeah?"

"The message was that there were boats launched to the north and south?"

"Right. Can't be certain of numbers. Dolphins don't seem to look at counting in the same way that we do. But I think more than one boat."

"They talk about disturbances?"

"Volcanoes and quakes and that stuff? Yeah, quite often. But it's real common around here. The Keys are at the center of a major fault line."

"Nothing new?"

Miranda shook her head at the question. "No." She paused. "But I've brought them all in for safety. To the inner harbor. Pirates shoot them as soon as look, and the bottlenoses are so damned friendly."

"There's none of them out there now?"

"No, Ryan. None. No need, is there?"

"Guess not. Just that the cloud over to the east is swelling real big."

His concern was set on a back burner when J.B. called out to him. "Here they come."

Yoville had learned his lesson about trying it small and quiet. This time it was big and loud.

"War wag," Krysty said.

"Two small armorer wags. One from the south and one in the dust behind the war wag. And twenty or thirty with blasters, skirmish line on foot." Ryan looked around. "Dean."

"What?"

"Sea. Go check out the horizon, all around, and report back to me. Like now."

The boy went from standing still to a flat-out sprint without any apparent intervening stage.

Yoville had chosen the direct route, as Ryan had figured he might.

There was only one minor obstacle between the attackers and the institute. The dirt road from the main highway crossed a creek bed, which was dry at this time of year. It was about forty feet wide and less than ten feet deep, with a wooden trestle bridge running over it from west to east. From the main gate of the institute to the bridge was roughly one hundred yards.

The wag wag stopped, its rumbling engine coughing and spluttering.

"Trader would've had someone's gut for bootlaces if one of our war wags had sounded like that." J.B. shook his head. "I hate sloppy. Hate it."

The wag looked as though it might have started life as an M-548-B tracked cargo carrier, built on an old M-113 chassis. But from the note of the engine it had obviously been converted, with only partial success, from diesel to gas. Ryan saw with immense relief that it wasn't one of that model of wag that carried either the Chaparral or HAWK missiles. There was the stump of an 107 mm mortar on the turret, but it looked to be sawed-off and defunct.

"Browning .5 machine gun," the Armorer said. "Normally carry about two thousand rounds of ammo. Do us some harm if they got the caliber. Not easy to find. Could mebbe try to convert it to something more common. Can't tell from here."

"Why've they stopped?" Tomwun asked. He was carrying an M-16, as were most of his people. At Ryan's insistence they'd all changed out of their habitual white coats.

"Just taking a look, I guess," Mildred replied. "I reckon I could put one through that ob slit at the front, Ryan. Worth a try, is it?"

He shook his head. "Hold back showing them what we can do. And I don't want the driver taken out. Not yet. Not until after they reach the bridge."

Obviously satisfied with what he'd seen, Red Jack Yoville had ordered his small army to advance. The war wag in the lead flanked the two smaller vehicles, kicking enough dust to conceal the men and women who were darting in behind them.

Ryan glanced back over his shoulder, seeing that the smeared pillar of golden cloud was being dissipated over the sea, meaning that the eruption had passed.

For the time being.

As far as he could tell, the plans that had evolved from their long meetings over the best hope of defensive success had been followed. All around the perimeter of the Mark Tomwun Institute of Peaceful Oceanographic Research were armed men and women. He and J.B. had paced out the walls together, seeking dead ground, finding the best points to defend, with the widest lines of fire.

Now everyone was waiting, fingers on triggers, crouched inside windows and behind walls.

Dean came running back, dodging to left and right, showing an uncanny sense of what was safe ground, out of sight of the heavy machine gun on the front of the war wag.

"Boats," he said, having to raise his voice to a shout so that his father could hear him over the roar of the advancing wave of attackers.

"How many?"

"Two south and one north."

"How far?"

"Mile or more."

"Fast or slow?"

"About twenty minutes away from us."

"Men?"

The boy shook his head. "Too far off to make them. But the boats don't look too big."

Ryan beckoned to Tomwun. "Three boats. One to the north and two to the south. Can you send any of your dolphins out after them? Turn them over?"

The scientist considered the question. For longer than Ryan welcomed. "Probably too little time. I'll see what Miranda can do with them."

"Worth a try."

"Close to the bridge, Ryan," J.B. warned.

The war wag was within a dozen yards of the far side of the flimsy wooden bridge. Ryan's first plan had been to cut it down, or weaken it. But his second plan, on the previous evening, had seemed much better. Another couple of minutes and he'd find out whether he'd been right.

Over to the right, he heard the faint snap of a rifle being fired, and he saw the tiny puff of smoke from the corner of one of storerooms.

"Waste of time," Dean said.

"Yeah," Ryan agreed.

Yoville kept his crew on a tighter rein. There hadn't been a single round fired toward the defenders.

The war wag's unseen driver was having a lot of trouble holding the engine in the low gear he wanted. It was clear that his concentration was wandering, as the tracked vehicle would suddenly shudder and kick sideways.

The speed had dropped below walking pace, the two smaller vehicles crowding in close behind the wag. The tracks chewed up the sand, throwing it out in a blinding sheet, obscuring the men and women on foot.

"Hold your fire!" Ryan shouted. "Don't waste the ammo on what you can't see."

Slightly to his surprise, Tomwun's people obeyed his order. They were all amateurs when it came to facing blasters, and Ryan knew the temptation to pull the trigger and keep pulling it, even when the hammer had clicked a dozen times on a spent cartridge.

The lead wag had just reached the far side of the trestle bridge.

Ryan picked up his SSG-70 Steyr bolt-action rifle, cradling the smooth walnut stock to his shoulder, sliding one of the ten full-metal-jacket rounds into the breech. The dawn was well advanced, and he didn't need the Starlite night scope, but the laser image enhancer was going to be useful.

To his left, someone's nerve didn't hold out and he heard a carbine crack, the bullet ricocheting off the armor plate of the war wag. It had been a wasted round, but at least it had been an accurate wasted round.

It prompted a response from Yoville's gang. The machine gun opened fire, a raking burst of lead splattering the wall and gate of the institute. A young woman standing next to Mark Tomwun dropped like a lead weight, a neat hole through her forehead, a much larger cavity blown out of the back of her skull.

"Keep down!" J.B. called. "Keep flat, behind the walls if you can."

The bullet that had killed the woman had driven clean through the main gate.

Ryan heard a voice artificially amplified, and he guessed it was Yoville, though he couldn't quite make out what the leader of the pirates was saying.

There was no further shooting from the machine gun, and the war wag began to roll ponderously toward the middle of the bridge, slewing dangerously to the left until the driver managed to correct the yawing movement.

Ryan leveled the Steyr, drew a careful bead on the ob slit behind which the driver was sitting, then let the laser sight drift lower, down the sloping armored front of the wag onto the scarred timbers of the bridge.

Lower still, into the shadows where there were uneven piles of sand.

"Over halfway," J.B. said.

"Yeah." Cheek against the stock, right eye squinting through the sight, he pulled the trigger.

"Missed," the Armorer said.

"Fireblast." He shot a second round.

"Missed again. Make it a couple inches right."

Ryan made the minute correction, then fired the Steyr a third time.

"Come on, Dad. Nearly off the bridge," Dean urged.

"Want me to open up with the Uzi? Spray them with a burst? Might be best."

Ryan shook his head at the Armorer's suggestion, for the fourth time aiming below the bridge, where nearly two hundred gallons of gas were buried in large cans. The problem was that they had to be well enough hidden so that none of Yoville's skirmishers spotted them and diverted the war wag away from the bridge.

But they were proving too well concealed.

Ryan couldn't work out precisely where they lay beneath a thin covering of sand.

And the war wag had stopped for a moment, two-thirds of the way over, one of the smaller vehicles close behind it, the second wag a few yards back.

If he missed again, the heavy armored vehicle would rumble unchecked into the institute, providing cover for the rest of the gang.

And the fight could well be over before it even got started.

Ryan checked his aim and pulled the narrow trigger on the Steyr a fourth time.

Chapter Thirty-Six

It was the kind of scene that would have driven any stickie over the brink of orgasmic delight, a combination of a deafening roar and a spectacular explosion of smoky orange flames that rose a good hundred feet into the Florida morning, enclosing the war wag in a sea of solid fire.

Ryan and J.B. had spent an extra hour the previous night, using some of the spare gasoline from the base's supply to splash over the dried timbers of the narrow bridge. It was time eminently well spent.

The fuel had soaked into the wood, catching and burning with a ferocious intensity, the roar clearly audible to the defenders of the institute.

Black coils of greasy smoke erupted from the fire, soaring high, blotting out the early sun, darkening the land and sea around. Over the noise of the raging flames, they could all hear the screams beginning.

"May the gods of earth and water have mercy on their souls," Tomwun muttered, crossing himself.

"Hot piping ace on the stripping line, Dad!" Dean yelled, dancing up and down, his heavy blaster waving triumphantly in his diminutive fist.

"Doesn't win it for us," Ryan shouted, obscurely angry that the success of his plan was being greeted with delighted cheering by the white coat scientists on both sides of him, feeling, oddly, more sympathy for the poor bastards who were being roasted alive in the iron war wag.

They were fighters, men and women who took what they wanted. They were a whole lot more like him and his companions, not like these ice-heart cold-eyes who tortured creatures to help try to win their own victories.

The driver of the war wag must have suffered hideous injuries, his ob slit open to the implosion of fire. Blinded and mad with pain, he'd stamped down and pushed the pedal to the metal. The engine raced, then choked and died, leaving the ponderous wag stranded in the sea of dancing fire.

The smaller vehicle was less well protected and immediately stalled, engulfed in bright red, yellow and orange fingers of surging heat.

"Shoot anyone who gets out," Ryan said, glancing sideways at Mildred and J.B., the only ones with weapons capable of doing serious damage at that range.

The gasoline exploding had been so horrifically violent and rapid that pirates traveling inside the two wags had no chance. Only one of them was even able to get free as far as the turret of the trapped war wag, appearing for a moment, standing upright amid the inferno.

It wasn't possible to tell whether it was a man or a woman. Just a dark figure, clothes blazing, hair flashing to a scorched stubble in half a second. The arms were raised, fingers spread, the blinded, blackened face turning helplessly and hopelessly from side to side.

Mildred had lifted her target blaster, steadying it, then lowering it again.

"Not a lot of point, is there?" she said quietly, watching the pirate fall to its knees, head hunching into the shoulders, before it rolled over like a charred collection of withered branches, vanishing into the burning lake of fuel. "Oh, God, my father..." she whispered, turning away.

The screaming didn't last very long.

In less than two minutes the desiccated timbers of the trestle bridge had burned through enough to allow the war wag to tip gracefully forward. Its glowing iron tumbled through into the dry sandy creek below, followed less than a half minute later by the smaller armored wag. There was no possibility of there being any survivors.

J.B. had called out a warning to all the defenders to keep low and under cover, guessing, rightly, that the attackers would open fire.

Which they did, with a prolonged burst of shooting, all along their front, accompanied by shouting and cursing. Most of the bullets were wildly aimed and flew wide or high. A few tore chunks from the walls, or shattered windows or ripped away long splinters of white wood from the gates.

But it was mediocre stuff, very poorly directed, and didn't cause a single serious casualty among the men and women in the institute.

Ryan heard a voice bellowing for an end to the shooting, a hoarse, angry voice that he recognized as being Red Jack Yoville. It was a disappointment that their trap had failed to chill the pirate gang's leader.

"What'll he do now?" Tomwun asked, lying flat on his face behind the wall, his hair sprinkled with stone dust. "Mebbe he'll go away."

Ryan touched a finger to his cheek, where a tiny shard of wood had nicked the skin and drawn a bead of blood. "No. No, he won't."

Thorund was next along the line. "They've took dreadful losses, Mr. Cawdor. Surely they'll see sense. See that we aren't a ripe peach to be easy plucked."

"No. Not the way it works. Man like Yoville has control through fear and power. He backs off from us, and he's lost his authority and his power."

J.B. nodded. "Ryan's triple-right. Yoville might as well suck his blaster as retreat from us. He'll come in again. Soon."

IT DIDN'T TAKE LONG.

Having lost his most potent weapon, as well as the small armawag, with probably a quarter of his total force, Yoville had to rethink his strategy. There was no point in the mindless sacrifice of sending in a skirmish line over a hundred yards of fairly open ground against armed defenders who'd gun you down from the safety of good cover.

Yoville chose to wait for the arrival of his seaborne attackers, knowing that this would force Ryan to divide his limited power and weaken the frontal defenses of the institute. The pirates went to ground, crawling through the dunes, occasionally offering a burst of sniper fire to keep the frustrated defenders pinned down.

It was a desultory few minutes, with nobody taking a serious wound, with the exception of a skinny pirate with one arm who made the mistake of showing himself for a moment too long. He was rewarded with a .38-caliber bullet through the chest from Mildred's ZKR 551.

Yoville, in the last of his wags, had retreated toward the ribboned remains of Highway One, reappearing on foot, his brilliantly crimson shirt and pants making him conspicuous among the rolling sand hills.

Ryan tried two shots at him with the Steyr, but the pirate baron was too wily, burrowing into the dips and hollows, gradually worming his way nearer.

"Not so good," J.B. called, sitting with his back to the wall, holding the Uzi in his lap. It wasn't the right weapon for that kind of cautious firefight, any more than the Smith & Wesson M-4000 12-gauge that lay at his side.

"You want to hold here, while I go out and take a look around the harbor."

"Sure, Ryan."

"Can I come, Dad?"

"Yeah. If there's a message to bring back to J.B., you can carry it."

Tomwun grabbed at his sleeve, nearly pulling Ryan off his feet. "You can't leave us."

"Do that again and you get to pick teeth out of the back of your throat."

"Sorry."

"Checking out those boats that was coming our way." He glanced at Krysty. "That *were* coming this way. Those sons of bitches out front aren't going to rush us."

"Suppose you're wrong?"

"Suppose I am? What the fireblasted difference will it make, Tomwun? They still got a big edge over us, and if their boats come in and they take possession of the quayside area, then we're in deeper shit than I care to think about."

He turned his back on the scientist and moved quickly away from the entrance of the institute, Dean jogging at his heels.

RYAN BUMPED into Miranda, who was walking quickly away from the docks toward him, the tension in her eyes reflecting her obvious worry.

"Ryan. I was coming to see you."

"What? You sent out some dolphins to try to wreck the boats before they reach us?"

"No. That's what I was going to tell you."

From where he stood, Ryan could see across the quayside into some of the pens. Every one of them had a dolphin in it, swimming around and around, thrashing the water into foam, showing every sign of disturbance.

"They know something. That it?"

She nodded. "They won't go. Nothing'll make them. I tried...I tried the electric prods and the goads. Never known them to refuse like this."

"They say anything?" Dean asked, staring past the young woman toward the narrow strip of the Lantic that was visible between two of the old warehouses. "Hey, I can see one of the boats out, and more of that stinky smoke."

Ryan looked, distracted for a moment from Miranda. The original dun cloud had long dissipated, but his son was right. This was like a prairie fire, covering a quarter of the horizon, as yellow as corruption, soaring higher than an eagle's wing. Far beneath it, dwarfed by the great column of smoke, was a small boat, heading directly toward them.

"The dolphins knew about that," the young woman said, her face as pale as parchment.

"How do you mean?"

She gripped Ryan by the arm, her fingers digging in so hard that it made him wince. "We get quakes and stuff all the time around the Keys. All the time."

"So? What's different now?"

Somehow he knew what she was going to say. An atavistic, primitive sense seeped into Ryan's mind, filling him with something that lay partway between awe and fear.

"This time it's big, Ryan. So big that it could be the end of everything. The pirates out there and us and the Keys and all."

"What've the dolphins been saying?"

"You know that the language we use and the way they seem to visualize things are totally—"

He put his face to hers. "Cut the science crap, Miranda. What?"

"They see darkness and a shaking and the fabric of the waters parting. Fires and a great rising of the sea." She shook her head. "That's the nearest I can get to it. Just like the end of the fucking world, Ryan."

As HE SPRINTED toward Krysty and the rest of the group, Dean panting behind him, Ryan distinctly felt a strong tremor shake the earth beneath his feet.

The shooting had stopped, as though both sides were aware of external forces beginning to threaten them all.

Krysty turned as Ryan joined her. "I've never felt anything as powerful as this, lover."

The smell of burning sulfur had drifted across the key, filling the nostrils and making the eyes prickle. The dawn had turned to dusk, with clouds towering in the eastern sky, blotting out the light, erasing all shadows.

"Upon my soul," Doc said. "It's looking uncommonly like the end of the world."

Chapter Thirty-Seven

The noise of breaking glass was sudden and total.

Ryan staggered, nearly falling as the ground rocked, then gave a savage jerk to left and right, throwing him against the main gate. Every single pane of glass in the place disintegrated simultaneously as walls and ceilings warped and flexed.

The air was filled with a deafening roar that swamped the ears with sound so intense and painful that Ryan pressed his hands to his head, then looked at his fingers, expecting to see them clotted with blood.

Ever since the great nukings of 2001, the planet had been struggling to get itself back into kilter. But the deep-seated damage to the tectonic plates of Earth wasn't that easily or quickly remedied. Now, a hundred years later, there were still constant quakes and volcanic activity.

Ryan had seen and experienced hundreds and hundreds of such events throughout the length and breadth of Deathlands, mostly very minor, scarcely even worth mentioning. But this one was in a different league.

Even above the thunderous crashing of the quake, Ryan was aware of a high-pitched clicking and whistling, as the dolphins all went crazy.

Out across the open expanse of scrub and sand, the gasoline fire had almost died away, with only occasional little bursts of purple and orange flames dancing around the blackened wreckage of the two wags.

Yoville and the survivors of his gang were out of sight, scattered among the dunes.

The earth's rumbling faded away until it sounded like a war wag tackling a steep grade in a low gear, but the ground was still vibrating and twitching.

J.B. looked at Ryan. "Think the worst of it's over?"

"Don't know. But the clouds out in the ocean look real bad. If it's happening under the Lantic as well, then there could be all sorts of shit coming our way."

One of the older male scientists lost his nerve, running like a headless chicken, mouth gaping open, straight out of the gate, which now sagged crookedly on broken hinges.

Mildred made a halfhearted effort to restrain the man, but the ground was still moving like it had turned to oatmeal, making it almost impossible to maintain balance, and she just missed him.

Ryan watched the staggering, stumbling figure, wondering how long it would be before one of Red Jack Yoville's gang of killers noticed him.

It was about thirty yards, and three blasters opened up more or less simultaneously, kicking the scientist onto his back into the shifting sand.

In the general confusion and near panic, the death went almost unnoticed.

The quake was now throwing up great clouds of blinding dust, making it impossible to see more than a dozen yards, with visibility shrinking all the time.

Tomwun appeared from the orange haze, shrieking out Ryan's name.

"What?"

"Harry says there's big waves breaking up the sea. Says the boats have all been turned over."

It occurred to Ryan that the natural forces were combining on their side to help them toward a possible victory—apart from the unfortunate fact that those same natural forces would also probably chill them all.

He beckoned the other six around him, shouting at the top of his voice to make sure they could hear them.

"Boats are sunk. War wag gone. They lost over half their men and women by now. Can't be more than fifteen or so left, plus the one small wag. Best chance we got is to stick real close together and go out after them."

J.B. nodded, holding on to his fedora with his left hand. "Might be they're ready to cut and run."

"Could try for that wag. Take it and head north. Straight out to the redoubt before the whole of the

Keys vanishes.'' Krysty's voice was hoarse, her eyes darting like a madwoman, the bright curls of hair strangely dulled, clinging to her skull like a fiery bathing cap.

Tomwun loomed out of the whirling insanity, staggering as the earth tipped and lurched to right and left. "You're leaving us! You can't."

He started to lift the M-16 and Ryan shot him through the chest, firing the Steyr from the hip, the force of the heavy bullet knocking the scientist off his feet. Tomwun tottered backward, arms flailing, disappearing into the sandstorm.

"Now!" Ryan yelled.

"Miranda's..." Michael began, stopping as he realized that he was speaking to himself.

He took a few hesitant steps toward the heart of the institute, nearly falling over the corpse of Tomwun. A jagged crack opened in front of him, splitting the concrete path into ten thousand splinters, revealing a deep, smoking cleft in the dirt beneath, releasing a strong gush of sulfur that made the teenager gag.

For a dozen tremulous, racing heartbeats, Michael stood still, keeping his balance against the moving ground as easily as he had on the reeling boat.

It was impossible. The pounding noise and the total blinding chaos convinced him that Ryan Cawdor had, as usual, been right in his instant decision.

There was nothing to do but run for it.

As he hesitated a moment longer, the quake stopped with a jarring abruptness, and he was able to see over the tangled wreckage of the tumbled buildings of the institute the open expanse of the Lantic.

"Mother of the Lord," he whispered.

It was as if the surface of the ocean were a huge sheet of gray green, being shaken by the giant hand of a fractious child. It was moving in monstrous ripples, some of which appeared to be forty or fifty feet high, swirling and tumbling in on one another, creating whirlpools a hundred yards across.

Michael spun quickly on his heels and began to head in the westerly direction taken by Ryan and the others.

THE UNEXPECTED STILLNESS caught Ryan leading the rest of the group at a dead run, across the open ground that lay between the ruins of the institute and where he figured the front line of the remaining pirates had to be.

The sand began to settle and the air cleared, though there was still a bone-deep rumbling some limitless distance far below their sprinting feet.

It was as though a curtain had been pulled back in the middle of a scene out of a play, with all of the actors frozen in their places.

Scattered among the dunes, most of the surviving pirates were standing upright, shocked from hiding by the abrupt horror of the big quake.

Moving fast, reflexes trained to a razor's singing edge, Ryan and the others had an enormous advantage over the startled group of killers.

J.B. was first, shooting the Uzi from a crouch, pouring a stream of bullets into the hills of sand and scrub. Ryan took his time, firing all nine remaining rounds from the Steyr, picking his targets, most at a range of less than fifty yards, killing six, wounding two and missing one.

Around him he was conscious of the boom of the Browning, the sharper sound of Krysty's double-action Smith & Wesson and the measured snap of Mildred's ZKR 551, each bullet chilling another pirate.

Doc's Le Mat had roared out its .63 scattergun round, blowing a charging woman's face into rags of torn flesh draped over a scraped skull.

Ryan glanced behind him, wondering what had happened to Michael, and saw him running flat out, his little .38 gripped in his right fist.

It was an absolute and shattering victory. There was barely a single round fired in retaliation from the shattered gang. Two or three raised their hands in a token of surrender. But either Ryan or J.B. shot them down where they stood.

While the others consolidated the area, Ryan ran on alone, aware that none of the corpses had been dressed in red, aware that the last of the wags had to be somewhere over the crest of the hill.

Less than thirty seconds after it ceased, the quake returned, with redoubled vigor.

Tripled vigor.

Quadrupled.

Ryan was lifted off his feet and hurled sideways, the empty rifle nearly slipping from his shoulders. If had hadn't been among soft sand, the rolling fall could easily have left him with a broken shoulder or ribs. But he managed to get up quickly, though the unbelievable violence of the earthquake had shaken him to the very core.

Once again the air was filled with dust and he blinked his one good eye, struggling to see what was happening. He stood on the highest point of the Key, with the ocean visible on both sides. But it was hardly recognizable, the Gulf of the Lantic both dappled with a shimmering layer of white foam.

To his right Ryan glimpsed the institute, a few figures scurrying about in the ruins, like tiny ants whose home had been disturbed by a careless spade. A little farther down the hollow, near the dry creek, stood Krysty, J.B. and the others, all fighting for balance. Even as he watched, Ryan saw Doc clutch at Mildred's arm for support.

To the left was the undulating length of the highway, its blacktop obscured by drifting sand. Less than a hundred yards away was the remaining armawag. And halfway toward it, crawling on hands and knees, was a figure in bright red shirt and pants.

Jack Yoville's back was turned, and Ryan realized immediately that the noise of the quake would drown out any noise he might make in closing with the pirates' leader.

It crossed his mind to stop and reload the Steyr, but that would take a few precious seconds. And with the quake making the land writhe like a broken-backed rattler, it could be a difficult shot, allowing Yoville to make it to the relative safety of the small armawag.

With Ryan Cawdor, to think was to act.

The rifle bouncing on its sling, he moved as quickly as he could, balancing like someone on a slack wire, closing the gap between himself and Yoville. He drew the panga from its sheath as he ran down the slope.

At the last moment the man sensed him coming and half turned, fumbling for a slate-gray automatic in his broad leather belt. Ryan had a momentary impression of a narrow foxy face, with long dyed red hair and curling side whiskers, tinted with white; a mouth opening in a snarl of bitter, defeated hatred, and eyes of the palest blue, staring fixedly up at approaching death.

Yoville made one last desperate attempt to parry what he guessed would be a powerful, hacking blow aimed at taking the head from his shoulders.

But at the last he guessed wrong.

Ryan changed the angle of the panga, using it with the probing delicacy of a surgeon instead of the clumsy brutality of the slaughterer.

He dived in, turning in the air, jabbing down with the eighteen-inch blade, aiming for the exposed angle of Yoville's throat, below the left ear. The honed steel whispered through skin and flesh, slicing open the walls of the artery.

Bright crimson fountained into the quivering earth, dripping all over the scarlet shirt and pants.

"You fucker," Yoville said in a normal, conversational voice, rolling onto his face and dying.

Ryan was on his feet, beckoning to the others to hurry and join him.

The earthquake was worsening, and the stench of the undersea eruption was becoming overpowering.

"I believe that the time has come to depart," Doc shouted as the engine of the small wag kicked into life.

Nobody argued with him.

Chapter Thirty-Eight

The weather changed the same day that Abe reckoned the cougar meat would be running out.

He'd skinned and gutted the monster predator, throwing the tripes a few yards from the cabin door, smearing the fresh snow with black gobbets. The good meat he tied up to the rafters of the cabin, where he took it down and cooked it over a small fire, a small fire that ceased to burn on the fifth day due to the lack of available fuel.

After that, Abe devoured the meat raw, washing it down with snow crystals. The skin and offal from the cougar had vanished in the first night, and he was careful to block the broken window so that no other creature could take him by surprise.

Now the temperature outside had risen by twenty degrees since the bleak dawning, and a warm wind blew from the west, tasting of the ocean that lay in that direction. The roof ran with meltwater, and the trees all around were dripping noisily, pitting the graying snow beneath their branches.

For the first time in an age, Abe was able to walk a few cautious, hesitant steps outside, taking in deep breaths of the clammy, thick air.

"Sure tastes green," he said, his voice louder than he'd intended, startling him.

The line shack behind him was cramped and dirty, smelling of blood, shit and darkness.

It was a relief for Abe to be out and on the trail again, moving the last miles toward the Pacific.

HE'D TRAVELED LESS than a mile when he smelled wood smoke and what was uncommonly like the scent of baked apples with cinnamon sauce.

The stainless-steel Colt Python was in his gloved fist without his even realizing that he'd drawn it. Food was people. People could be good news.

Or bad news.

He picked his way carefully through the melting slush, hearing a stream somewhere below the trail, already roaring with the swelling water that was coursing down from the mountains all around.

The path was slippery and treacherous, with pockets of glazed ice and wet snow overlaying each other.

As he worked his way lower, the wind changed a little, veering easterly, and the warm smell of cooking vanished. Abe stopped, sighing, aware of the damp already penetrating his worn combat boots, trickles from the pines finding their way beneath the collar of his coat.

"'Oh, do you remember sweet Betsy from Pike, Who crossed the wide desert with her lover, Ike?'"

The voice was flatter than a snake's dick, but it had the loud confidence of someone used to singing alone.

Abe still kept his blaster ready, but he felt little sense of immediate danger.

The song stopped abruptly as Abe's foot cracked a fallen branch, concealed beneath a thin layer of dull snow. "Someone there?"

"Yo, the camp!" Abe called, spotting a thin trickle of light gray smoke filtering up through the trees ahead of him. The smell of the apples was suddenly stronger, making him salivate with the sharp hunger.

"Come ahead. On your own?"

"Yeah. You?"

"Sure am. Wouldn't be exercising my muleskinner's bray like that if I'd known there was anyone close."

Abe holstered the .357 Magnum. It was rarely a good idea to enter someone else's camp with your blaster drawn and cocked.

Now he could see the owner of the worst singing voice in the Northwest, perhaps in the whole of Deathlands.

The man was around six feet tall, wrapped in so many layers of ragged furs and clothes that it was impossible to tell if he weighed one-twenty or two-fifty. He had on a balaclava helmet made from dark blue wool that covered all of his face except for his mouth and a pair of bright green eyes.

A rope belt was knotted around his midriff, with what looked like an antique Colt Navy cap-and-ball pistol with broken grips stuck into it.

"Come ahead, friend," he shouted. "Just baking me some apples I found in a barn a couple weeks back before the snows came closing in on me."

"Smells good."

"I'm Floyd. Floyd Thursday."

"My name's—"

"Abe, if I don't miss my bone-cracking guess. Yeah, you'd be Abe."

"How do you know that?"

"Lean as a whipcord and a mustache. Said he couldn't understand why you bothered to cultivate something so downright ugly under your nose when you got plenty more hair than that growing wild around your ass." Floyd slapped himself on the thigh and cackled with laughter. "Only sort of joke the old guy made." He paused. "If it was supposed to be a joke."

"Trader," Abe breathed.

"Called himself that. Carried an Armalite so old it looked like Noah himself used it to blast the dove out the sky. Left a letter for you, Abe."

"Letter?"

"Sure."

"Wait a minute." Suspicious, his hand dropped over the butt of the Colt. But the other man didn't seem to notice the gesture. "Trader couldn't fucking write."

"Correct. But I can. Next question is, can you read, Abe?"

"Sure. Got taught by a breed woman out near Sonora. Got a knife in my thigh in a sort of disagreement in a gaudy. She looked after me. Fed me shit-tasting soup and my letters. Don't know which was the worst."

"Well, here it is."

"How did he know I was around these parts, Floyd? How could he know?"

The man grinned through the damp slit in his woollen hood. "You know him. That answer the question? Yeah, I surely guess it does."

The paper was brown, looking like it had been used to wrap greasy food.

Abe took it and angled it toward the morning light, trying to read the faint words.

"Sorry about the paper," Floyd said. "Kept my fatback bacon in it."

Abe, glad the mutie bobcat didn't chill you. Always sleep with one eye and two ears open. Known for some weeks you been on my trail. Should've known couldn't just walk out on life like I hoped. Still rather been lost and stayed lost. No point weeping on account of a spent round. Time you read this, I'll be moved on some. But not far. Reckon we might meet soonish, Abe, and jaw over old times. Like old men does. Watch your back. Trader.

Abe folded it carefully and tucked it into an inside pocket, intending to read it several times when he was alone. "Mighty grateful, Floyd. Reckon I'm about ready to tackle those good-smelling apples now."

He felt more cheerful than he had in a long while.

Chapter Thirty-Nine

It was a trip through the outer edge of hell.

The wag was underpowered and had a gearbox that drove like it had been old before skydark. It was a tight squeeze for all seven of them to cram into the cramped vehicle, forcing Mildred onto J.B.'s lap and Dean to lie hunched up between the two front bucket seats.

Ryan drove as fast as he dared, peering out through the narrow ob slit hacked out of a single sheet of corroded iron. All around them, it felt like the world was ending.

They got off the dunes and onto the bucking ribbon of the northbound blacktop, but the earthquake was so severe that it was almost impossible to hold the wag on the highway. None of them had ever experienced a shaker that went on and on, each shock following right on the heels of the one previous, seeming to get stronger and fiercer.

Dust blew around them, and it sounded like a hurricane howling outside. With the fine sand that seeped in through every crack in the wag, combined with the foul miasma of sulfur, the air was almost unbreathable.

During the crazed journey back toward the redoubt, hardly a word was spoken, everyone aware that time was closing in on them.

There was a brief pause between shocks, and Ryan stopped the crowded armawag, the gears grinding in protest. "Going to take a look," he said, banging on the door to force it open.

There was nothing that he could recognize.

The road had virtually disappeared under the sand, and the light was like late dusk in a dank November. Black clouds whirled across the lowering sky, and the strange golden haze from the sulfur floated beneath it.

He glanced across toward the Gulf on their left.

"Fireblast!"

There were waves fifteen feet high crashing down on the beach, creeping ever higher toward the center of the key. And out to sea, Ryan could see plenty of even bigger waves, gathering themselves ready to rage across the low-lying land.

Though he couldn't look over the Lantic from where the wag was parked, he had no doubt that exactly the same things would be happening on that side, perhaps even more terrifying, as the first ominous signs of the current holocaust had appeared far away to the east.

"Bad?" Krysty shouted, as he clambered back into the driver's seat.

"Worse than bad."

It felt like the sand was filtering into every single mechanical part of the decrepit vehicle, and Ryan was surprised that they actually managed to get moving again.

"CAN'T RECOGNIZE where we are." Ryan pulled on the hand brake so hard that the frayed cable parted. But they were on level ground so it didn't much matter. "Too much dust, and the quake seems to have altered the landscape."

Krysty leaned across and looked out, blinking her eyes. "There's some mimosas. Saw some like that just after we left the redoubt. Didn't see any more anywhere else, lover. Must be close now."

The engine of the armawag was spluttering, seeming like it was about to give up completely. Ryan turned off the ignition. "All right, folks. Walking time."

It didn't seem any distance from the shattered remains of the blacktop to the crest of the dunes on the west of the key, barely a hundred yards. But the earth was moving so rapidly, shifting under the feet as much as eighteen inches in a single violent jerk, that it was hard going.

Dean proved quickest, skipping around, grinning broadly with excitement, hands out to maintain his balance. He was several paces ahead of any of them as he reached the ridge and stopped, turning to beckon to the others.

Ryan could just catch a small part of what he was shouting. "Right place! But out...sea..." The rest was torn away by the incandescent bedlam of noise.

It *was* the right place, the stretch of golden beach, now pounded by ferocious surf, and the pile of tumbled rocks that marked the ruins of the hidden redoubt, rocks that were being covered by the highest of the waves now raging in.

But that wasn't what caught all of their eyes.

It was farther out, much farther out, across what had been the Gulf of Mexico. Ryan's instant calculation told him it had to be forty or fifty miles away, at the center of an unbelievably vast underwater eruption. The cloud of smoke and steam reached to the upper limits of the atmosphere, boiling, lanced with great darts of silver and purple lightning.

Below it was the wave.

Ryan closed his eye and looked again, one part of his brain trying to do sums that another part of his brain steadfastly refused to accept.

There simply couldn't be a wave that was well over a hundred feet high, *two* hundred feet, white-topped, black as jet beneath the foam.

"How interesting!" Doc shouted, last to arrive and stare at the spectacle. "A tsunami. A giant tidal wave, hundreds of feet high, racing along at sixty to a hundred miles an hour. And I do believe that it's heading in our direction."

"Be here in something around twenty to thirty minutes," J.B. called, holding on his fedora against the rising wind. "Wash away the whole shooting match. Won't be anything left on the Keys but some bare rock and a few grains of wet sand."

Ryan looked again at the cluster of jagged stone where they'd have to climb before they could make the hazardous plunge into the turmoil of water to try to find the entrance to the redoubt. His heart sank at the thought of the ordeal.

Even in brilliant sunshine and a calm sea, it was a stern challenge.

"Do we have to, Dad?" Dean yelled, clutching at his sleeve. "Do we?"

"Must be some other way!" Michael's face was the color of gray river clay, his eyes sunken into dark pits of fear. "I don't think I can."

"No other way, and time's racing by. No argument. You come and have a good chance of survival. Or you stay here and die." Ryan looked around at his six companions. "Same for everyone."

EVERYONE HAD A BELT looped around their left wrist, the other end gripped by the next in line. It wouldn't save them from anything like the giant tidal wave, but it served its purpose and kept them together onto the outcrop of boulders, though everyone was completely soaked by the time they reached the point that overlooked the dark cavern.

The day wasn't cold, but Michael was shivering as though he were in the grip of some ferocious ague, his teeth chattering and his fingers clenched tight, nails biting deep into the palms of his hands.

"Here?" J.B. looked around, showing uncharacteristic uncertainty.

One patch of rocky coast looked precisely like another. If they were wrong, then there wasn't going to be time to try to locate the right place before the tsunami struck.

Already the tidal wave was visibly much nearer, now looking closer to five hundred feet high.

"I'll go last," Ryan said, hanging on to a splintered pinnacle of rock.

"I'll take Michael!" Krysty shouted.

"Me and John go with Dean." Mildred even managed a smile for the boy.

"And I shall plunge beneath yonder foam like stout Anchises. No, I mean Orpheus. Or was it... Let it pass." Doc's thinning silvery hair was pasted flat to his skull, and he looked like a revived corpse.

"Go," Ryan ordered.

Michael wasn't given enough time to refuse. His wrist linked to Krysty, he was jerked into the massive, white-topped swell, both of them vanishing.

The rest waited and watched, flinching as a large wave broke over the rocks, nearly washing them away.

"Go," Ryan shouted, and Mildred jumped with J.B., the slight figure of Dean between them.

Doc and Ryan were left alone, staring into the surging blackness below. There wasn't a sign of any marine life, no friendly dolphins to bid farewell from the Keys, no giant mutie serpents to pluck them to their doom.

Unless, Ryan thought, the snakes had already coiled around Krysty and the others, dragging them to their undersea lairs while more waited for himself and Doc.

"Go!" Ryan yelled, grabbing at the old man's arm and pulling him into the sea.

His last glimpse before he hit the water was of the gigantic tidal wave, looming above him and obscuring the horizon with its frothing bulk.

THEY HUDDLED TOGETHER in the corridor while J.B. opened the sealed sec doors. The usually smooth gearing and counterweights sounded rusted and damaged, but they worked.

"Least we're safe now we're down here," Mildred said, rubbing her hands together. "Wave can't get us."

Doc shook his head. "Not necessarily true, dear lady. The pressure when that wave hits the shore will be incalculably powerful. It will certainly force the sea through the narrow passage and into this corridor with the most extraordinary pressure. It will remain intensely dubious whether even these steel sec doors will protect us."

"Shit!" Ryan hadn't thought about that. "Let's get this jump made triple-fast."

The quake and the storm had done further damage to the already-ravaged control room. A scummy

layer of brackish water covered a quarter of the floor,
salt stains on the ceiling and walls showing where it
had found its way through from the sea above. The
cracks all around the room gave mute support for
Doc's fears for the effect of the tsunami.

The pale yellow walls of the gateway were hardly
visible in the poor light. Only about one-third of the
lights seemed to be working in the complex. As they
made their way toward the heart of the mat-trans
unit, there was a severe jolting shock, and another
bank of neon tubes plunged into darkness.

"By the three..." Things were moving too fast.
Ryan led the way to the open armaglass door of the
gateway chamber, ushering the others through.

His mind was filled with the image of the tidal
wave, bigger than anything he could have imagined in
the deeps of a jolt nightmare, plunging toward them.
How close was it now? Ten miles still?

Or five?

Or one?

"Has to be close," Krysty said, as though she could
read his thoughts.

"How close?" Ryan asked, not even realizing that
he'd spoken out loud.

"Close," Doc replied, still finding a moment to
give him a friendly pat on the shoulder as he joined
the others in the chamber.

Ryan hesitated a moment, wondering whether there
was still time to go back and drop the sec doors.

"No," he said.

Everyone was sitting on the floor, backs against the walls, waiting for him to join them.

For a fantastic fraction of a second, Ryan realized that he truly wanted to know what would happen when the tidal wave struck the Keys. Was Doc right? Would the gateway suddenly flood with sea water, under such pressure that it would crush flesh? It would be amazing to see that.

"Lover," Krysty said quietly in the stillness, a stillness so profound that he could hear the faint ripples of the tiny wavelets out in the corridor.

He went in, glancing once around the room at the others, smiling as he did so.

"Might one ask what is so profoundly amusing, my dear Cawdor?" Doc asked.

"Just thinking we look like a warren of drowned rats." He paused, his hand on the heavy door, ready to pull it shut and trigger the mat-trans system that would propel them into elsewhere. "Here we go, friends."

He sat by Krysty, with Dean on his left. Doc was opposite, lying on his side, knees drawn up to his chin. Everyone else had assumed the positions that they knew from experience would be most comfortable for the jump.

Ryan took Krysty's hand in his.

The lights outside dimmed, and he heard the crackling of a major electrical circuit malfunctioning. The metal disks in floor and ceiling began to glow, and the pale yellow armaglass started to pulse with the familiar misty light.

The inside of his brain was beginning to float in the nauseous way he hated so much.

"Something's wrong."

The voice was his father's. Couldn't be. Old man. Doc. Something was wrong.

Felt wrong.

Ryan tried to grip Krysty's hand more strongly, but they were suddenly wrenched apart with a dreadful force and violence.

He could hear the roaring of a mighty water, and his breathing was being choked.

"Wrong."

The darkness swam around Ryan, and he realized with a chilling terror that he was completely alone.

"What's happening?"

The thrills come cheap...so does death.

JAKE STRAIT BOGEYMAN

by FRANK RICH

In the ruthless, manic world of cheap pleasures and easy death, professional bogeyman Jake Strait has stayed alive the hard way, and like everything else, he's available for a price.

In Book 4: **TWIST OF CAIN,** Jake Strait is hired by one of the rich and powerful to find an elusive serial killer called Cain—a collector of body parts who is handy with a nail gun. In this action-packed fourth and final book, Jake Strait wanders into the playground of the rich, only to find that he has been set up from the start.

Are you looking for more

DEATHLANDS ®

by **JAMES AXLER**

Don't miss these stories by one of
Gold Eagle's most popular authors: